Entrapped

Entangled Book 2

A Novel by Carlie Yates

Cardinal Moon

978-1733264914

To Zachary, Marcus, and Jacob.
Thank you for teaching me about unconditional love.

CONTENT WARNING!!

This book contains emotionally sensitive
subjects and situations.

PROLOGUE

Safe

Now you'll be safe.

Those were the last words Catherine had said to Brody before he'd gotten in his mother's car, and they swirled around his troubled mind.

"Are you going to tell me what happened?"

He looked over at his mother as she drove, her eyes firmly on the road ahead of her. "He decided not to hide where he hits me."

"He who?"

Brody's eyes narrowed. "Frank. Who else would I be talking about?"

"What happened?"

"Fist." Brody held up his fist. "Face." He pointed at his face, then his eyes dropped back to the camera he held in his hand.

The camera Catherine had given to him.

"What started it, though? You know how he gets."

Brody couldn't suppress his eye roll. Of course she would take Frank's side. She always had.

"Well?"

"Don't worry about it."

"It's in the past, anyway," his mother agreed, as unwilling to talk of Frank's actions as she'd always been. "We're going home now. Different house, but home."

Home.

He wasn't sure he knew the actual meaning of the word.

He had just begun to feel a sense of what it could be, with Catherine.

"And we're safe," Tyler added from the back seat.

Safe.

As Brody stared out the windows at the passing scenery, he wasn't confident in Tyler's assessment, or in Catherine's. It didn't matter that Frank was now officially in their rearview mirror; with all the anger boiling in his veins, Brody felt that he was with him always.

CHAPTER 1

Four Months

You have a bad attitude, Brody.

Those words spoken by his coach just a few hours before still had him seething, even as he walked down the hall with the coach's daughter. It was bad enough they'd called him down to the counselor's office just the day before, but today he was told this, in front of every person in his history class.

What a way to fuck with the last day of his junior year.

"Ah, just look at those lucky bastards." Max elbowed his way between Brody and Catherine, putting his arms around their shoulders. "Right over there. See them? Seniors. They never have to come back to this place"

Brody glanced to his right where his best friend's mocking scowl was prominent for the world to see. "You do realize that's us next year, right?"

"And I'm so known for my patience, aren't I?" Max's scowl was replaced with a grin as he stepped forward, leaving Brody to pull Catherine closer. "Speaking of... woman!" He called out to Sarah, who despite being much further down the hall paused at the sound of her boyfriend's voice. Max turned without breaking stride. "You two lovebirds behave now. Later, bitches."

Brody shook his head at Max as Catherine took his hand in hers. He felt the calm wash over him, even in the middle of the chaotic hallway.

"I'm supposed to go with Jen to the mall."

He glanced down at Catherine, who was still looking straight ahead. "I remember."

"I can cancel."

"Don't." He said the word with a smile, knowing what was coming next.

"I was just thinking we could spend some more time together. Maybe at your house this time."

That was Catherine, always wanting to spend time together. He was aware that this wasn't due to insecurities; rather it was their lack of time pushing them both to strive for every moment they could. It was the thought of her coming to his home that made him pause, made his heart race for a moment before slowing down. "It's okay." He shrugged, calmer as he remembered. "My aunt canceled, so I need to stay with Ty and Sammi. Mom has a late night ahead of her."

"Then I will definitely come over."

"Don't cancel your plans, Cat." He had to force himself to speak calmly, coolly as they paused by their lockers one last time, gathering the last of their belongings before summer break. "You don't get time with your friends, either."

"Friend," she corrected him, raising her index finger for emphasis. "Singular. Unless I count you, of course."

"And Max and Sarah."

"They were a package deal with you." Catherine sighed as she leaned against the lockers, staring at the students moving quickly towards the exits. "I do like them, I just feel like maybe they're *obligated* to like me or something."

"I assure you that's not the case." Satisfied that the only things left in his locker were unneeded papers, he slammed the door shut. "They didn't like my last girlfriend and let her know it."

"Bethany met them?"

Brody paused for a moment, then shook his head. "No, no... sorry. Audrey."

"*Benson?*" Catherine's repulsion was evident in her tone alone. "You dated that snooty girl? And wow, rebound much? And... how did I not know this?"

"You did." He took her hand as they walked towards the exit where Catherine was to meet up with Jen. "I just didn't mention her by name."

"You didn't tell me you dated someone as soon as you got back here."

"It was before I left."

"Oh." She drew out the word, her eyes softening. "She's the one who didn't want to do long distance."

His smile was tight. "Yeah, something like that."

"I know, I know, I'm all twenty questions girl." They paused just outside the front doors and Catherine stood on her toes to kiss his lips softly. "I won't stop until I am well versed in all things you."

"Only if it comes from me," he added for her... for the both of them. They'd felt the sting of what gossip could do, how damaging it could be for the soul let alone its destructive power over relationships.

"It's been four months today."

He smiled. "I know."

Four months since she'd walked into his photography class.

Four months since they'd shared that kiss in the equipment storeroom, sealing their bond.

Four months of integrating into each other's lives in their new normal, one that didn't include hiding from the world.

Four months of him wondering why she was with someone like him, when he was as far from perfect as they came, when he was someone she once thought of as plain and ordinary.

She squinted up at him, the afternoon sun's rays hot and nearly blinding compared to the building they'd just exited. "I promise. And I'll have my cell phone on me, so… call?"

"Absolutely."

"And then after the mall, I can have Jen drop me off at your place."

The light in her eyes matched his, and he felt a warmth not contributed to the sun flow through his veins. "If it's late enough, we can go to the park, sit under the stars."

"Brody,"

"But only if you're sure."

He wasn't talking about the park.

"I'm sure."

And neither was she.

"Jeez, you two." Jen grabbed Catherine's arm and began pulling her down the steps, away from Brody, the pastel purple streaks in her hair the subject of more than one rude comment. "I'll send her back to you when I've turned her into a raging lesbian," she called over her shoulder. "With fuchsia hair. You hear me? *Fuchsia hair!*"

Brody's laughter was genuine, his heart as full as it could be as he watched Catherine and Jen, two people who couldn't be more polar opposite, but had become extremely close. Jen often hung out with the two of them to the point where one of the rumors around the school was that Jen was sleeping with Brody right under Catherine's nose. Said rumor had made the three of them laugh hysterically, although they hadn't bothered to tell anyone why.

"You laugh as if I'm kidding!" Jen yelled, which only made him laugh harder.

Jen herself was, as she put it so kindly, a 'raging lesbian'.

Brody's smile lingered as he thought back to the Catherine he'd met almost a year ago... she would have never spoken a single word to Jen, let alone be climbing into a car to go to the Valley Mall, which was far 'beneath' the one she frequented when she lived in the house on the hill.

Back when Catherine swore she had many friends, only to find out none of said friendships had been genuine, just as he had told her.

"Got a minute?" Coach Garner was beside him now, his expression serious. Brody nodded and followed his coach—Catherine's father—back into the building, to the offices. Unlike the emptying hallways, the offices were still full of staff finishing up their end of school year work, perhaps even preparing for the next. He followed Coach back to one of the conference rooms, the air conditioning going full blast leaving a chill in the air. He took a seat in one of the empty chairs, his eyes watching Coach Garner's every move as he took the seat across from him.

"So, the trial starts soon." It was a statement, not a question. Brody nodded, but remained silent. "I'm sorry for you and your family that he refused a plea bargain, but at the same time..." Coach's voice trailed off as he scratched the back of his neck uncomfortably. "I never got the chance to apologize, Brody."

This caught Brody off guard. "For?"

"Had I been more active in Catherine's life, had I pushed the issue and inquired about what was going on, this would have been taken care of much sooner."

Brody stiffened, himself uncomfortable with the memories of Frank.

The abuse—physical and otherwise—had started long before he'd been forced to move to the house on the hill the prior summer, away from his mother in whatever hospital she'd been admitted to, away from his friends.

But the escalation, the isolation, the fear had been so prominent.

Overwhelming.

"It isn't your fault." Brody repeated the words to his coach that had been lodged in his brain, spoken over and over by prosecutors, officers, therapists.

Words he tried to repeat to himself.

Words he tried to believe.

"Did you give any thought about our talk yesterday?"

The talk.

Where Coach had brought in the school counselor, where they discussed his angry outbursts with team members. Where they discussed locker doors and walls that had been hit and kicked. Where they discussed team and attitude and issues. Where they said words like 'trauma' and 'anxiety' and 'depression' and 'perhaps medication.'

"As your coach, I'm going to tell you that if you have a repeat performance, you won't be playing on my team."

Brody wondered if that would make everything easier for him, for the team.

For his mother.

"As a father, I'm going to tell you that seeking help is non-negotiable if you want to continue dating my daughter."

Brody nodded and stood, needing out of that office as he felt himself break into a familiar sweat. Coach was silent when Brody opened the door, still silent when he looked over his shoulder.

"Thank you, Coach."

Coach Garner's smile was warm despite the conversation. "Anytime."

"No, for..." His hand tightened around the doorknob. "For finding the memory card, for taking it to the police."

The memory card that held a video of Frank's final assault on Brody, the bloody mess it had left him.

"I was told what to look for."

Brody nodded, knowing that Catherine had confessed everything to her father.

That Catherine had saved him, once again.

With words swimming in his brain, screaming to get out, Brody was silent as he left the office and the school to the first afternoon of summer break, an icy fear gripping his heart.

Not just over knowing he would be coming face to face with Frank soon.

Because of the anger, the all-consuming rage he felt at the thought of that monster.

What if history was repeating, and he was becoming a monster himself?

He shook it off as he stepped outside, the emptying parking lot before him, and sighed. He was so used to driving to school that he'd forgotten that his mother had needed the car. It was far too late to catch the bus now, so he began the walk on cracked and crumbling sidewalks to his home.

He'd lived in this small town nearly his whole life, aside from the few months he'd been forced to leave. Most people couldn't wait to get away, even if they weren't going far, just to have a change of scenery or more to do. For the longest time, Brody had been the same way, but for far different reasons. Now there was no looking over his shoulder, no wondering when the next time he would set Frank off was coming.

There would be no punishment for missing the bus.

A few giggling girls were entering the dance studio as he passed and he waved to them, making them gasp and hurry inside. Catherine worked part time at the studio and had even encouraged the manager to start gymnastics classes as well. The students would often giggle and blush when he would visit Catherine there; she even told him once that he only stopped by to feed his ego.

The 'ego' that he insisted he didn't have.

The 'ego' that Frank had accused him of.

A car slowed down on the other side of the street, and Brody looked over to see Max sticking his head out the driver's side window. "We're heading over to see Brian. Wanna go?"

See Brian.

They couldn't *see* Brian.

He was six feet underground where they'd left him to rot after he'd splattered his brains across the room he'd shared with Brody.

"I have to get home."

"You sure?"

It was Max, Sarah, and some kid he knew had hung out with Brian but couldn't remember. There was room for him in that car; he could easily get in the back seat, make the drive just out of town, stare down at the stone and scream at someone who would never hear him.

How dare he leave Brody to go through this shit alone.

How dare he not say anything... *anything* to him before he put that gun to his head, taking all of the answers with him.

"I'm sure."

He watched Max nod and wave, not moving again until they had driven off. Only then did he realize he could have at least asked for a ride home. There was no rush, though. He had an hour before Tyler and Sammi would be home, and that was plenty of time to walk.

To observe.

To think of how his life had been turned upside down and inside out, robbing him of his sense of home, security, warmth.

Love.

Without realizing where his feet were taking him, he made a wrong turn, one that had been right for years, until he stood in front of the house that he'd once lived in. The canary yellow front door was still there, its color cheerful, hiding the hell within. The other side of that door most likely still had a dent in it from where Brody had been slammed for missing the bus.

"You think you're so smart, boy? You can't even make it to the bus in time. How fucking stupid do you have to be to miss the fucking bus?"

"I missed the bus today." Brody muttered the words softly. "What are you going to do about it, asshole?"

He turned from the house, his footsteps more hurried as he approached the street he had to take to get to the house he lived in now, angry words and angrier fists playing over and over in his mind.

But Frank was gone.

Frank was in a jail cell awaiting trial, awaiting divorce, awaiting the sentence that the judge was sure to send down.

He wouldn't be behind the door of Brody's house waiting with whiskey on his breath and threats of harm and demands of silence and obedience.

"You're going to learn respect if I have to beat it into you."

He'd tried to.

Over and over he'd tried to.

In the end, Brody lost any respect he may have had for Frank when he was younger. He wasn't like Brian; he couldn't make excuses for Frank, no matter what he'd done to provoke his anger. And since he'd found there was nothing he could do right in what was legally his father's eyes, why not be as bad as he had been told he already was? Why not be defiant? Why not drink when he'd been accused of it before he'd ever touched a drop?

Why not be the polar opposite of his mirror image?

Until his mirror image was gone.

Remember to be back before the kids get here

That was the text on his phone from his mother, who wouldn't berate him for missing the bus much less ask why he wasn't home yet, so long as he would be there for the kids.

No mention of how he was just a kid himself, either.

I will be

He shot back the message as he slowed his pace. He had plenty of time, and the town wasn't nearly as large as the sprawling housing development that he'd lived in a few short months before. When his phone buzzed again, he expected it to be another text from his mother. Instead, it was a picture of Catherine with a wild pink wig on.

He smiled.

Catherine... somehow, she always brought him joy. Peace. Comfort.

Don't think I won't was the caption. He quickly snapped a picture of two dogs frolicking in the park he was passing and sent it to her followed by his dare of her to go through with it.

Not that he wanted her to. Not that he even had to think about it, because he knew Catherine wasn't about to do it. She wasn't nearly as daring as Jen, who she would still gush about to Brody, her newfound understanding of what friendship really was still confounding her.

The car was gone from the driveway as he finally arrived home. He still had a good fifteen minutes before Tyler and Sammi would come through the door, full of energy, leaving a trail of shoes, book bags, and various papers behind them. Their mother had promised him that all he would need to do was heat up whatever dish he pulled out, feed them, and, in her own words, make sure they didn't burn the house down.

Instead, as he finally got the lock to let loose and walked inside, he saw that everything she'd promised she was taking care of hadn't even been touched.

He let out an irritated sigh along with a muttered curse word as he surveyed the small living room, the smaller dining room, and the cramped kitchen, each space more cluttered and dirtier than the one before. He'd offered to take care of it the night before, but his mother had insisted that he just relax.

Relax.

He hadn't gotten to relax in... had he ever?

With another sigh, this one of resignation, Brody began his summer with less freedom than he'd had in school.

CHAPTER 2

Something Like That

The moon was nearly full, bathing everything it touched with its silvery light. It had been the perfect means of Brody finding his sure footing as he crawled upon the rooftop, settling just above his bedroom. Shingles scratched his hands as he leaned back and tilted his head to the sky, its stars barely visible. He was sure that if he were in the country, or perhaps by that lake that he'd gone to on his last birthday, he could see hundreds of them dotting the horizon in intricate patterns.

He and Brian had shared many late nights on the roof of their old house talking about their futures. There in their old house, the roof above the room they'd shared had faced the east, and many times they would watch the sun rise, hurrying back to their beds before their absence had been noticed. Here, the bedroom he shared with no one faced the west, so if he was still up on the roof, the sun would rise behind him, edging out the darkness piece by piece.

Here, he wouldn't have to hurry back to his bed, pretending that he'd been there all night instead of facing Frank's wrath.

Here, beneath the light of the moon, he could rest.

Here, he could escape from dreams that haunted him, taunting him with memories long forgotten.

Tonight's dream had been the worst.

It hadn't been one that made no sense but left him anxious nonetheless; instead, it had been about the old house, when his mom and Frank had first brought Sammi home. They'd all been so happy, basking in the joy of this new bundle who'd been pure love from the moment she was born. Tyler had been small then, still in diapers, but even he had fallen in love with his baby sister, insisting on helping every time she needed changed. And Frank...

He'd been so different.

He'd smiled all the time, talked about how their family was complete, and shared his grandiose plans for the future. He'd been kind and generous to a fault, showering all of the children with gifts that Brody now knew couldn't have been afforded. He'd felt safe, though... safe and loved. Frank would often tousle his hair, calling him his 'wild one,' saying how Brody was just like him.

That's when Brody had woken up that night, cold sweat across his forehead, his heart racing.

Unable... unwilling to sleep afterward, he had opted for his sanctuary upon the rooftop, the moon and stars keeping him company as he pondered his future. It had changed since he was younger; he no longer dreamed of being a BMX racer, although he still longed to travel the country. Now it would be with his camera—the one that Catherine had gifted him with for Christmas... for his freedom.

The one with the memory card now held by authorities, marked as evidence in the upcoming trial.

He'd thought that he'd done something wrong that first day of his photography class when someone from the front office came in to say they needed to see the contents of the memory card, and demanded to do so immediately. Hell, he hadn't even put it together that the history teacher was Catherine's father; she resembled her mother so much that the looks wouldn't have given it away. Brody also had never imagined that Catherine's father would be a school teacher, much less a new member of the faculty at Valley High.

Or that Catherine would have told him everything.

Brody was amazed that Coach hadn't kicked his ass, considering he most likely had seen what had led to the altercation with Frank. He heard all about the talk Coach had with Catherine, who shared it with Brody along with the horror of her father attempting a birds and bees conversation. Just the thought of it had Brody laughing softly in the darkness, easing the tension from his shoulders.

Catherine was his saving grace.

His comfort.

The light when his mind grew dark.

He wasn't sure if she knew how much happiness she'd brought to him.

For a moment, he wondered what would happen if he didn't have that light. Would it all be too much for him? What if he didn't have Tyler and Sammi depending on him?

Would he give up, too?

Would he be in the grave next to his brother, the time between the dates cut short?

Sixteen years... that was all there was between the first and last date on the tombstone for Brian, the tombstone that he hadn't seen. He'd looked for it that day, as they laid his brother to rest, his mind fixated on how TV shows had it all wrong: first they bury the body, then eventually, maybe when the family comes up with a few hundred dollars they couldn't afford, a tombstone would be put in place.

Did Brian even have one?

Brody hadn't been back to the cemetery to see. He'd heard his mother's pleas for them to get him 'something nice,' and Frank—who had always put Brian up on some unreachable pedestal—had told her that Brian didn't deserve it.

The rest of that day was a blur, with only pieces and fragments that stuck out.

Mostly, though, he'd just felt alone, no matter where he was, no matter who he was with.

His phone buzzed in his pocket, and his brow furrowed as he pulled it out. It was a Facebook notification, which was all the more curious. He only had one person set to give him alerts, and she certainly shouldn't be up.

Then again, neither should he.

As her status was a bit open-ended, stating she wasn't able to sleep, his added comment about sitting on his roof wasn't out of context. It did, however, warrant a call from her, his phone buzzing in his hand as her smiling face lit up his screen. "Hey." He nearly whispered the word as he answered.

"What are you doing on your roof? Or are you not, really?"

"I am, really." He stretched out again, lifting his face to the silvery light of the moon the way one would lift theirs to the sun. "Just came up here to think."

"Am I interrupting?"

He opened his mouth to tell her that she wasn't, then smiled. "You're the most welcome interruption I've ever had."

"I'm going to refuse to read into that and just bask in the glow."

His smile remained as he stared upwards, still wishing more stars were present.

Wishing she were present.

"Does Coach know you're up this late?"

"Around my house he goes by the title 'Dad,' and no, he doesn't. I'm spending the night at Jen's."

"How did you get sweet, quiet Jen to be all loud and boisterous?"

"She's not, not really. I mean, I know I didn't know her before, but... I dunno, she just needed a friend." He could hear her covering her phone muffling something to her friend, her soft laughter edging its way under his skin, trying to fill a void that had been there for so long. "And we are both bitches for talking about her when she's within earshot."

It was Brody's turn to laugh, albeit softly. "Wait, isn't there some sort of phone etiquette that says you're not supposed to be talking to me when you're there for the night?"

"One would think, except this hussy with her purple hair keeps messaging some hottie and won't tell me who. Yeah, Jen, I'm talking about you. Best friends, my ass." Again, Catherine's laughter washed over him, calming the storm within. "And you."

"What about me?"

"I miss you."

His eyes slid shut. "I miss you, too."

"We don't get to see each other enough."

Because they both worked days, but now his nights were with Tyler and Sammi instead of spending them with Catherine, the way they'd planned. Not to mention Coach wasn't about to let her come over when his mother wasn't home, which had increased greatly in the two weeks since school had let out.

"I could come over now. That way, Jen could go see her hottie, and we could finally spend some time together."

He should tell her no, tell her not to defy her father's wishes like that.

Except her father had told her she couldn't be there when his mother wasn't home, and she was... sound asleep in her room, but she was.

"Brody?"

"How good are you at climbing trees?"

He could hear her smile when she answered. "We're about to find out."

His interest was piqued as he watched Catherine survey the tree from below. He'd reached a branch from his window to get him to the roof; she, on the other hand, was in his back yard, contemplating the branch that was far above her short stature. "You sure that..." She held up her hand to stop his question. "Okay." He held up his hands in surrender. "I'll leave you to it."

The wind was rustling the leaves as Catherine walked back to the fence line, and Brody wished he could see her face more clearly. He could envision the determination in her eyes as she took off running, jumping without the springboard she was used to, and in pure Catherine fashion, she reached the lowest branch, gripping it as she swung her body upward. "Ugh." She paused between branches that she was moving through with ease. "I am out of practice."

"That's considered out of practice?"

She looked so endearing, her blonde tendrils falling from the messy bun she'd thrown her hair into, framing her beaming smile. Her eyes left his to survey her choices before her, which branches would be the most conducive of achieving her goal. He enjoyed watching her features at those times the most, the way the shadows rose and fell with each arch of an eyebrow, curl of her lips either up or down, the slightest change in expression just as she came to her conclusion. The rest of her climb was made with ease and as much grace as she had with every movement she ever made.

He wanted to photograph her this way.

"What's on your mind?" Catherine wasn't winded in the least as she settled in beside him.

"You."

He'd said the word without hesitation as his eyes traveled the length of her body, up across her collarbone where the light and shadows made his stomach tighten, to her upturned face, its heart shape one of the first things he'd noticed about her. It had chilled him to the bone when she'd first looked at him with her green eyes full of loathing and disgust, but now he saw tenderness. Caring. Understanding that mirrored his own.

She actually 'got' him.

Not many people did.

And he knew her so well that he could tell by just a flash of emotion— be it from those eyes that he adored, to her lips twitching, either up or down—what her reaction was to any given situation. But the best thing about her...the best thing about them... they talked to each other.

About everything.

"Nightmares?"

"Something like that." He stretched back and she followed his lead.

"Was it bad?"

He paused as he contemplated how to explain this dream, the memories, the feelings attached. "One of the worst." A smile touched his lips as he felt her hand on his arm, urging him forward. "It was when they brought Sammi home."

"He was that awful with a baby in the house?"

Brody shook his head. "He was amazing." His brow furrowed as the memory taunted him. "That was the worst part. He would be so attentive. In the best way, I mean. Then he would take it all away and I would be back to feeling like I couldn't do anything right."

"But you can, and you do."

"JJ blamed me for Brian."

Catherine sat up then and turned to face him. "That wasn't your fault."

"Wasn't it?" His gaze returned to the moon, wondering if Brian was stuck somewhere, reliving whatever hell had gone on in his own mind that he'd never shared.

"No. Brody, look at me."

He turned his head, his eyes meeting hers in the silvery moonlight. Once again, he wished he had his camera, this time for the vulnerability and tenderness in her gaze.

"What happened to Brian isn't your fault."

"It didn't happen to him; he killed himself." He paused briefly, the pain washing over him. "He put a bullet in his brain, and I wasn't there to stop him."

"Brody,"

"I'm surprised Jen let you leave." He changed the subject abruptly, looking back up at the moon as he did so. He heard Catherine sigh as she laid back as well. Sometimes she actually let him divert the conversation, and this was one of them.

"Like she had a choice. Besides," she grinned at him, "she's sneaking out to see whomever it was she was texting."

"Did she at least tell you who?"

"No, the bitch didn't."

"She's changed a lot, you know. Jen. Since she met you."

"She has, hasn't she?"

"Was that a project of yours?"

Catherine shook her head. "Strictly her own doing. I'm pretty sure we're all seeing the real Jen now, the one who isn't as worried about what others think. Phoebe was my last project, anyway, and I'm not going down that road again."

"Did I meet her?"

"No, she moved away before."

"What went so wrong with her?"

"I didn't believe her… or maybe I did and just didn't want to."

"About?"

"Mitch." Catherine said the word with just as much venom as she had for months. "She'd told me about how he'd tried to get her to sleep with him, about how creepy he'd been."

"Creepy? Mitch? Nah."

"Easy on the sarcasm."

"Does it make me too much of a jerk?"

They shared a smile under the moonlight, one that held their memories as their hands met, fingers entwining.

He knew there was nowhere else he'd rather be, no one else he'd rather be with.

She moved closer, leaning her head against his shoulder and he left a kiss in her hair. "I'm glad you're here."

"Me, too. Not that I'd necessarily pick being up on a roof," she added. "At least you're not riding your bike off of it. I feel bad for calling Max a liar, by the way."

"Sometimes you can't tell if he's bullshitting or not. He's just Max that way."

"Yeah, well, he told me to ask you how you got the scar, that one in your eyebrow. I'd always assumed that it was…" Her voice trailed off, her sentence not needing to be finished.

"No, it wasn't him, but I got my ass beat for that stunt. I suppose I deserved it."

He felt her stiffen. "No, you didn't."

"Cat, I was,"

"A child."

"This didn't happen all that long ago, you know."

Her frown deepened. "I know, I heard. And why haven't I met JJ?"

"He moved away just after Brian's funeral, to wherever his Mom is living now. He did that a lot, but he always came back."

"Just not this time."

"Not until now."

"And it was the four of you, right? That must have really sucked for Max when you left."

It was Brody's turn to frown even as Catherine settled in closer, nestled against him. "I guess I didn't think much about it, which means I suck as a friend."

"You had a lot going on." Catherine shrugged. "I wouldn't say you sucked, just that the situation did. This roof isn't comfortable at all, by the way."

He leaned his head against hers. "How long before you have to leave?"

"Jen said she'd call when she was on her way back to pick me up. She didn't say how long, though."

"Here." He sat up and inched away from her, towards the edge of the roof, reaching for the closest tree branch. "Follow me."

"After I just climbed up here?"

The soft laughter that left him was genuine, heartfelt.

This girl made him feel like he could fly, even when her voice dripped with sarcasm or a touch of annoyance.

He looked over his shoulder, his eyebrows raised as his gaze met hers. "Would you prefer the discomfort of the roof?" He watched mesmerized by her grace as she sat up and reached out for a larger branch, swinging her legs up and around before settling on it, facing him with one eyebrow raised. "Show off."

"I'm amazing, admit it."

"You are."

The sincerity in his voice softened her expression, and the smile on her lips—all he wanted to do was capture her this way.

Happy.

Carefree.

"I'm going to photograph you. Not tonight," he added as he read her expression, the one that said she wasn't wanting her picture taken this way. "But someday."

Without waiting for her response, he descended onto the next branch and reached out, opening the window to his room, its lack of a screen providing easy access. He stepped in, using both branch and windowpane for support before leaning down and entering his room. The chair he had by the window was less than stable, so once in, he turned to help Catherine, easily taking her into his arms and slowly lowering her to the floor.

"Oh."

The word left her lips, breathless and full of wonder.

And he kissed her.

She tasted of strawberries and summer, sweet and wild. Still, he took his time with her, their tongues dancing languidly as his fingertips slid up her sides. Their hearts beat wildly together in stark contrast to their slow movements, light touches sending chills down his arms.

"Cat," he whispered against her lips as he lifted her effortlessly. When she locked her legs around him, his heart constricted in his chest, the sweet pain melding with the nervous flutter within him. They smiled together and he kissed along her jaw as she growled in frustration while reaching for her phone. "That better not be Jen."

Her shiver at his whisper in her ear urged him on, and he nibbled gently at her neck, her shuddered sigh bringing forth another smile.

He smiled much more with her.

She pulled away slightly, her arms and legs still wrapped around him. "She's watching a movie with her hottie."

His eyes searched hers. "So we have time."

She nodded before leaning in, leaving one soft kiss on his lips as he lowered her onto his bed. "Where were we?"

He kissed her breathless as he fumbled blindly with his hand through his nightstand drawer. Capturing her sigh with another kiss, he braced himself on his arms, pulling away just enough to stare deep into her eyes, so green, so beautiful.

"Brody?"

He smiled. "Chapter eleven."

"You really didn't read ahead?"

Her question made him laugh softly as he lay beside her, curling his arm around her as she settled in with her head upon his chest. "I told you I wouldn't." The fingers from his free hand played with the silky strands of her hair as he opened the book, its placeholder falling beside him as he began to read out loud.

CHAPTER 3

Not Now

Three loud knocks on the door startled Brody awake and blinking, slivers of daylight filtering through his windows as Catherine stirred in his arms.

"Oh, shit!"

His exclamation had her sitting upright, eyes wide, and they shared a look of panic.

"Brody, open this door, now." His mother's voice was firm, angry, accusatory.

With reason, and a good one.

"Catherine's father is here."

Brody cringed and watched as Catherine's expression went from panic to a mixture of horror and dread.

"What do we do?" Her eyes were pleading with him for an answer, a way out, but Brody knew there wasn't any.

"Relax," he whispered before turning towards the door. "It's not locked, Mom. It's just stuck."

"Unstick it, then, just open this…"

The door was open before Brody or Catherine were off the bed, and Coach was filling the doorframe. "Young lady, get out of this house and into my car." He paused a beat, his eyes never leaving his daughter's. "Now."

Brody's heart began racing at an uncomfortable pace no matter that he knew this was Coach, not Frank.

Not Frank. She's okay.

"We fell asleep reading, Dad." She was in full-on Catherine mode, the girl that Brody had known before. She slid off the bed and fluffed her hair, her expression now one of bored indifference. "It's no big deal."

"You don't want to do this here."

"Maybe I do." One of her eyebrows was up, challenging her father.

Here.

In front of everyone.

To have an argument that Brody couldn't bear to stand witness to, knowing he'd immediately jump in between them, and…

He's not Frank.

"Cat." Brody's voice was softer, calmer than his pounding heart, and she glanced over at him.

"No," she snapped, "if he's going to have an attitude with me over something so trivial,"

"Trivial?" Coach's voice was raised now, and Brody felt the fear, the dread, the anticipation deep within him. "You lied about where you were, you spent the night with your boyfriend, and do not interrupt me, it isn't about what you did or didn't do beyond that. Get to the car."

"Coach,"

"I'm not your coach right now, Harris, I am Catherine's father." He stepped to the side as Catherine huffed her way past him and down the hall.

"Mr. Garner, then." Brody stood, eye-to-eye with the man who had far more reason to beat the shit out of him than Frank ever had. "I'm sorry."

"That's a five-letter word."

"It won't happen again."

"How very rehearsed of you."

And it all came rushing back, hitting Brody like a train, taking the air from his lungs as he clenched his fist along with his jaw. "Fuck you, then." He couldn't hear his mother's exclamation of how she didn't raise him to be that way, of how he knew better. His focus was directly in front of him as he glared at Catherine's father.

Coach's eyes narrowed. "What did you just say to me?"

"My apologies. Fuck you, *sir*."

He couldn't hear what his mother was saying as she stepped between the two of them. The rhythmic whooshing of blood filled his ears drowning all other sounds away, muffling them, until his mother turned his face towards him as Coach turned to leave.

"Are you listening to me, young man?"

"Not really, no." His voice was far calmer than he felt.

"What is going on with you? You... you've always been irresponsible, but this anger,"

He stopped listening as he turned away from her, feeling said anger boiling in his veins. "Not now, Mom."

Not now when he could snap, when he could turn on her with all the rage and venom he felt within. Irresponsible? He'd kept

Tyler and Sammi safe. He'd taken care of them, made sure they were fed and bathed and entertained while their mother had slept her days away, and he was doing so again so that she could work, and...

"Yes, now. You snuck your girlfriend in to spend the night with you."

Catherine...

Fuck, what have I done?

He turned again to face his mother, try to explain. "That wasn't our,"

"No, of course you didn't mean to get caught," she cut him off as she turned around, hands thrown up in the air.

"Yeah, we're so fucking horrible that we fell asleep reading. How *irresponsible* of us." He said these words as he texted feverishly to Coach, one after another.

Please don't take this out on Catherine

It was my fault

I was out of line, and I'm sorry

Coach, please don't take what I said out on her

His mother turned back around and placed her hands on her hips. "It *is* irresponsible, Brody. When you lie, and you sneak around, and... that girl is a horrible influence on you. You start dating her, and... and you're getting in fights in school, lying to everyone, and,"

"I've never been in a fight in school."

"At your last school, that one when you were..." She waved her hands. "I know about the suspension. Did you think I wasn't going to?"

Brody crossed his arms and narrowed his eyes. "Have you been talking to Frank?"

"I'm not under interrogation here."

"Neither am I."

"Hey!" She stopped him from closing his door. "You brought your girlfriend into this house without asking, without even *telling*, and had her stay the night. You bet your ass you're going to answer to me. I know about your outbursts, I know about your talk with the counselor and with Mr. Garner. I know why you said you needed to go back to the therapist, and I agreed because this isn't you. You're... acting out, or something."

"Acting out? I'm not twelve."

"Then stop acting like it. You need to set a better example, you know? You need to be..."

"Like Brian," Brody finished for her when she stopped herself. "A lot of good that did him." This time when he shut his door with a bang, his mother didn't stop him, and he locked it to ensure she wasn't coming back in.

One single text came from his coach.

She's safe

Of course she was safe. This was Coach, not Frank, but what the hell had he been thinking?

The book he and Catherine had been reading was on the floor, haphazardly lying there opened where it had either dropped when he'd fallen asleep or in their scramble to get up. He leaned over and picked it up, leafing through the pages, trying to remember where they'd left off.

"Fuck." He muttered the curse as he threw the book down on the floor. Of course this would happen. Of course his one source of comfort would be threatened. She was the one thing in his world that was light and laughter and as close to normalcy as he had ever been.

She knew everything.

And she accepted him anyway.

He closed his eyes while counting down backwards, his breaths choppy and labored, his hands fisting in his hair.

10, 9, 8

The smell of her perfume—light, floral, feminine—was on his shirt, permeating his fractured mind as his warring emotions raged on.

7, 6, 5

The kids were up now, rustling about their room, dresser drawers opening and shutting, their echoes so clear through the paper-thin walls.

4, 3, 2

He pulled at his hair telling the rage to stop, stop, stop.

1

The rattling of the wall adjoining his and the kids' room stirred the contents of his bookshelf, drawing his attention to where a small strip of photos sat, taken at a booth just a few weeks before. He walked over and reached for it, a smile touching his lips at the faces Catherine had insisted they make.

She'd asked him that night why he'd been more moody than usual, what was up with the bullshit after and sometimes during his baseball games.

He'd told her not to worry about it.

He'd told her it would pass.

He wasn't sure of that anymore.

"Grounded?"

Brody shrugged as he opened his front door further for Max, who walked in to shrieks and hugs from Sammi before he sat on the couch.

"Yeah, what can I say?" Brody sighed as he sat back down on the floor, unpausing the game so he could continue. "I'm a rebel."

"With access to Xbox still, so I'd say you got off easy."

"And my phone." Brody never took his eyes off the screen. "Don't forget that one."

"And you can go to the park," Sammi spoke up.

"Nice try, kid. You know I can't leave the house except for work and stuff."

"Which punishes us, too." Tyler walked into the living room, baseball and mitt in hand. "Thanks for that."

"You're welcome." Brody sighed as he lost another life in the game and held up the controller, which Sammi gleefully took from his hand.

"You got off easy." Max shook his head in wonder "If my mother walked in on me doing my girlfriend,"

"I wasn't 'doing' her, shithead." Brody brought out a couple cans of soda from the fridge and handed one to Max.

"You were seriously just sleeping? Brody, my dude... don't let that get out."

"What's doing mean?" Sammi asked.

"Nothing you need to know," Brody replied before turning towards Tyler. "Where are you going?"

"Out back. Or am I not allowed outside, either?"

"Don't leave."

"If... if Max is with us today, can't we leave with him?" Sammi asked.

"You're staying here until I get back." Brody checked his back pocket for his wallet and front pockets for change. "I think I've got everything. Why didn't Sarah come?"

"Well, Mr. Grounded, my awesome girlfriend got that lifeguard job at the pool."

"Can we go see her at work?" Sammi asked, jumping up and running towards the couch, video game forgotten.

"Not today," Brody said before Max could reply. "I shouldn't be gone long, I don't think."

"You don't think," Max quipped. "Now there's a first."

"Fuck you." Brody said the words with a grin, knowing that Max would continue to milk his grounding for everything he could. "I have to get going. Ma said no cooking for you, Max. She doesn't want the house burnt down."

"Hey, my culinary skills have grown since the seventh grade, unlike yours."

"Yeah, well…" Brody messed with Sammi's hair as he walked towards the door.

"Don't leave me hanging, dude. Yeah, well… what?"

Brody flipped his best friend off and left to Max's laughter and his baby sister yelling that he wasn't being very nice.

The walk to the bus stop wasn't long. It was a route he'd taken quite a few times during the court-ordered evaluation, where his answers to the therapist had been short, rehearsed.

Rehearsed.

Like Catherine's father accused him of this morning.

Like Frank had accused him of for years.

The streets were quiet this morning, devoid of children walking to school, fewer cars passing him as rush hour to a normal 9 to 5 job had passed. The lawns were patchy, the lack of rain they'd had over the spring impeding growth, but the residents here weren't as concerned about appearances; he'd learned as he grew up that food and electricity were hard enough for lower income families to pay for, and increasing their water bill for lush, green lawns wasn't on their mind.

Except for Max's mom, who waved from her porch, their full lawn in contrast with the others on their street. His parents took pride in their home, in what they could do to give their children everything they could. Brody smiled and waved back at her, an inkling of jealousy gnawing away. Max's family was the exception, complete and thriving in this neighborhood that they said they loved.

Brody's bus arrived ahead of schedule, and he broke into a jog to ensure he didn't miss it. The city buses weren't much different to him than the school bus, other than its occupants being quieter. If he'd had his camera, he would have captured the young woman staring at the passing scenery with a sadness in her eyes, or the older gentleman looking down at his hands as he muttered incoherently. He hadn't brought his camera, though, or a book, so he settled back into his seat with a sigh, counting the bus stops until he'd reach his destination one town over.

"Tell me about Catherine."

Brody's therapist sat across from him, notepad in hand, a serene smile on her face. He opened his mouth to answer, to tell her everything that Catherine meant to him. "She's my girlfriend," he said instead before looking down at his hands, wondering why they had a slight tremor to them.

"I get that much."

His therapist… Laura. That was her name. He remembered being her before, telling her he had everything under control.

What a lie that had been.

"What is the first word that comes to mind when you think of her?"

"Comfort." He'd said the word without thinking and closed his eyes.

"Is that so bad?"

"No." He smiled softly, and it quickly faded as he opened his eyes. "But we fucked up."

"How?"

"She came over last night." He shifted in his chair, his eyes on the floor, memorizing the patterns in the rug. "And instead of staying on the roof, we went into my room."

"The roof?"

"Yeah." He shrugged. "It's… it's my place, I guess."

"Not a very safe one."

He huffed out one short laugh. "It's peaceful. Not very comfortable, but peaceful." He shifted again, a scowl returning on his face. "But I fucked up and fell asleep, and… and then, it was morning, and her father was at my house to pick her up. Fuck, I don't know how he knew." He ran a hand through his hair, resisting the urge to pull it. "But he did, and he's pissed, and my mom's pissed, and I tried apologizing." He shrugged again and began to pick at a loose thread.

"You were caught in bed with your girlfriend, Brody."

"Not like that," he snapped, then forced the calm back into his voice. "We fell asleep reading."

"You'd said reading aloud to her is your," she checked her notes, "definition of joy."

He nodded, still picking at the thread, even though he didn't remember saying that to anyone. Maybe it had been at one of the earliest appointments, when he'd decided he was going to be done with being under a microscope as soon as possible.

"Brody, why are you here?"

"Because I have to be."

"Who says you have to be?"

"The counselor, Coach, my mom."

"Why?"

"They say I have anger issues." He raised his eyes to meet hers, his gaze steady and level. "I'm fine, but I said I'd come."

Laura leaned forward, a soft smile touching her lips. "With everything that's happened to you, if you didn't have anger, or sadness, or grief to work through, I might question your sanity."

He almost smiled.

"Whatever issues you have, though, I can't fix for you. But if you give me a chance, I'd like to help you work through them. Will you do that for yourself? Not anyone else. Let's put the focus on you. Deal?"

He shrugged. "I don't like being..." He looked back down at the patterns in the rug, his jaw clenching as he shifted again.

"Give me a month, okay? One month, and you agree to follow up with the doctor downstairs about medication. If you aren't comfortable talking with me, we can get you another therapist then."

"I don't want a different therapist," he muttered. Or medication, but that was an argument to save for his "meds doctor." His psychiatrist. The one who would officially label him and medicate him and take away his ability to feel. He didn't want to stop feeling, to lose the joy in his life.

To lose what he was feeling for Catherine.

"It's okay to not be okay, Brody. You're seventeen years old, and you're going to make mistakes. You've lost your brother, your stepfather was an asshole. Yeah, I said it. And you've had the world on your shoulders since you were a small child. So your coach is making you go to therapy. So what? You have the opportunity to take care of yourself here, and no matter what you've been told your entire life, you are worth it."

He blinked several times as his eyes began to burn, the therapist's words bouncing around his head, trying to burrow in no matter him saying he didn't need this at all.

"What do you say?"

He inhaled sharply, burrowing his feelings deep down inside, the devil in his mind telling him that he was being weak.

Then he thought of Catherine, and of Tyler and Sammi.

They deserved better than what little he had to give.

"Yeah," he finally said, his voice hoarse with emotion. "I'm in."

CHAPTER 4

I Like Your Plan

"This is just the best time I've ever had grocery shopping."

Brody was grinning despite the evil eye he was giving Max, and he continued bagging the items without saying a word.

"I think I'm going to come here, like, every day, only buy a couple of things, and request you as my bagger."

"He did request you today," the cashier—Brody wasn't sure of her name—called over her shoulder.

"And you," Max grinned, "can't even call me an asshole until you're off work."

"I don't work forever."

"Ah, you do speak still."

Brody finished with the last of the bags, placing it in Max's cart. "Yeah, I speak."

"You must excuse him," Max said to the cashier. "He's been grounded from his girlfriend. Makes him a bit cranky."

"So I heard," she replied with a laugh. "You can go on break now, Harris."

Just Harris.

There would be no more mistaking which Harris he was.

"What if I want him to load these in my car?"

Brody smirked as he walked past Max. "Sorry 'bout your luck. And I wasn't grounded from my girlfriend."

"Yes, you were. And I'm requesting that you load my groceries next time," Max called to him, making him laugh softly as he walked through a door by the entrance, its 'Employees Only' sign worn, the words barely visible. He clocked out before sending a text to Catherine.

On break

Max was still loading groceries into his car when Brody made it back outside. "My mom is so happy that you're working here."

"Because you're doing the shopping for her."

"Yep." Max closed the trunk and pushed his cart towards Brody. "Be a good boy and put that up, would you?"

"Fuck you," Brody replied with a laugh, but he pushed the cart into the small island set aside for them. The last thing he wanted to do was retrieve carts that had been abandoned around the lot.

"Am I supposed to tip you or something?"

"Nah."

"Good." Max's grin faded slightly. "You okay, man?"

"Yeah, yeah, I'm fine."

"Just missing out on your summer."

Brody rubbed his temple, which continued its slow, steady throb. "Something like that."

"Dude, come out to the pool tomorrow. I know you won't be grounded anymore, so no more hiding behind that."

"I wasn't hiding."

"You didn't even go before you took off last summer. You know what I mean," he added before Brody could correct him.

"I.." Brody's voice trailed off and he grinned. Fuck it. "I don't work tomorrow."

"Sa-weet."

"I think my mom does, though."

"So? Bring them."

Brody considered it, knowing that Tyler and Sammi would have fun at the community pool.

He also knew they couldn't afford it.

"Dude, I got you."

"Man..." Brody drew the word out, the familiar guilt and shame creeping in. He couldn't keep accepting handouts from his friends just so he could be around them, too.

"Nope, you're not backing out. Besides," Max grinned, "I got passes."

"Using your girlfriend for passes." Brody shook his head. "That's a new low."

"Dating the hottest lifeguard has its perks."

"Is she working tomorrow?"

"Of course. Lady Cath-er-ine!" Max's grin widened as Catherine walked up.

"You're lucky I like you," she said to Max as Brody turned to her, his body warming in the unseasonable chill of the morning.

Max's arms were wide open. "Bitch, you love me. Bring it in."

Catherine laughed as she hugged him. "You're my favorite ginger. How's that?"

"Makes my day."

Catherine then turned to Brody and wrapped her arms tightly around his waist.

His tension dissipated.

"I was just telling your boy here that we need to go to the pool tomorrow."

"Isn't it kinda cold for the pool?"

"Tomorrow, blondie. You know, when the 80s return in all their... that's it!" Max clapped his hands together and rubbed them. "We all dress in 80s fashion."

Brody shook his head as Catherine was telling Max there was no way she was teasing her hair. "Forget it, dude."

"Miami Vice, man."

"No."

"Sarah will be working, so she'll have the Baywatch thing going."

"I have Tyler and Sammi tomorrow."

"Figure something out."

"Max," Catherine began, but he held up his hand.

"Gotta go, there are perishables in the car. See you two tomorrow, high noon, to celebrate your ungrounding. Sorry, you *four* tomorrow."

"There's no talking him out of it is there?"

Brody pulled Catherine closer as Max drove away. "Nope. We could always show up as ourselves and he'd look ridiculous."

"I like your plan." She turned to him and stood on her toes, reaching up for a kiss.

He'd missed her kisses.

"So," she asked as she stepped back and pushed her hair out of her eyes, "we're going to the pool tomorrow."

He grinned. "Yep."

"Actually spending time together, and not just me going on and on over the phone while you interject with a word or two."

"I've liked our phone calls." He reached out and took her hand in his, interlacing their fingers.

"But it isn't the same."

He looked down at her, his pulse quickening as he took in her beautiful features. Her eyes which had once been hardened with contempt for him now looked at him with earnest.

With adoration.

Her small hand in his, her sun-kissed skin soft, her grip firm, did more for his darkened mood than anything else could. He'd never had this comfort before; he was always the one comforting, the one consoling, the one hurting all the while.

"Thank you," he said to her, feeling it down to his soul.

"For?"

He smiled briefly and kissed the tip of her nose. "For everything."

"For making a quick trip to the store to see you on your break?" They began walking hand-in-hand to the entrance, paying more attention to each other than their surroundings.

"Yes."

"For rescuing you from Max?"

"Oh, definitely, yes."

"For telling my dad I needed feminine hygiene products so he'd give me the keys to his car even though I'm grounded until tomorrow?"

His head tilted back as the laughter hit him full force. "Especially that, Cat. Especially that."

"Brody!" Sammi's excited voice rang out as she ran into the living room that night with her swimsuit on, plastic sunglasses, and a play feather boa. "I'm wearing this!"

"You're not... on second thought, yeah. It's perfect." He smiled as she twirled around, red feathers trailing behind her.

"If she's wearing that, I'm not going."

"It's a Max thing, Ty."

Tyler's face lit up. "Oh, I've got this."

"Thought that might change your mind." He sat the last plate on the table. "Dinner's ready."

"Coming." Sammi ran to her chair, but Brody stopped her.

"No way, kiddo. Go change. And no pouting about it," he called after her as she ran back towards her room.

"I'm not pouting!"

"She was totally pouting." Tyler sat down at the table, staring at the warmed-up casserole. "Is this really what we're eating?"

"Yeah." Brody sat beside him, adjusting his seat as he grinned. "And no pouting."

Tyler picked at his food with his fork as he chewed on his lower lip. "Brody?"

"Yeah?"

Tyler sighed as he continued moving his food around, his eyes on his plate. "Nothing."

"Dude."

Tyler looked up at Brody then, his gray eyes troubled. "Is there... can there..." He placed his fork down. "Do you think that... I mean."

"It's okay." He smiled at Tyler, being his safe space as he always had been.

"Brian... he had those sunglasses, and that... that coat."

"Like from Risky Business?" Brody asked, and Tyler nodded.

"Do you think they're in one of the boxes?"

Brody swallowed over the lump in his throat. "They are." He knew this because he'd been the one to pack the boxes, put all the clothes, the mementos, the personal belongings of his other half into. Frank had screamed and ranted about it, and his mother… she had just cried.

So he'd done it.

Alone.

"Brody?"

"It is. They are, I mean." He took a bite of the casserole, telling himself he could keep it down.

"Do you know where?"

Brody nodded.

"Can I wear it? Tomorrow, for the Max thing."

Brody could think of a million reasons to say no: He didn't want to get into the attic, he didn't want to make a mess that would be left to him to clean up, the jacket would never fit Tyler anyway…

They were Brian's.

And Brian was gone.

"Please?"

His smile was tight. "We'll see."

"Cool."

Cool because he'd always given in. He'd felt that he had to, that somehow, he needed to make up for the innocence they'd lost, he needed to be someone they could count on because he was all they'd had for so long.

"Because I am not wearing a feather boa."

"What's a boa?" Sammi asked, finally coming to the table, back in her regular clothes.

"What you had on."

"I had on a swimsuit."

"No, dummy, the thing that,"

"That's enough."

Brody barely recognized his own voice when he interrupted their bickering, and it echoed off the walls in the silence that fell across the table afterward. The children were looking at him—Sammi with fear, and Tyler with anger—but neither of them said a word. He set down his fork and rubbed his palms against his jeans.

"No fighting, remember?" he asked as his own heart thumped uncomfortably.

"We weren't fighting," Tyler snapped.

Brody felt a surge of rage.

One he couldn't act on.

One he *wouldn't* act on.

"It's...no name calling, okay?" Brody sat back in his chair, the words *stay calm* repeating in his head.

"Oh." Tyler shrugged and looked at Sammi. "Sorry. But it is a boa."

"It's a swooshie."

"Boa."

"It's both," Brody cut off Sammi's reply, a smile threatening to creep forward.

"Brody..."

Sammi's voice was a bit higher, and he knew she was about to ask his permission for something. He nodded in her direction.

"Do we really have to eat this shit?"

"Samantha Jayne!" He knew he shouldn't be laughing, but trying to stop it was like telling Tyler to pause his video games.

Catherine was right; he needed to watch his swearing around them.

Tyler, of course, was howling with laughter and had even high-fived his baby sister, who still looked at Brody with questioning eyes. "That's what it looks like," she said with a shrug, making Tyler stop and look at his plate.

"It does... ugh, I'm not eating this now. No way."

"It doesn't..." Brody paused and looked down at his plate, grimacing at what he saw. "It's the same stuff we've eaten for... forever."

"And it's gross." Tyler crossed his arms as he shook his head.

Sammi sighed. "I miss Greta."

Greta. The housekeeper who was so much more in that house on the hill.

Greta who had cooked the meals, cleaned up after everyone, looked after the children so that Brody could have some peace and maybe get to be a teenager occasionally.

But it had cost him dearly.

"You need to learn how to cook."

Sammi's sweet voice made him smile. "Yeah, yeah, I know." He was about to ask if they would settle for peanut butter and jelly when there was a soft knock at the door. "Hold that thought."

He crossed the living room that he'd had to clean again after his mother had left for work and, after wrestling with the loosened doorknob, opened the door.

"Hi."

Catherine was smiling up at him, the sun shining on her golden hair giving her the ethereal look of an angel. His eyes roamed down her small frame, taking in her tight black spaghetti strap tank top, her small torn jean shorts, her tanned legs, and her chunky sandals that made her roughly two inches taller.

How did he get so lucky?

Did he deserve to be so lucky?

"Are you going to just stare at me, or can I come in?"

She'd said it with the laugh that always made his heart sing.

"Catherine!" Sammi's excited screech had him stepping aside so his baby sister could jump into his girlfriend's arms as she walked through the door, the pure affection between the two of them a stark difference from Catherine's callous behavior in the beginning.

"Hey," Tyler said to Catherine with a slight smile. He was still sitting at the table, arms crossed, refusing to touch the cooling food before him.

"Come see!" Sammi was pulling Catherine to the table as Brody finally remembered to shut the front door. "We're eating shit!"

"Ohmygod." Catherine stopped to stifle a giggle as Brody corrected Sammi's language.

"But it looks like it."

"It, um… what is it?" Catherine looked over at Brody as he walked closer.

"It's a casserole of some sort. Aunt Sheryl had sent it over, frozen and stuff, so… I heated it up."

"She sent us a *lot* of it," Tyler interjected.

Sheryl had cleaned out her freezer before their move so far away, leaving Brody tied to this house, tied to the children, having to be far more grown than his 17 years.

"Can we go to the gym?" Sammi asked excitedly jumping up and down, and Brody watched as Catherine's expression fell for the briefest of moments.

"I'm sorry, but… no, we can't."

"Why?"

"It's… well, I don't live there anymore."

Catherine's smile didn't reach her eyes.

Did she miss the house on the hill, even though she'd sworn she didn't?

"Are you… Where are you practicing for your cheerleading?"

The blush in Catherine's cheeks was slight, but Brody noticed it anyway as he walked past her. "I'm not in cheerleading anymore."

Brody watched from his chair as Catherine again tried to hide the sadness of everything she had lost. He knew she'd been offered a spot on the squad, as she'd been a varsity cheerleader at Davis High, but she'd turned it down.

And she never told him why.

"I get to dance, though." Catherine was smiling as she took the fourth seat, the one their mother would sit at on the few nights she didn't work. "At the studio that I work at."

"And tumble?"

"And tumble." Catherine's head tilted to the side. "I can bring you there some time, if you'd like."

"Brody, can I?" Sammi's eyes were lit up with excitement.

"I think we should ask Mom," he answered, and Sammi shrugged.

"She'll just leave it up to you."

He kept his eyes on Sammi, even as he noted Catherine's inquisitive look. "We'll ask her."

"Do we really have to eat this?" Tyler slouched, his eyes on his plate of food.

"Can't we just get a pizza?" Sammi added, and Brody tried to hide his sigh.

"I don't,"

"Sure." Catherine smiled as she reached into her black bag that she always carried with her. "Let's do it."

"Cat, don't."

"Let me do this, please."

Her eyes were as gentle as her voice.

"I don't feel right."

"It's the food," Tyler piped up, and Brody bit back a laugh with a soft curse. "He knows I'm right, Catherine. I'm all for pizza."

"Then it's settled."

"Cat,"

"Majority rules." Catherine's triumphant smile had him smiling in return as she pulled out her phone, its pink case a little worse for wear, and called for a pizza.

And even ordered it with mushrooms, although she loathed them.

"Can we throw this away now?" Tyler asked.

"I've got it." Brody stood and took the plates, emptying them one by one in the sink, along with the rest of the casserole, the garbage disposal drowning out the excited talk of going to the pool the next day. Ty and Sammi had always had fun at the pool, especially when he and Brian would take turns picking them up and tossing them about, and...

And this would be their first time there without Brian.

"Hey."

Catherine's arms were around him as she leaned against his back.

"Hey to you." He stood up straighter, placing his hands over hers as he did so. "How'd you get out of grounding a day early?"

"I can be very persuasive."

He turned around, pulling her close into a warm embrace. "Yes, you can."

The store.

The discount clothing store at the overpriced mall.

The one he'd made her take him to in that godawful pink car.

That's when he'd started falling for her, despite her horrid insults and shitty attitude.

Because he saw through it, saw that somewhere deep inside, she was hurting, too, even if she didn't see it.

"Mmmm, this is what I've missed." She cuddled closer and inhaled deeply.

"What, the rank stench of teenage boy?"

"You always smell good." She smiled up at him. "Pizza will be here soon."

He nodded, still in awe that she was here, that she was with him.

He didn't think he'd ever understand it.

"And when it gets here, you can tell me all about this pool we're going to tomorrow. Deal?"

The pool.

Where he'd see her in a swimsuit.

He wondered if she would wear the small white bikini he'd seen her in the summer before, admiring her body from afar as he'd helped Tyler with his batting.

"What is that sly look for?"

She asked the question as she trailed her fingertips across his back, sending a chill through him.

He answered with a smile.

Her lips formed an 'o' even though the word never left her, and she reached up, her glossed lips feeling like a slice of heaven against his.

He hadn't kissed her like this—a soft, gentle promise—in nearly two weeks.

That was two weeks too long.

He longed to hold her to him, drown in her comfort, never surface again to this world that kept taking one thing after another from him.

Instead he just kissed her, as if she were the most precious gift in this world that he'd ever received.

Because she was.

She was.

"Whatcha doin?"

Sammi's question, even though she knew the obvious answer, interrupted the couple. Catherine's breathlessness, the wonder in her eyes was enough to get him through one more night, one more week, one more month until the promise of change was fulfilled.

"They were sucking face, duh." Tyler squeezed by them with an apology as he refilled his glass of milk.

"Hey,"

"It's okay. I won't tell Mom."

Brody led Catherine out of the kitchen by the hand. "What's there to tell Mom?"

"That you were subjecting us to watching you make out with your girlfriend in the kitchen. What else would I tell her?"

Catherine half-snorted in laughter as she and Brody sat side by side on the couch. "Oh, that child is so just like you."

"I've never been like him." Brody was smirking as he said this.

And his smile fell.

Because he had been.

And Frank…

"Brody?"

"It's nothing."

Catherine pulled back from him, one eyebrow raised. He shook his head and moved closer to her, folding her into his arms as he kissed the top of her head.

"It's nothing," he repeated.

Maybe if he said it over and over, it would be the truth.

The box Brody retrieved from the attic sat unopened on the floor of his bedroom. It had been sitting there for well over an hour as he stared at it with tightness in his chest. Most of the boxes containing Brian's belongings hadn't been touched except to move from one place to another. Still, Brody remembered the majority of what he'd packed up as well as each box's contents.

He couldn't forget, even on the days where he wanted to.

"It's not going to open itself."

Catherine's voice broke into his thoughts, bringing a soft smile to his face which widened when she took his hand in hers.

"Do you want me to open it?"

He shook his head. "I've got this." The tape he'd used was easy to peal back, and he crumbled it after he removed it, then tossed the ball into his trashcan. "Two points," he mumbled, the words that Brian would have used had he been in this room.

"Are you sure that wasn't three?"

"Small room," he replied, his heart hammering as he opened the box. This one contained Brian's books as well as the jacket and sunglasses he'd worn that Christmas Eve to JJ's party. Brian was the one who collected yearbooks, even though his mother had said the ones she'd spent money on had been for the both of them.

They'd shared almost everything.

They'd even been close to the same size, although Brody's build had always had more muscle. Brody was the athlete who loved literature and Brian had been into music and theatre. Brian had also been the more outgoing of the two, always smiling, always laughing.

Staring down into the box brought an onslaught of memories along with a fresh wave of anger.

Why?

Why hadn't Brian said anything to him? Brody was sure he would have caught subtle signs, sure he would have talked his brother out of ending his own life. Instead he'd walked into their bedroom that Christmas Day, almost ready to ask Brian why the coat and hat had been laid on his bed...

And he'd seen him.

He'd seen his own face staring up at him, lifeless. Still. One bullet hole in his forehead, his hair spread out behind him, blood and brain matter spattered on the floor... the bed... the wall.

Had Brody screamed? Had he cried?

He couldn't remember.

He couldn't remember if he'd called 911, or if everyone had come home first.

But he couldn't forget his face.

He'd been so sure that Frank had killed him, but he'd left a note.

The note had been tagged as evidence.

He didn't know if his mother had retrieved the note or not.

And Frank... he had... *cried*. He grieved for the perfect boy that he wanted Brody to emulate, and his coldness towards Brody had escalated, and...

"Yes!"

Tyler's exclamation as he entered the room, seeing the coat in Catherine's hands, snapped Brody back to the present. His breath was ragged, shaky as he stared back down in the box.

10... 9... 8...

"Is that what you're wearing tomorrow?" Catherine's voice sounded so far away, as did Tyler's.

"Yeah, and these."

Tyler's hand appeared before Brody, reaching into the box for a pair of black sunglasses.

7... 6... 5...

"How very *Risky Business* of you."

"Now I have something for the pool thing tomorrow. What are you wearing?"

"Probably a bathing suit."

"Good call."

4... 3... 2...

"Oh, wow, this one's old. Hey, who went to Davis High? Frank?"

The sound of that name snapped Brody's head in Catherine's direction. "He's from here." He took the yearbook from her and frowned down at the cover.

"Then that must be your mom's."

"Cool!" Tyler exclaimed. "Let's see!"

"No." Brody's eyes narrowed as he looked at the worn cover, suddenly realizing he had no idea about his mother's side of the family. She never spoke of them, he'd never met his grandparents.

Brody hadn't known his mother had gone to school in an affluent area.

"Brody,"

"I know," Brody snapped at Catherine, then closed his eyes. "I'm sorry."

His real father had been an exchange student. He'd never been told his name, but he was most likely within the pages of the book Brody held in his hands.

He'd never looked through this book before. He hadn't even paid any attention to it while he'd packed up Brian's things.

Was the answer within the pages?

If it was, Brody knew he wasn't ready to find out. He placed it back in the box and closed its top, folding the last edge beneath the first, and pushed it and every emotion it evoked aside.

CHAPTER 5

Running to the Edge

Audrey Benson was the last person Brody thought would be at the community pool, but there she was, all golden caramel skin and dark ringlet curls, her full pouty lips almost mustering half a smile. "Hello, Brody."

"Hey."

He had no reason to be mean towards her; they'd broken up the day he was taken from his home and forced to go to the house on the hill. That seemed like a lifetime ago, and since then, he'd found happiness. And Audrey... well, she'd found notoriety in dating him, the twin of Valley High's golden-boy-turned-tragedy.

She'd used her notoriety well.

"I heard you would be here."

"From?"

"Kate."

That caused Brody to stop short. "Evans?"

"Yeah, who heard it from JJ, who heard it from Max. You know how it goes." She ordered a water from the concession stand behind him before turning towards him, her full breasts nearly spilling out of the top of her bathing suit.

"JJ."

"Yeah, he's back. Kinda like you. Kid sitting still?"

His eyes wandered over to Ty and Sammi, who sat on their towels fumbling with the sunscreen, laughing at something Max had said. "Yeah."

"Heard you're working at Mack's."

"I get it, you hear everything." He wasn't being mean when he said the words, his laughter showing so.

"So where's, um… what's her name?"

"Catherine." He squinted through the early afternoon sun. "She'll be here soon. And stop pretending like you don't know her name."

"Catherine, right." Audrey took a drink of her water. "Well, Kate and I will be over on the other side of the pool." She pointed to the deeper end, where most of the teenagers were congregated. "You can stop by and talk to us. You know, if you're not too busy."

Brody refrained from rolling his eyes. To Audrey, he'd always been too busy.

Audrey didn't know what he had been going through.

"Yeah, well, we'll see."

The pool was busier than usual that day, with a fresh blast of hot air coming in and the summer break finally getting underway. Brody knew most of the people there, if not personally, then at least by name. Most of them were friendly, waving, and saying their hellos, but there were the few who still liked to stare and whisper.

Yeah, his brother was dead.

He had been for just about a year and a half now.

This was his first time back to the pool since then, having chosen to stay away from large crowds, and then being uprooted without much notice. Not much had changed, other than everyone growing older, and some of them growing apart.

Brody spotted JJ on the other side of the pool, his hair bleached out now, a tattoo that had most likely been illegally obtained adorning his left shoulder. JJ had been Brian's best friend and had barely spoken to Brody since the funeral.

Not since he'd told Brody that it was his fault that his brother was dead.

"So." Max greeted him with a grin when he sat on a faded towel alongside Tyler. "They all got into the theme. What about you?"

"I'm here, aren't I?"

"Yeah." Max looked out across the pool where his girlfriend sat high in a lifeguard's chair. "You're here."

"Why didn't you tell me JJ was back?"

Max shrugged. "He comes and goes. Besides, I didn't think you two were talking."

"We're not."

"Should I fix that?"

Brody laughed softly. "Nah, I'm good."

"Can we get in the pool now?" Sammi asked.

"I hear the water is really cold," Max said with a grin. "I don't think Brody here has the guts to get in."

"Dude, really?"

Tyler gave Brody a small shove. "That means you have to dive in now."

"Can you not see the signs that say no diving?" Brody was grinning when he asked the question.

"In the shallow end, chicken."

"Tyler just called you a chicken," Sammi giggled.

"Okay, I see how it is." Brody accepted the challenge and took his shirt off, tossing it to the side before walking over towards the deeper end of the pool. Despite the warning of cold water, many were already in, swimming and splashing around, with the words 'Marco' and 'Polo' being shouted at different intervals. His mind wasn't on any of this, though, as it drifted to years past.

He and Brian would yell to clear a path.

Then they would take off running, a straight shot for the deepest end of the pool.

And they would see who could dive the farthest.

But there were no shouts today, no running to the edge.

There was just Brody, staring down at the water for a moment before diving in, the icy water nearly knocking the breath out of him that he was holding. He emerged, shaking his head, water beads shooting out everywhere. Refusing to let his teeth chatter, he called out to Max, "It's fine! Stop your whining and get your ass in here."

Brody ignored Sarah's calls at him to watch his language, choosing instead to watch as Max ran towards the deep end and cannonballed in, only to come up sputtering.

"Brody, you bitch!"

More calls for behaving themselves were drowned out by Brody's raucous laughter as Max went into great detail about his balls attempting to crawl up to his throat. "Dude, that's Sarah's problem, not mine."

And as Max dunked him underwater to silence his laughter, Brody wondered for the briefest second what would happen if he would simply not hold his breath.

That lone thought had him rising quickly, sputtering for air to Sammi's laughter and Tyler's grin just before he followed Max's lead and cannonballed.

What would have happened to them without him?

They'd needed him for so long. His entire world had revolved around making sure they were good, they were fed, they were clean.

They were safe.

Tyler emerged, immediately kicking more water in Brody's direction as he took off swimming towards his friends on the opposite side of the pool, leaving only Sammi standing at the edge.

Sammi, who looked so sweet, so innocent and young, even as she dove in gracefully.

Like Brian.

So much about this little girl who loved her art and her dancing and her tumbling was just like Brian.

Even her beaming smile as she asked him how she did.

"Perfect." He grinned at her as he treaded water. "Stay close to me."

"Okay." She swam closer and scrunched up her nose slightly, an expression she'd learned from Catherine. "My friends are on the little kid side."

"That's because your friends aren't little fishes!" Max had snuck up behind Sammi and lifted her easily into the air before tossing her.

Just as Brian would have.

If he were there.

Sammi was still giggling as she swam beside Brody towards the side of the pool. "Where's Catherine?"

He scanned the crowd, not seeing any sign of Catherine, or Jen, who probably would have been easier to spot with her brightly colored hair. "Not here yet, I guess."

Sammi contemplated for a moment as she held onto the side of the pool, kicking her feet, the crowd drowning out whatever Max was yelling up to his girlfriend in her lifeguard chair. Her face suddenly lit up with a smile that had her gray eyes twinkling in the sun. "Can I ride on your back? You know, like I used to?"

He returned her smile, his shoulders relaxing as he turned. "Hop on."

With Sammi's arms around his neck, he took off swimming across the pool, worries forgotten as he immersed himself in the joy of simply being a teenager.

"You brought a book to the pool?"

This was Catherine's greeting as Brody was searching through his bag almost 2 hours later. He grinned up at her and shook his head. "I mean, yes, but... no." He finally pulled out the sunscreen and handed it to Tyler before he leaned back. "You're late."

"You know me and... entrances." She shrugged as she sat down beside him. "Or lack thereof." Her grin was slight as she shrugged off her comment, but he knew the last thing Catherine Garner was accustomed to was her appearance not causing even a ripple in the crowd. "Jen's getting something from the concession stand. She'll be right over."

"Hey, don't,"

"No, it's fine." Her soft kiss on his lips wasn't reassuring, but he welcomed it anyway. "Need some help?"

"I got it," Brody said as he took the sunscreen back from Tyler and motioned for Sammi to sit down beside him.

"Hi." Sammi was far from jovial as Brody rubbed sunscreen onto her back.

"What's up with you?"

"We had to get out of the pool."

"Everybody had to." Brody gestured towards the empty pool. "It's break time."

"Tyler said it's because someone peed in it."

Brody bit back a laugh. "No, you know they have breaks." He shifted his gaze towards Catherine, whose expression showed she'd taken the child seriously. "They really are just on a break, Cat."

She pushed her sunglasses back up, shielding her eyes. "If you say so."

"Catherine, the scrunchy... I love it." Max had walked back over, his hand on his heart as he took in Catherine's contribution to the 80's theme.

"I couldn't let you down, Max." Catherine's flirty nature, one that she'd shown at Davis High when doting eyes had been upon her in crowds, wasn't lost on Brody. "I even found these." She reached into her bag, her eyes lit up with excitement at the assorted flavored lip balms that she pulled out.

"Is that Orange Crush?" Sarah had joined them, sitting beside Catherine as she took the lip balm from her.

"Yes! You can have that, if you'd like."

"Women." Max plopped down beside Brody and nudged him. "Shiny, pretty smelling things, and they're done for."

Brody laughed softly and laid back, soaking in the sun. "At least we have ideas of how to appease them."

"Douse ourselves in glitter and perfume?"

Brody closed his eyes. "No thanks. Have at it, though. It suits you."

"What does?" he heard Sarah ask.

Voices muffled and the air around him shifted, the soft orange scent flowing over Brody as Catherine lay beside him.

"Is it okay for the kids to be over there?"

"Hmm?" He looked through one half-closed eye and saw Tyler and Sammi with a few of their friends. "Oh, yeah. They're with the Mathews kids. They're good." He grinned at Catherine again before closing his eyes once more.

"Are you sure?"

"Their parents are over there, Cat. I'm sure."

"Ouch. Okay, cranky."

"I'm not cranky." He peered over as she sat up and removed her shirt, revealing her white bikini top that glowed against her tan skin. "It's just some of us don't get tan just by blinking."

"I don't know where this comes from, aside from it's my dad's family. Theresa pays a lot of money to get this way." She stretched out her legs and tilted her head back, her eyes closed. "Will we be staying in the shallow end?"

He let out a short laugh. "Those kids? Shallow end? No way."

"So you'll be helping them?"

"Tyler and Sammi could do laps around me, no problems."

"I didn't know they were good swimmers."

"Because you wouldn't let us in your pool."

Their silence was filled with the voices of the crowd, so loud it could drown out anything they would have said to one another. Brody glanced over at Catherine, who had turned so she wasn't facing him. He hadn't meant for his reply to be rude; he'd simply been stating the facts. Neither he nor his siblings had been permitted in the pool, and there had been no explanation given.

"Cat,"

"I know," she called over her shoulder, but a smile was in place as Jen joined them.

"Holy long lines for a drink." Jen handed the cup to Catherine, who took a big sip, then shuddered.

"What is that?"

"Dr. Pepper." Jen flashed a grin. "JJ got me hooked on it."

"JJ… the blonde with the guitar?"

Brody sat up slightly, propped on his elbows. "You met JJ?"

Catherine turned her head slightly, and he knew her expression. She was pretending to be in a good mood, pretending to be happy that she was at a public pool.

Pretending she wasn't angry with him.

"He's really nice."

Brody let out a short huff of a laugh. Nice? JJ was far from nice. JJ was the asshole who turned on him when his brother died. That's all he'd ever be to Brody now.

"What is this?" he heard Max say, drawing his attention from his pissed off bikini-clad girlfriend. "Where's your 80's tribute?"

Jen smirked. "I am the tribute."

"Dude." Max's eyes lit up. "You're *Jem*."

"Hardly."

"But you're truly outrageous."

Jen's smirk became a smile. "Yes. Yes, I am."

And Jen had officially become part of their group. Finally, Brody noted, which would make time with his best friend easier. Perhaps with Jen's acceptance, Catherine would understand that she had been accepted, too, even though she still held herself at a distance. Sarah had once called it an 'air of superiority.'

That was just Catherine, though.

To Brody, it was something he'd grown used to, but mostly something he could see through. He knew her insecurities, he knew how traumatized she had been when her group of friends had turned on her the way they had.

He also knew her deep remorse over acting the same.

Today, though, Sarah paid it no mind as she laughed at something that Catherine had said while she stood, whistle in hand to signal that break time was over.

"JJ said there was a party at his house tonight." Jen grinned at Catherine.

"Who's going to be there?"

Brody's eyebrow twitched at Catherine's answer. That was the Catherine he'd known before, the one whose main agenda was appearances and staying atop the social ladder.

"Everyone." Jen shrugged.

Sammi ran over to Brody as the whistle blew, signaling the break was over. "Brody, let's go!"

"We're going, we're going." He was laughing at his sister's enthusiasm, her pure joy of being there, when he caught Catherine's expression.

She was staring at the pool—or, more accurately, at the crowd of people occupying it—as if everything about this place was beneath her.

He held out his hand to her. "Are you coming?"

She smiled up at him, but he knew that smile. He'd seen it months before.

"Maybe in a little bit."

Of course.

"Brody, c'mon." Sammi was tugging on his hand. "Please."

"Okay, short stuff." He turned from Catherine and walked with his baby sister to the deep end of the pool, where Max and Tyler were already swimming, splashing, laughing at each other. "Hey, Max." As Max turned to him, he lifted Sammi, who screeched with delight. "Catch." After Sammi's big splash landed her next to his best friend and she emerged, giggling as she treaded water, he dove in to join them.

CHAPTER 6

That Girl

"The trial has been postponed."

Brody wasn't sure he'd heard his mother's words correctly. "What?" His heart pounded an uncomfortable rhythm as he walked closer towards her.

"The trial." Sandra smiled at him as she busied herself with wiping down the counters in the kitchen, which he had cleaned an hour before. "It's been postponed."

No... no, no, no.

This couldn't be happening... not now, not when he was just getting used to not looking over his shoulder.

When he was just getting used to the idea that Frank might actually get what he deserved.

"Why?"

She glanced over her shoulder before returning her attention to the kitchen. He knew it was busy work, knew she was hiding her expression. What was she hiding? Was it more than this? "I'm not sure. Something his lawyer has done or filed."

"He has a court-appointed attorney."

"Not anymore."

"Fuck." Brody ignored his mother's insistence that he watch his language, focusing instead on calming himself any way that he could.

She hadn't even asked how their day at the pool was, hadn't inquired about Tyler and Sammi's behavior or wellbeing.

If she didn't care about that, then she obviously wouldn't care about what this news would mean to Brody, or what it would do to his fragile sense of safety.

Trial postponed.

New lawyer.

Frank didn't have that kind of money, otherwise he wouldn't have had the court appointed attorney to begin with.

But he knew the people who did.

"I'm going out," Brody announced, again ignoring his mother who was this time questioning where and why. Sure, she cared about those things, but certainly wasn't concerned about leaving her 17 year old son home to raise her kids. But, hey, Frank had a new lawyer, and she seemed rather pleased to hear that.

He changed into jeans and a black t-shirt and ran his fingers through his hair, half to rearrange it, half to calm himself down. He hadn't intended on going to JJ's party, but his mother's revelation had changed that.

He needed to talk to Catherine, and this time it would be about a subject she'd refused to address.

Her grandfather.

He knew she hadn't talked to him since leaving the house on the hill, nor did she plan to despite his numerous attempts to lure her back. As much as he hated putting her in the middle of this situation, the only other option was to go to see the man himself.

That would be disastrous for everyone involved.

His walk was brisk as he made his way to the front door, pausing only when his mother called out to him.

"Tell me you're not going to see that girl tonight."

He turned to his mother, his eyes once again narrowed. "Her name is Catherine, and she's my girlfriend. And what's your sudden dislike of her? All this time you've been happy for me."

"You've just *changed* since she moved here."

"Not really," he said. "You just didn't notice me before. I'm going to JJ's," he added, drowning out her questions, her denials as he walked out the door.

This wasn't the first party at JJ's that Brody had been to. The last had been held two Christmas Eves ago, and Brody had already been hammered before he'd ever walked in the door. He and Max had gotten into a bottle of whiskey that Brody had found hidden in a cabinet whose lock was easily picked, and they'd shared most of it before Max had passed out cold leaving Brody to go to JJ's party alone.

This night, Max was already there with Sarah, laughing raucously at Jen who was losing at beer pong.

To Catherine.

This seemed to be Catherine's element, one drink in hand, commanding an audience as she moved with grace and ease sinking one ball after another.

"Can I at least finish this one? God, what is this shit?"

"Some bottom shelf piss water that my grandma calls whiskey." JJ was close by Jen, his bleached hair sticking out wildly. Brody could see that the tattoo JJ had gotten was a shadow of a guitar with a gray ribbon wrapped around it. Brody admitted to himself that the tattoo was badass, as much of a badass as JJ had apparently become in the time since he'd seen him last.

"Brody, you made it!"

He wasn't sure who'd said it since he'd been too immersed in observing, his normal habit since losing his other half. He pushed himself off the wall beside the door with a grin in place and accepted a freshly opened beer from one of his teammates.

"Wait a minute, I'm on a roll," Catherine called out to him just before landing another shot and throwing her hands up in the air. "And I retire on top!"

Jen downed the shot and smirked. "Bitch."

"Queen bitch." Catherine had a good enough buzz going on that her eyes were hazy when Brody finally reached her. "Tell her, Brody. Tell her I'm the queen."

"She is." He missed what Jen said in return as the music volume rose and everyone's voices along with it. He did notice, though, the way JJ rolled his eyes and turned, leaving the beer pong area and mingling in with the crowd.

"See?" Catherine was still grinning as she placed her arm around Brody's waist and leaned into him. "I'm still the queen."

"Did you ever doubt it?" He placed a kiss in her hair and held her close, her soft floral scent calming him.

"Do I need to answer?" Her eyes were shiny, a bit glazed over. He shook his head, also recalling the unceremonious way her former "friends" had dethroned her. "But it's different here." She gestured with one arm. "Everyone's here. Like everyone. And they're all talking to each other, and... it's like..." She shrugged.

"A community?"

"Yeah." She looked up at him in wonder before scrunching her nose. "It's weird."

One corner of his mouth lifted in a smile. "Depends on your perspective, of course."

She leaned against him with a sigh and took his hand in hers. He marveled at the smallness, the softness of her hand, even with the strength he knew she possessed. Tiny and fierce, that was his girl.

"I suppose Davis was weird to you, then."

He barely heard her words above the music and motioned towards the back door so that they could talk. They wove their way through the crowd hand-in-hand, only letting go once they reached the door. Brody accepted an unopened beer from someone—he couldn't see who—and then walked out onto the back porch with Catherine close behind him. The music and voices muffled the moment he closed the door behind them and he guided her off the slab of concrete that was the porch into the small back yard.

"I thought you weren't coming," she said as she looked up at him, her face illuminated by the light filtering through the windows.

"I wasn't."

"I'm glad you did."

His grin was tight as he opened his beer and took a long drink. There was no Frank at home to throw him into a wall, to tell him he was worthless, that he wouldn't amount to anything.

"I'm spending the night with Jen, and I'm really surprised my dad said yes. I think he had a date or something."

"The trial was postponed." Brody was looking up at the cloudless sky, the dotting of the few stars visible holding his attention.

"What? How?"

He looked at her then, his shoulders relaxing slightly. Catherine's shocked expression was genuine; she hadn't been told anything.

"I thought it was clearly open and shut."

Brody shrugged and took another drink. "He got a new lawyer."

"How did he…" Her voice trailed off and he watched as anger filled her eyes. "Oh, I know how," she said as she pulled out her phone, but she stopped from going any further as Brody's hand touched her arm.

"It's after midnight," he said, his voice low. "Plus you've been drinking. Don't give him ammunition."

"I was going to call my mother." Her nose scrunched up slightly and he couldn't resist kissing her there, right in the crease. "You distract me, you know."

"As you do me."

"I'll call tomorrow." She sighed and tucked her phone back in her pocket. "What if he gets out, Brody?"

"I won't let that happen."

"Hey." Her warm hand against his unshaven face eased another trickle of his anxiousness away. "What if you don't have a choice? What if he gets back together with,"

"She won't take him back," Brody cut her off. "Not after what he's done." His eyes slid shut as she rubbed his scruff.

"I hope for your sake you're right."

He opened his eyes and smiled at the vision she made bathed in moonlight and a slight spotlight from the street light in front of the house. "I'll believe it for now."

For now, when he didn't want to feel the weight of the world on his shoulders.

For now, when he was with this girl, who made him feel like he could accomplish anything, live through anything.

The music and voices were suddenly louder as the back door opened, a small group of girls coming out with cups in hand, laughing at whatever had been mumbled by the tallest girl—Brody's ex, Audrey. Catherine bristled beside him and he gave her hand a small squeeze as the door was shut, again muffling the sounds of the party within.

"Are we interrupting?" Audrey asked with a laugh.

"We were just going in." Catherine's reply was met with a smattering of giggles from the girls. "Is there a problem?"

"Cat, don't," Brody said, his soft voice tired. "Not tonight."

"I thought you were a cheerleader," Audrey said, walking a few steps closer. "You didn't even try out."

"I didn't want to." Catherine's words were clipped, and again Brody tried to calm her the way she did him.

"Where did you go to school before?"

Brody couldn't tell if Audrey was truly trying to be nice to his girlfriend, or what her motives were. She didn't set off the alarms in him that others did, but trying to explain that to Catherine wouldn't go over well at all.

Catherine stood a little taller. "Davis."

"Oh, so that's why you don't talk to anyone," one of the other girls piped up.

Catherine's mouth dropped open. "I talk to people."

"Not really," Audrey corrected her, and Brody groaned inwardly.

"I talk to…" Catherine turned to Brody. "Holy shit, I really don't talk to anyone, do I?"

"Oh, wow, thanks," he said with a laugh to diffuse the tension.

"Wow." Catherine stood there, her eyes wide. "I'm a total bitch, aren't I?"

His laugh was genuine. "Nah."

"Well, we figured you felt like being here was slumming." Audrey shrugged, and the other girls quickly agreed.

"I live here, and… it's a culture shock." She shrugged. "It's… like, everyone is here."

Brody watched as Catherine stepped towards the girls, being the open, party girl he'd seen the previous summer. She had them enthralled in a matter of moments with talks of dances and routines, along with talk of how at her former school there had been such a closed-off feeling, the best of the best refusing to mingle with those they felt inferior. Of course that wasn't the way she worded it, but that was the way Brody had perceived the whole situation there.

He'd hated it.

He'd hated that he'd been told by his then-girlfriend, Bethany, that he couldn't invite his friends from chemistry class to the Lake Party, or the post-Homecoming party, even.

He'd never understood it.

Catherine smiled at him and shook her head as he motioned that he was going back inside for another drink. He kinda loved that about her—yes, she liked to get her party girl side out, but she didn't need to continuously have a drink in her hand. Then again, she was showing them some gymnastics moves. He admired her form for another moment before heading back into the house, the blast of music and voices causing him to shake his head.

"Brody, my man." Max threw an arm around his shoulders. "C'mon in here." He led him into the small kitchen where JJ and Kaitlyn Evans stood with several full shot glasses on the counter. Max took two, handing one to Brody as JJ and Kaitlyn each took one. "To Brian."

"Brian," JJ repeated as he held out his glass. The clink the shot glasses made echoed in Brody's mind, even above the noise of the crowd as he downed his shot and was handed another.

"And to Michael," Max said, and Brody's eyes widened.

"What?"

"We lost him this summer," JJ replied, his first words to Brody since Brian's funeral.

Now JJ had lost a brother, too.

"To Michael," Kaitlyn said as she held out her shot glass.

"And fuck cancer," Max added before their shot glasses clinked again. Brody hesitated only a moment before downing the shot, his eyes still on JJ.

Now it made sense why he'd left.

"I had no idea," Brody began, but JJ brushed him off as he walked past, becoming lost in the sea of people in the small house that cheered loudly as the music changed to something harder, pop music left behind.

"Excuse me," Kaitlyn murmured as she followed after him leaving Brody and Max in the kitchen alone.

"I thought you knew." Max was looking at Brody, his eyebrows furrowed. "I could have sworn you knew. Dude, are you okay?"

Brody nodded despite his pounding heart.

Brian should be there, at that party. He should be the center of attention the way he always was. Audrey should be following him around the way she did before he'd put a bullet in his head and sent her following after Brody, who'd mistaken her attention as affection for him. Brian and JJ should be talking loudly about going to New York after graduation and talking JJ's brother, Michael, into joining them. Brian should be daring Brody to do something wild that would most likely cause physical harm, and Brody would oblige, showing that he would never back down from a challenge, and he would talk Max into joining in.

"Brody,"

"I just need some air," Brody said, setting the shot glass down with a loud thud before pushing his way through the crowd and out the back door. Catherine was still out there, talking animatedly with the girls gathered around her as if she were holding court.

"Maybe we shouldn't be so loud," she was saying with a laugh. "The cops could get called or something."

"Don't sweat it," Max called out to her, startling Brody. He hadn't noticed he'd been followed. "The sheriff's in there having a beer."

"Really?" Catherine asked, and she was quickly assured that he was, and that she could even go see for herself. "Weird," she said then, her eyes again filled with wonder as she and the girls, who were now following her instead of staying back with Audrey, made their way inside, where Brody knew that she would, indeed, see the sheriff there having a beer.

"Where did the bench come from?" Max asked Audrey as he straddled it and sat.

"I think from Randall's," she replied, then looked at Brody. "She certainly likes attention."

"It gravitates towards her," Brody said with a slight nod, knowing that Audrey was referring to Catherine. "Does that bother you?"

"Now that she's not acting like a snob, nothing really bothers me about her."

Brody said nothing in return as he took a seat on the acquired bench while Audrey bid her farewells and went back inside.

"I swear I told you about Michael." Max looked up at the sky. "Not that we knew him well, but he was still JJ's brother." After a beat, he added, "You haven't been back here since, have you?"

Brody shook his head. No, he hadn't been back to JJ's since that Christmas Eve party, where he had been incredibly drunk, where he'd argued with Brian telling him he didn't give a fuck about the consequences.

Where he'd stormed out, stumbling his way to the park where he fell asleep beneath an old oak tree, only waking when the first snowflakes began to fall on Christmas morning. He hadn't even hurried home, figuring he was going to get the beating of his life, possibly even where the bruises would be visible. Maybe he was going to finally go to someone afterwards.

If only he had told someone before.

If only he had gone home to face the music.

Maybe JJ was right.

Maybe it *was* his fault.

"Brody, dude... you listening?"

"I have to go." Brody stood and began walking quickly, bypassing the house, calling over his shoulder for Max to tell Catherine he left.

He couldn't stay.

CHAPTER 7

Alone

"I'm grounded again. Can you believe that?"

Those were the words he woke up to at 7 the next morning when he answered Catherine's phone call. Peering through one eye, he glanced around his room for a moment, shifting to waking mode as he listened to her.

"Can you? I mean, obviously Grandfather has something to hide, but instead of calling me, he berates my father because I must have been drinking. Which I was, since I must have called him and don't remember, but really?"

"Are you still at Jen's?"

"No, I got the 'get your butt home' call just after six. I don't even get to enjoy my day off, and there goes our plans for later. Do you know he even had the 'it's because I love you' talk with me? I mean, I've heard about other kids' parents giving this lecture, but oh, the guilt! What about you? And hey, you could have come in to say goodbye to me, you know."

"Hold on, hold on. I haven't had my coffee yet." He stretched with a groan before he stood and stretched again, listening to Catherine all the while.

"You and your coffee. You're like a 30 year old man sometimes, I swear. And we haven't had us time at all yet this summer, except for that one time that we got busted in your room. My dad still doesn't believe we haven't had sex, by the way. Ugh, the horror of the birds and bees talk with my dad. Did your..." Her voice trailed off about the time he'd reached the kitchen.

"No," he replied sleepily. "Frank never had the talk with me." He pulled down a mug and poured his coffee, a slight scowl on his face when he realized it was already made.

His mother was up already, on her day off.

He suppressed an eye roll as he realized he was most likely about to receive a lecture, too.

"You understand more about sex and how it should be than most adults out there."

He smiled at her declaration. "I'm glad you think so."

"Oh, you would go there," she said with a slight laugh.

"Hey," he countered after his first sip of coffee, "it's your mind that went there."

"And we will... go there... some day, and I sound completely stupid talking about it, so subject change. What was up with your disappearance last night?"

"I..." He closed his eyes, remembering Brian's face the last time he'd seen him alive. "The last time I saw JJ wasn't so great, and I didn't want a repeat. I'll tell you later," he added, knowing that Catherine would want a full play-by-play.

And knowing he could trust her with it.

"How are you on your phone if you're grounded?"

"I did the reverse of the silent treatment. Dad was not impressed. So, voila, I can vent to you and talk to you and you know what?"

"What?"

"I miss living with you. I miss going downstairs and talking most of the night."

He smiled as he touched his chest, swearing he could feel his heart beat faster. "I miss that, too."

"It was more comfortable than the roof."

"That's my place, though. Here, that is." He straightened in his chair as his mom entered the dining area, an automatic reflex as his mind waited for the bark from Frank to sit up straight. He was watching her as she moved to sit at the other end of their small table, her hands folded in front of her. "Can I call you back in a little bit?"

"Of course. Leave a message in case I'm asleep."

"Or on the phone with Jen."

"Or that. I'll talk to you soon."

He said his goodbye and hung up the phone, still looking at his mother. "Is he here?"

"Your father is still incarcerated."

"He's not my father." Brody's eyes narrowed as he watched her shift slightly. "What?"

"Your tone is what. You walking out of this house last night is what."

"I told you where I was going."

"And I know everything that goes on at Nan's." She always called JJ's grandmother Nan, the way that most of them did. "Your attitude keeps getting worse the longer you see that girl."

"Catherine."

"She's not from around here, and I know how privileged girls from her upbringing are."

He thought back to finding the old Davis High yearbook. "Because you were one of them." He hadn't expected her look of shock, even though it only lasted for a moment. "I haven't changed. I still like to read books and take pictures, and yeah, I like this girl. I really like this girl. We screwed up, but that's what kids do. They screw up and they learn from it."

"You've never been so... mouthy."

"You never got on my case. You sent Frank in to do your dirty work." He stood, done with the conversation. "I have to get ready."

"I'm going to be leaving,"

"For what?" He gestured widely with his hands. "For what, Mom? This is your day off. Here's an idea, try being their parent today."

"Brody,"

"I have an appointment," he muttered as he brushed past her, his phone in his hand. He sent an apologetic text to Catherine before gathering his clothes, drawers slamming shut as he pushed against them with more strength than needed. Emerging from his room, he pushed past his mother, ignoring her words as he shut and locked the bathroom door to take a shower and get out of the house.

He couldn't do it fast enough.

"You seem agitated."

Brody glanced at his therapist through the shock of hair that had fallen across his eyes. He pushed it back with his hand, running his fingers through his hair. "Yeah," he finally said. "I am."

"What's going on?"

Everything.

He wanted to scream that word at the top of his lungs. Instead he shrugged. "Name it."

"Catherine."

"Grounded. Again," he added as he shifted in his chair.

"And you are as well?"

He shook his head. "Her father found out she'd been drinking at the party last night."

"At your home?"

"JJ's."

"Is this the same JJ who had told you that you were to blame for your brother's death?"

Brody picked at a string on the hem of his shirt. "Yeah. He..." Brody's eyes narrowed as they dropped to the carpeting, memorizing the patterns. "He lost his brother, too. To cancer."

"Did you know him?"

"Not well. Michael only visited here. He lived in... Chicago? I think? Maybe. Somewhere around there."

"Did you talk with JJ about Brian?"

"No."

"So what happened at this party?"

"I went to talk to Catherine, to see..." To see if her grandfather was the one pulling the strings to get Frank's trial postponed, possibly even get him out of jail.

"Brody, I can't help you if you don't talk to me."

"I think she's seeing him. My mom," he said with a shake of his head. His thoughts were jumbling together, clouding his clarity. "I think she's been going to see Frank, and..." He swallowed over the lump in his throat, the one threatening to close his airway. "I think that he may be getting out soon."

"Oh." He heard the scribbling of her pen as she jotted down notes. "Is this what you went to talk to Catherine about?"

"Yeah, sort of." He looked back up at Laura, whose head was tilted slightly to the side. "Her grandfather is the only one that I can think of who would pay for Frank to have a lawyer. Who knows what Frank has over Catherine's mother, there's such a fuck ton that he could say. He's good like that, you know? Manipulating people."

"And you feel that Frank is manipulating your mother."

"What the fuck else is he doing? He already had her put in some hospital for months and moved us in with Catherine's mother. And he must have been banging her for some time behind my mother's back."

"Brody,"

"Language, I know, but it's true." Brody only then noticed his hands had balled into fists, and he watched them as he straightened his fingers out while counting backwards in his mind.

10, 9, 8

"It bothers you that Frank was having an affair."

7, 6, 5

"That's the adult way to put it, yeah." He sat up straighter and rolled his head from side to side. "But I found out some shit about my mom, too." He paused his counting, saving it for later. "I don't know if all the shit she said about her parents being dead is true, but that yearbook I found... I know it's hers. And it's from Davis."

"Brody." Laura was smiling then. "She said your father was an exchange student she went to school with. You have his name now, right?"

It felt to Brody as if the air had left the room. His *father*. His real father. The man his mother never talked about, and now he had the means to find shit out on his own.

The thought had never occurred to him before.

"I didn't..." He swallowed again. "I didn't look through it."

"Do you want to?"

He did.

He did with everything in him.

But that yearbook had been in Brian's possession when he'd died. Brody had found it tucked beneath his bed and had put it in the box with the rest of his brother's books, along with various other items that were all Brian.

And he'd never mentioned it.

"I don't know," Brody finally said.

"Why is that?"

"What if..."

What if his birth father was worse than Frank? What if he found they'd never been wanted at all? What if, what if, what if... The questions swirled around in his brain, one after the other, a kaleidoscope of what his life could have been.

"It's okay to finish the question," Laura said after some time had passed.

He sat back in the chair and rubbed his temple where a headache was beginning to throb. "Let's just leave it at that."

He didn't even want to go home, let alone go through that box of Brian's things again to find the yearbook. For all he knew, his mother had gone into his room, gone through his things, taken the yearbook to hide again, her past remaining a mystery to him. No, not just to him—to Tyler and Sammi as well. Didn't they deserve to know?

"Can we wrap this up, please?"

"Not until I know that you're okay."

"I'm not going to harm myself or others. Can we wrap it up?"

"Do you want to?"

"I wouldn't ask if I didn't."

"Harm yourself," Laura said, and he looked her in the eye.

"No."

"Do you have feelings or ideations of hurting others?"

"No."

"I can't help you if you don't talk to me."

"So you keep saying, but it isn't like you can change everything that's happened, can you?"

"No, but I can help you through the aftermath, teach you how to help yourself."

"How about next week?" He stood then, showing her that he was truly done with his session. "Yes, I'll be back, yes, I am taking my meds."

"What do you want most right now?"

"To be alone for just… just a little while. Please," he added. When she nodded, he was out of her office and down the hall.

The air was heavy and stagnant with humidity high enough to make breathing difficult if he moved too quickly. Once off the bus, he took his time walking to the park near the center of the small neighborhood. It was devoid of children who were either indoors enjoying air conditioning or at the pool.

He was alone.

With heavy footsteps he made his way to the large tree he had slept beneath that Christmas Eve. The carvings in the trunk of those who were there before him were still visible, though not as plainly as they had been when he would climb this tree with his brother, taking dares from JJ and Max as to who would climb highest and jump farthest.

Brian used to always win, until Brody had gotten into sports. "That's like cheating," Brian would say to him, but Brody would just laugh.

He could finally win. That was all that had mattered back then.

He would take every win back if it could change the outcome.

Brody shook his head, unable to sit by the tree, unwilling to let the memories tell him all the mistakes that he'd made, every time that he'd failed his brother. Instead, he walked to the lone picnic table that remained of the three that had been here when he was Tyler's age. He sat there, his fingertips brushing against the artwork that Brian had carved into the table. Art and theatre were two things that Brian did on his own, excelling in them the way that Brody had with baseball.

Theatre was where Brian had met Audrey.

Brian had introduced Audrey to Brody.

And when Brian was gone, they turned to each other in a way Brody had thought was love.

He knew better now.

Laura had said that sometimes people talk out loud to the ones they've lost, as if they were right beside them. Had Brody done that? He doubted that he had, aside from calling out to show him something only to be reminded that he wasn't there anymore.

Just like this piece of his artwork would be gone when this picnic table met its demise.

Everything began to blur as tears stung Brody's eyes, and he covered them with his hands, trying to will them away. Even after the first sob broke through, he was sure he could control it, sure that he could push it all back down for another day.

He couldn't stop them anymore than he could hold back his screams when he looked down at his own brother—at the face that mirrored his own—with the blackened hole where the bullet had gone through, his cold, dead eyes staring up, up, up...

"You asshole," he muttered before another sob tore through him.

And another.

And another.

"You fucking asshole," he cried into the crook of his arm as he laid his head down on that table, beside the art his brother had carved, unsure if he was talking to Brian or himself.

CHAPTER 8

Sandykins

It was late in the afternoon before Brody walked into his home, only going there after he'd received a text from his mother stating the kids were with their friends and that she had gone out to run errands. He wasn't sure what he would be walking into when he opened the door to his room, but it was the same as he'd left it, including clothing being thrown over the box of Brian's things. That didn't mean his mother hadn't gone searching for the yearbook; she could have easily replaced objects she'd moved. The only way he would know is if he looked himself.

And then he could look through its pages, find his real father's name, see his face for the first time that he could recollect. It wasn't even a subject that could be spoken about, at least for as far back as he could remember. Frank was their father, or so he would scream whenever Brody would remind him that he wasn't. The last time he'd asked what his real father's name was had been when he was 10, and it had resulted in his mother stating that their birth father hadn't wanted them.

Was that the truth?

He'd never thought of his mother to be dishonest. She'd often looked the other way, but he hadn't known her to be deceitful.

Or had she been all along?

Or… or maybe this was Frank's doing, too, making her say something that wasn't true.

Brody inhaled sharply before closing his bedroom door, knowing that it would stick and should his mother come home, she wouldn't be able to open it. He pulled the clothing off the top of the box, tossing them into the dirty clothes basket before he sat beside the box, his own hand writing along the side.

Brian

He pulled the box open and pushed the top contents aside, finally reaching the books beneath. The yearbook stuck out, one white corner bent downwards, and Brody lifted it out, sitting it on his lap. If Catherine had been there, she would have come up with some dramatic sound bite or a witty remark to make him smile, to calm his racing heart.

But she wasn't there.

It was just him and the book that looked like it had barely been looked at over the years. Judging by the year on the cover, and the fact that his mother had told him she'd dropped out of school when she was pregnant, she would be an underclassman. He started back through the Freshmen, no Sandra Montgomery present. Moving up to the Sophomores, he scanned the pages, stifling a laugh when he saw Catherine's mother.

"Theresa Davis," he said aloud. "Fucking figures. School probably is named after their family."

He flipped a few more pages, finding Catherine's father, unable to stop the laugh. Coach with a mullet; this was priceless.

He took his phone out and captured a picture of it, making a mental note to send it to Catherine as soon as he found what he was looking for. Again not finding his mother in that class, he moved up to the Juniors.

No Sandra Montgomery.

This had to be a mistake. She'd told him that their father was a foreign exchange student and that she'd dropped out of school. There was no way that she'd been a senior the year this had come out.

But there she was, within the colored pages, big hair and even bigger smile, an absolute radiant beauty. She looked relaxed, happy, with the brightest of futures ahead of her. Long before she'd watched her husband throw her second eldest child into their front door with a hallowed expression, long before she'd buried her oldest child.

For so long, Brody had felt a twinge of guilt over even being born, hearing often how his mother couldn't finish school due to her pregnancy. Apparently it hadn't happened in high school, though, as he saw a picture of her receiving her diploma towards the back of the book, only then remembering he hadn't looked for anyone resembling himself. Neither he nor Brian looked anything like their mother, and judging by the way Frank would sneer at him, Brody always assumed he looked like his biological father.

Maybe he was wrong about that, too.

When he heard the front door open, followed by Sammi's excited chatter, he stood with the yearbook in his hand and shoved it under his pillow, in case his mother came looking for it. He wasn't ready to give it back to her just yet; he wanted answers first.

He tugged his door open and walked down the hallway, the smell of fast food hitting him in the face, reminding him he hadn't eaten in quite some time. "What's going on?"

"I got your usual," his mother said as he entered the dining room, where she was pulling sandwiches and fries from the bags and setting them around the table. "I figured you'd be hungry."

Sammi's jovial mood as she sat smiling triumphantly in her spot had him smiling as well. "I asked for this, see?" She held up a French fry. "I'm brilliant."

"Oh, so that's the occasion," Brody remarked.

"Mom didn't want to cook," Tyler spoke up as he opened the wrapper to his sandwich. "And you can't, so we all win."

Brody threw a fry at his little brother. "I can."

"You suck at it, though."

"Shut it." Brody was smiling, which turned into more of a smirk when his mother told them to settle down.

"We are going to have a nice family dinner together." She emphasized the last word, and Brody felt an edge of guilt sliver into his subconscious.

"Of course." He grinned slyly, unable to let part of his revelations slide. "Sandykins," he added, and Tyler began to laugh.

"Sandykins?" Tyler held up his hand, which Brody high-fived.

"What's a Sandykins?" Sammi asked.

"Ha ha, very funny, you two." Sandra's deadpan reaction only had Tyler and Brody laughing more. "I would like my yearbook back. And how did you end up with it, anyway?"

"Brian had it." Brody's laughter was gone even though he somehow kept his smile intact.

"Is that so? Hey, no phones at the table," she added as Brody pulled his out to see what the buzzing notification had been for.

"It's just Max."

"I don't care, put it down."

Brody stole a quick glance at the text. "I'm going over there after dinner."

"What happened to asking?"

"Sandykins, may I?"

Tyler was doubled over with laughter, and even Sammi was giggling at this point.

"Very funny. Be back before 11."

"I was going to spend the night." Brody watched her expression as he ate a few of his fries, seeing if she'd had any plans that she'd failed to mention. If she had, she didn't let it show.

"Don't you work tomorrow?"

"No, I don't."

"Be home before noon. And no, this doesn't get you out of family dinner. Phone away, it's time to eat."

Sammi threw a fry at her mother. "Chill out, Sandykins."

"See what you two started?" Sandra asked above her children's laughter. "No throwing food, Samantha. Don't pay attention to the heathens."

"What's a heathen?"

"Never mind, just eat."

"I'd stop asking questions like that if you'd just buy me a dictionary."

"You wouldn't even know how to work one," Tyler said.

"Do so."

"Do not."

"Children." Sandra was trying not to laugh along with them. "Let's… all of you, eat," she added as the home phone began to ring.

"No phones at the table," Tyler piped up as Sandra picked up the receiver.

"Very funny," she said to him as she stood. "I have to take this."

Brody watched her through slightly narrowed eyes as she answered the phone, taking it with her down the hall towards her bedroom. The only way to see if she was accepting a phone call from Frank was to listen in, so he stood, taking his own phone with him. "I'll be back."

Tyler and Sammi's laughter and conversation was muffled once Brody made it back to his room and shut the door, although not by much. The walls were rather thin, making it easy for him to hear his mother's side of her phone conversation.

"Yes… I know, but he's asking questions, and I don't think I can just put it off, or not answer them."

Brody stiffened, knowing she was talking about him, about his questions regarding his real father.

"He's not going to take that for an answer anymore, and… yes, I know." Sandra sounded nearly defeated, as she did so often. "They're good. Samantha wants a dictionary."

Samantha… not Sammi, or even just Sam. Another sign that she could be talking with Frank.

Deciding to be productive with his time, he grabbed his backpack and began filling it with items he would be taking with him to Max's for the night. As he heard his mother recount his therapy and hopes that it would help his anger, he scowled. According to Laura, his anger had been justified. His life wasn't full of sunshine and rainbows, instead holding pockets of despair and tragedy sprinkled with tiny lights of hope, flickering distantly.

He could be done with all of this soon.

He would be 18, and then he could get away from there, only be responsible for himself instead of carrying the weight of parenting his younger siblings and holding himself to someone else's standards of who and what he should be.

If his mother was going to let Frank back in, would he allow himself that freedom?

As he heard his mother's exclamations of disbelief at the mess that Tyler and Sammi had made in his absence, he grabbed the yearbook and stuffed it inside his bag.

He had a lot of decisions to make, and the time to do so was running out.

"Am I a shitty friend?"

Brody asked Max the question out of the blue as they played their video game late that evening.

"Where is this even coming from? Dude, you just shot me. We're on the same team. Not cool."

"Just thinking is all."

"Oh, that's a change for you." Max's voice dripped of sarcasm. "And no. It sucked that you left, but I get it. And I get that you didn't have your phone and shit like that. Nice shot," he added as Brody took out one of their online opponents.

"JJ was gone, too," Brody added, without having to say they'd also lost Brian.

"Which I also got. At least he had his phone. Fuck Frank, by the way. Glad he's gone."

Brody grinned slightly. He'd never gone into details with anyone other than Catherine, and she only knew because she'd witnessed Frank's actions firsthand. "Yeah, I second that."

Still, Brody felt like he'd let Max down. Would Max have simply stopped all communication because some asshole had told him to? Probably not. The short emails he'd sent when he'd been at school hadn't been any more than 'I'm alive,' and Max deserved better than that.

All of Brody's friends had deserved better than that.

And yet, he hadn't kept any lines of communication actually going, hadn't turned to his friend when his own world turned darker than it ever had been.

Instead, he'd turned to Catherine.

Had he done so simply because she'd been there? No, he knew better. He wouldn't have opened even the slightest crack of a door to her had she not shown her heart to him.

Had Frank not uprooted them, had he not been screwing around on Brody's mom, where would they be then?

"Never thought your mom would do it. Get rid of him, I mean."

"Right?"

His mother hadn't had a choice, though Brody often thought that she never would have gone that far. Frank had decided for her, shipping her off to a mental facility while he took Brody, Tyler, and Sammi away from the only home they'd known.

"Good for her," one of their opponents spoke up. "Are you lovebirds done?"

Max shot at the person's character, missing. "Not even close."

Another player showed up, joining their team, and Brody smiled as he recognized the player's name. Queen C, which suited Catherine in more ways than she knew, took out the opponent that Max had missed. "What would you two losers do without me?"

"Lovebirds," Max corrected her. "Or did you miss that moniker?"

"Nope. I figured I'd catch both of you on here, since neither one of you are answering texts."

"Your father does not understand the concept of grounding, does he?" Brody asked with a grin.

"Don't tell him that when you two get your butts over here. That's an order, by the way."

"Don't fuck with the queen," one of the opponents spoke up, which Catherine soon agreed with.

"We have a purple haired princess over here celebrating a birthday," she continued. "Don't even shoot that at me, peasant." She took out another enemy character.

"Is there cake?" Max asked.

"Not yet. You need to bake it, so hurry."

"I get to bake?"

"Pansy," an opponent called out, and was soon taken out by Brody.

"Let's get this done, so says your queen."

Brody smiled. "As you wish."

CHAPTER 9

Over the Threshold

B rody felt the first wave of calm the moment Catherine opened the door and jumped into his arms, her legs wrapped around his waist and her arms around his neck as she showered his face with tiny kisses. He held her there, his arms around her waist instead of having his hands on her ass right in front of her father.

"Hey Coach," he said with a sheepish grin.

"Hey yourself. Are you seriously carrying my daughter into the house?"

"Over the threshold," Catherine said with a giggle, then kissed Brody's unshaven cheek one last time before releasing her hold on him. He still held her waist and they shared a smile as he lowered her to the ground.

"Yeah, no thresholds. And no touching the beer," he added as Max walked towards the kitchen. "I'm not about to lose my teaching license."

"No shenanigans, Mr. Garner." Max held up one hand. "Scout's honor."

"That's not even the scout's salute."

"Minor details, JJ, minor details."

Brody walked over towards the couch where Jen sat beside Sarah, her smile beaming. "Hello, birthday girl," he said to her as he set his book bag down and unzipped it. "You must wear the birthday boa." He pulled out Sammi's red feather boa and draped it around Jen's neck.

"That's a swooshie," Max called from the kitchen.

"Sorry, you're right. Birthday swooshie." Brody shrugged and sat down beside the couch. "Happy birthday."

"And Jen's the baby," Catherine added as she sat beside him. "She's just now turning 17."

"Dude." Max stepped out of the kitchen, carton of eggs in his hand. "You're only going to be 17 when you graduate next year?"

Jen lifted one shoulder in a slight shrug. "It has its perks." She moved as Sarah got up to join her boyfriend, who went back into the kitchen.

"The mix is on the counter, Max," Catherine said over her shoulder.

"Oh ye of little faith," he replied. "I can make it from scratch."

"We know what your hand's been scratching," JJ shouted over the girls, which was met with laughter and Coach saying he didn't want to know before walking back to his bedroom.

"I'm telling you," Max continued, "there are all of the ingredients here for me to make a cake, a real cake. And doesn't our Jen deserve the best? By the way, Jen, had we known you were this awesome, you would have been *our* Jen for years."

"I've known," JJ said as he nudged Jen's knee.

"You're my cousin, that's bias right there. And besides, we all know Max is intimidated by my photographic prowess."

Even amidst the multiple conversations going, Brody was able to tune them all out when Catherine snuggled up against him. He draped his arm around her and held her close, leaving a soft kiss in her hair before resting his forehead against hers.

"How did you talk your dad into this?"

"It wasn't that hard." She smiled and crinkled her nose. "I kinda started crying when Jen told me she'd never had a birthday party."

That's the Catherine he'd fallen for. Her compassion, once she'd tapped into it, was overflowing. She would risk everything to help.

He knew this firsthand.

"I didn't even have to ask, really. I just told him why I was crying, and that was it. He's using the whole faith thing letting Max into his kitchen, but Sarah swears he can bake."

"I wouldn't know. He did set the kitchen in our old place on fire making mac and cheese, though. Don't worry, Cat," he added when her eyes grew wide. "We were 13 at the time."

"Has he baked for you?"

One corner of Brody's mouth lifted. "He must not think I'm special enough." His smile grew as her hand caressed his cheek, but he refrained from kissing her. "I'm glad your dad agreed to this."

"Me, too. Oh! JJ was playing some of his music for us. He's really good, you know? Like professional good."

"I haven't heard him play in awhile."

"Did you know Jen before?"

"Yeah, kinda. She was really quiet, kept to herself."

"She's definitely not quiet now."

"No, she isn't," he said with a soft laugh. "I'm happy for you, you know?"

"It's so weird learning what friendship really is, or what it's supposed to be. I mean, Chelsea and I... we did practically everything together, but it was always a contest."

Brody pushed Catherine's hair behind her ear, caressing her cheek with his thumb. "No contest."

"And this... you." He felt her take his hand and the rest of the world melted away a fraction more. "I know how this is supposed to be, how it's supposed to feel."

"This is real." Refraining from kissing her in her home with her father walking around was more difficult than he'd anticipated. "And we'll get our time, our night out."

"If I quit screwing up and getting grounded."

"Just a hint, Cat." He glanced around before looking into her eyes once more. "Again, I must tell you, this is far from grounded."

Her grin was mischievous. "I still know how to get my way."

"As always." He teased her lips with the softest kiss, one he couldn't resist giving her.

"Easy on the PDA, lovebirds," Mr. Garner said as he walked past them. "Max, what are you looking for?"

"Food coloring."

"What do you need that for?"

"The cake. Trust me, Mr. Garner."

"Famous last words," JJ muttered.

"Okay, now that *that* is taken care of..." Mr. Garner stood in the living room with a box in hand.

"Is that an actual VHS tape, Dad?"

"Yes, my darling daughter, it is." He removed the tape from the box with a smile. "The *original* Star Wars."

"No way," Brody said with a touch of awe as he stood, and he and the rest of the boys gathered around Coach, their eyes wide as if they were seeing the actual Holy Grail.

"Where do you think I got my love of Star Wars from?" Catherine asked from behind them.

"Does it still play?" Brody asked.

"Check with the birthday girl to see if she wants to watch it first," Coach suggested.

"Oh, I'm in. Sarah?"

"Hell, yes."

"That's my girl," Max said, beaming with pride as he walked past her towards the kitchen. "Wait until I have this in the oven."

"Hey, I'm the birthday girl. What if I don't want to wait?"

"I still have to get this contraption hooked up."

"I got it, Coach," Brody said, stepping in to hook up the VCR. "Old school plugs and everything."

"Here's the converter. It isn't as hard on you to get up and down off the floor as it is this old man."

"Dad," Brody heard Catherine say, "are you seriously going to be out here chaperoning?"

"I'm here for the movie. Scout's honor, and I actually was a scout."

"Here are the chips," he heard Sarah say just as he finished. Catherine was now sitting on the other side of the room, closer to JJ. Brody smiled when she stood to give him room, and this time when he sat on the floor, knees drawn up, she sat between his legs and leaned her back into him. When he wrapped his arms around her, she took her hands in his, interlacing their fingers together.

Brody leaned in, speaking as discreetly as he could. "Kinda bold move in front of your dad."

"Bold would be turning around and…"

"Cake is in!" Max's exclamation cut off the rest of Catherine's sentence, but she and Brody shared a knowing smile as Coach hit the play button.

"Nothing beats the original," Max was saying as he and Brody were helping gather dishes to take them to the kitchen. For Brody, it had almost been like seeing the movie for the first time. He hadn't even watched the enhanced version since he'd walked into Catherine's room in that house on the hill.

"If we could get that on digital,"

"No, man, just like that." Max nodded his approval at his own statement. "Yep, just like that."

"I don't have a VCR."

"Yeah, neither do I. I didn't even know they had remotes back then."

"Heard that," Coach said as he brought in a few cups they'd missed. "You're lucky you can bake so well. I may hire you for the holidays."

"Really?"

"No, not really, but it was still good. Thank you, Max."

"Anytime, Mr. Garner," Max said with a proud grin before walking out to the living room to say his goodbyes to his girlfriend. The sun had long set, and the boys were all getting ready to leave, despite wanting to stay.

Brody was rinsing the dishes and handing them to Coach who was placing them in the dishwasher. "Did you know my mom back in high school?" The question was innocent enough, and Brody figured it would be the perfect place for him to start.

"I didn't hang out with her, but yeah, I knew her. Or of her, I should say. She was a couple years ahead of me."

"What about my dad?"

"Frank didn't go to school there."

"Not Frank." Brody paused for a moment. "My real dad."

Coach stood up and studied Brody's expression. "Have you talked to your mom about this?"

"So you did." Brody rinsed off another dish and handed it to him, not wanting to say how little he'd been told.

"I was Theresa's date at their wedding."

Brody almost dropped the glass he was rinsing out. Another lie… how many had she told? "What wedding?"

Coach shook his head. "Ah, kid. You're fishing for information, and I played right into it."

"Coach, please." Brody could feel the familiar sting in his eyes. "I don't know anything about him. I… my mom told me she dropped out of school to have me. Us, I mean us, me and Brian." How could he slip like that? Brian had existed.

And so did their real father.

"She probably did."

"But it was college."

"It would have been, yes." Coach sighed and placed a hand on Brody's shoulder. "I didn't know him personally, just as a guest at a wedding in a ballroom full of people I had nothing really in common with, and I drank myself stupid."

Brody nodded, his eyes downcast to hide the threatening tears. "What about a name?"

Coach was silent, but gave his shoulder a squeeze.

"I just want to know."

Coach nodded as he stepped back, closing the dishwasher. "I'll call a few old high school friends, see if they remember anything."

"You don't know his name?"

"Something Greek, I believe."

"So at least that part was true."

"You're a good kid, Brody. Don't let your parents' mistakes rule your head, or your heart. I know the situation sucked, but I'm glad you were there for my daughter. And I'm here, if you need to talk."

"I'm back with that therapist, the one the court wanted me to see before."

"Good." Coach smiled at him. "Good."

"Dude, what the hell is in your bag?" Max asked from the living room. "It weighs a ton."

"Oh, right." Brody grinned at Coach. "Maximilian, I have something to show you."

"This better not be gross, or you can't show him here," Catherine warned as Brody walked out to the living room and took his backpack from Max.

"Judge for yourself." He was still grinning as he pulled the yearbook out and flipped to the page he had marked, handing it to Max.

"Mr. Garner! You had a mullet?"

"What are you... ah, hell." Coach was shaking his head with a grin as the yearbook was passed around before Catherine grabbed it.

"I'm *dying*," she said, her eyes wide with amusement. "Brody, how could you have not told me about this?"

"I was going to, I just got distracted." His grin was subtle as he reached for the yearbook, which Catherine was examining more closely.

"A mullet *and* a mustache? Dad, please."

"I was trying to grow it all out. That was a total failure until college."

"I should have looked through this when we first found it," Catherine continued as she reached in her back pocket for her phone.

"I already took a picture of it; I'll send it to you."

"Wonderful. Great. You're going to show all of your friends that your old man succumbed to the times and listened to metal all at once."

"Yeah, what's… Slayer?" Jen asked as she took one last peek before Brody reclaimed the yearbook, placing it in his backpack.

"Don't get him started on his music," Catherine warned. "Besides, we still have *Goonies* to watch."

"You're making us leave when they're watching *Goonies*?" Max placed a hand over his heart. "That's harsh."

"Kaitlyn's on her way to Nan's," JJ said. "I'm out."

"Boys…"

"Yeah, my mom's asking where we are. Embarrassing." Max shuddered before starting his round of goodbyes.

"Coach?"

"We'll talk soon, Brody."

Brody smiled. "Thank you."

After he'd hugged Sarah and Jen, making sure to squeeze the birthday girl extra hard, he walked outside with Catherine, hand-in-hand as they waited for Max to stop telling Jen, who'd never seen *Goonies*, exactly why she'd love it. "What was that all about?"

Catherine looked up at Brody, her face illuminated by the porch light.

"Apparently it's all about *Goonies*, which I have a feeling is going on as soon as we get back to Max's house."

"With my dad."

"Oh, that." He squeezed her hand. "He's going to see if he can find out about my dad. My real one, the one... Apparently they were married, and I'm kinda fucked up about it." He knew that was an understatement, but had no other words for it.

Married.

He hadn't been the bastard that Frank had sworn he was all the times he used it as a weapon.

You're just a bastard anyway.

"Married? In high school?"

Brody shook his head. "After, and... it's a long story," he said as Max finally walked out the door.

"Ready to go?"

"We'll talk about it soon, I promise," he said, and Catherine smiled as he leaned down to kiss her.

"I'll see how soon I can get out of grounding."

"This is not being grounded, FYI," Max piped up. "Don't let your dad talk to my parents. They'd set him straight."

"The cake was amazing," Catherine said as she threw her arms around Max. "You're so my favoritest ginger ever."

"Hear that, world?" Max stepped back. "Queen C has dubbed me top ginger."

"Have fun," Brody said to Catherine, kissing her one last time before he left.

He was close to having answers, he could feel it.

But if they were what drove Brian over the edge, would he really want to know them?

CHAPTER 10

Sounds Contagious

Spiking temperatures kept Brody and the kids inside on what would have been the day Frank's trial started. The air conditioning wasn't set to a cold temperature, but at least taking the humidity out of the air made their house tolerable. Brody didn't even mind that his coffee was cold as he sat at the kitchen table scrolling through Facebook as the sun filtered through the thin curtains.

"Keep everything closed up as much as you can," his mother was saying as she slipped her shoes on. "I'm not sure how late they'll keep me there tonight, so don't wait up."

He nodded, not much for words without proper caffeination.

"I'm running errands before work."

Again, he nodded, even though one eyebrow jumped upward at his mother's statement. She'd been 'running errands' a lot lately. His phone began vibrating and he looked down, seeing Catherine's name pop up.

"Haven't finished my coffee," he mumbled when he answered.

"Nikos Kostopoulos."

"Sounds contagious."

"Very funny. That's his name. Nikos Kostopoulos."

He wasn't sure if his mother could hear Catherine, but if she had, she said nothing as she left. Brody's own silence was born of shock.

He knew his father's name.

"Are you there?"

"Yeah, yeah. That… that's… wow."

"You're definitely Greek. Oh, and dad said that he was a P.K."

"Preacher's kid? Wow, how did Mom end up with him?"

"Think of what school your mom went to, Brody. Not preacher's kid; producer's kid."

"What else did you find out?" He was suddenly awake and full of questions. "Did he go to Davis? Is he here or in another country?"

"I don't even know how to spell it yet. Give me time, though. I'm a master sleuth. I can probably tell you his mother's maiden name before the day is over."

"Really?"

"Probably not, but if he's on social media, I'll find him."

He sunk back in his chair, trying his best to wrap his head around the news.

"Brody, are you listening?"

"You said you'll find him."

"Wow, you really are asleep. I said our air conditioning is out and Jen isn't home. Is it okay if I come over?"

Technically the standing rule after their earlier debacle was that Catherine couldn't come over unless his mother was home. At that moment, though, in his shock that was mixed with anger over his mother's deception, he didn't give a damn what her rules were. "Yeah, of course. I'll leave the door unlocked."

"I can't just walk in."

"You can if I say so." He took another sip of coffee, deciding then he didn't like it cold. "I'm going to take a quick shower."

"She's not home, is she?"

"No, she just left with another set of errands that she comes up with nearly every time I have a day off."

"So we're rule breaking. What rebels we are. Trust me, I can't get out of this sauna of a house quick enough. I'll be right over."

The kids were restless, but willing to play video games as Catherine searched the internet on her laptop. There was plenty of room on the couch, but Brody sat in the newly acquired beanbag with Catherine on his lap, his arms around her, drawing in her comfort.

"You know," she was saying as he nudged her hair back with his nose and began leaving soft kisses, a trail from her jaw down to her collarbone. "I thought... I can't think straight when you do that... I thought that you and JJ were fighting or something."

"Or something," Brody murmured against her skin, smiling as a shiver ran through her.

"You seemed fine the other night."

"He ignored me the other night," Brody whispered in her ear, not wanting to talk about JJ or any of the myriad of emotions that he kept bottled tightly inside.

All he cared about was her.

"He did, didn't he? I didn't notice."

"We sat wrapped up like this."

"Similar, only this time your brother and sister are in the same room."

Brody growled his frustration and rested his chin on her shoulder. "I know."

"What, is the show over?" Tyler asked, his eyes never leaving his character on the screen.

"Funny," Brody mumbled.

"I think I figured out how to spell it. Here."

In the search bar of her account, Catherine had typed Nikos Kostopoulos, and a small amount of search matches listed below. Brody's heart hammered as he looked at the profile pictures one by one.

This was it.

After years of wondering, he could potentially take a glimpse into his birth father's life.

"Should we look at this one?" Catherine asked, pointing to a profile picture of landscape with an older stone building in the corner.

"Can we wait?"

"Whatcha looking for?" Sammi, always the curious one, asked.

Catherine shut her laptop. "Just things." She stood and stretched, and Brody watched the hem of her tank inch up. He had an idea of just things, being a hormonal teenage boy incredibly infatuated with this girl.

Just like every other day, though, he had obligations and responsibilities that, to him, belonged on the shoulders of the mother who didn't seem concerned enough to stick around.

"I should probably go." Catherine turned towards Brody as he shook his head. "No? What if your mom comes back and I'm still here?"

He shrugged and took her hand, leading her down the short hallway to his room. He honestly didn't care if he was caught, not at that moment. His anger towards his mother for the secrets she'd obviously been keeping his entire life overrode his reason, the way it had been doing whenever he allowed himself to think of how his entire life had been a lie.

That was more often than not as each piece of truth edged its way in.

Once in his bedroom, he pushed the door to, without closing it all the way, and silenced Catherine's question with a kiss, one he poured his heart into as he cradled her face in his hands.

"I can't get over that, you know." Her breathlessness brought a touch of a smile to his lips.

"Get over what?"

"You treat me like I'm precious."

He allowed his fingertips to linger against her skin as he pushed her hair back. "You are. Hey." He kissed her temple. "That's not supposed to bring tears to your eyes."

"I can't help it." Her lips turned up in a trembling smile, one that melted his heart. "I don't know if I'll ever get used to someone treating me like I matter, like I'm not some horrible human who they only want something from."

"I want your happiness. Does that count?"

She wrapped her arms tightly around his waist and rested her head against his chest as she held him close. He couldn't find words at that moment, the ones that would tell her that she did the same for him, that she made him feel alive, warm, safe.

Loved.

Even though she'd never said the words to him, the same words he was still learning to accept despite believing he was unworthy, he felt *loved*.

He held her close, reveling in emotions swirling within, warmth and comfort chiseling away at words yelled at him in anger, in rage.

Can't you do anything right?

You are such a waste.

Maybe if you were more like Brian, you wouldn't be a disappointment.

Just get out of my face. You make me sick.

But Frank's voice was nowhere to be heard when Catherine turned her face and left a kiss over Brody's heart. "I'm so happy that you're in my life."

He inhaled deeply, her soft floral scent permeating his senses, and he left a soft kiss in her hair. "You're the best thing that's ever happened to me, Cat. Ever," he added before he pulled back and lifted her chin with his fingertips. Their eyes met, searching for the confirmation that this was real, that they each had meant what they said. He leaned down and rested his forehead against hers and lifted his lips in a whisper of a smile. "Tiny and fierce, that's you. When you care about something or someone, nothing stops you. I've always admired that."

"Always?" There was a hint of sarcasm in her voice that made him laugh softly. "Even when I was a raging bitch?"

"Like you were so enamored with me when we first met." He kissed the tip of her nose as she crinkled it. "And that is so fucking adorable."

"My nose?" She giggled as he kissed it again.

"That expression." He dropped a soft kiss on her forehead. "Everything about you. The way you move... it's mesmerizing."

Her head tilted to the side. "How so?"

"Every movement flows together with ease, with grace. It's..." He gazed up at the ceiling trying to gather his thoughts, the right words as his heart urged him on. "It's everything, Cat. From the way you walk to the way you do a cartwheel or a handstand, to the way you climbed that tree in my back yard. I don't think you realize that confidence—you know, the thing you swear you don't have anymore—it shows. And it's a beautiful thing. *You're* beautiful. Everything about you is,"

His words were cut off as she kissed him with such gentleness that his own eyes stung with unshed tears, the way hers had.

Was this really love?

Would she turn against him in his time of darkness, when he needed her the most?

"Hi, Mommy!" Sammi squealed with delight from the living room, and Brody groaned.

"Fuck," he muttered, then looked down at Catherine.

"Do I have time to hustle out the window?" He knew she wasn't serious, especially with that touch of sadness in her eyes. Her laptop was out in the living room, and there was no mistaking that it was hers.

"Brody?" His mother's voice was angry, sparking his own anger, that sense of betrayal he now felt any time she was near.

"Don't." Catherine placed her hand against his cheek, only this time he didn't feel her warmth.

"What?" That was all he said as his mother pushed his door open.

"It's time for you to go home," Sandra said to Catherine, her eyes cold.

"Needed to anyway," Catherine said nonchalantly, then she turned to Brody. "I'll see you soon. Let me know what you find."

"I promise," he replied, then placed a soft kiss on her lips. "Excuse us." He said those words to his mother, who put her hand out.

"No, you stay put. I need to have a word with you."

Once she passed Sandra, Catherine turned towards Brody, mouthing the word "please." He knew she was asking him to keep his temper in check, and he was trying.

He was trying his hardest.

"What part of she's not allowed here when I'm not home did you not understand?"

"It's pushing triple digits outside and their air is out." He shrugged. "I was being gallant."

"You were being disrespectful."

There was that word again, being hammered into his brain with a pair of angry eyes on him. Was that a look of disgust on her face?

"I was being a good boyfriend."

"As compared to a good brother who wouldn't have been back here with his door shut having sex with his girlfriend." She gestured towards his unmade bed as Brody heard the front door close.

There was no keeping his promise to Catherine now.

"Fuck your assumptions, *Sandykins*." His voice was low and controlled even as he felt the rage begin to boil, as if he were a timebomb tick, tick, ticking away as his explosion neared. "This bed isn't made because I haven't been in it for two fucking nights. I've sat on that fucking roof waiting for the sun to rise so that fucking *monster* that should have been on trial today doesn't haunt me in my dreams."

"You watch your language and your tone, young man."

"And you sound just fucking like him!" He was yelling now, letting off some steam in a way he hadn't been able to do. He was so focused on keeping his own anger in check that he almost missed her hand as she swung to slap his face.

Just almost.

He held her wrist in a tight grip. "Will that make you feel better? To fucking hit me, just like he always did? Huh?" He pushed her away from him. "Try it again!"

"What is wrong with you? Why can't you,"

"Act like Brian? Look what fucking good that did him! Is that what you want me to do?"

Her tears didn't affect him, not the way that Catherine's did.

In front of him he saw the one person who should have protected him, should have stepped in.

Should have been honest.

"Brian was a brilliant actor," she said. "But you, you've never acted. I just want my sweet boy back. And you were, always, so sweet."

"He's sweet now, Mommy." Sammi ran past her and straight into Brody's arms.

"It's okay, kiddo," he whispered to her as she cried into his shoulder.

"See what you've done?" Sandra gestured towards him. "Do you see?"

"Newsflash for you: this wasn't all me." He moved to shut his door, with Tyler nudging his way into the room with him and Sammi. He muttered another curse, hating himself for his sister's tears, hating himself for the look of sadness in Tyler's eyes before he wrapped his arms around the both of them.

"Please don't yell anymore." His brother's words were muffled as he had his face buried in Brody's shirt. "Please."

Brody adjusted his arms so they were around both Sammi and Tyler. "I'm so sorry. I lost my temper, and you shouldn't have seen that."

"We've seen worse," Tyler reminded him.

"Doesn't make it right." Brody kissed both of them, holding them close, praying for the demons haunting him to go away.

Just go away.

"Will you say sorry to Mommy, too?" Sammi asked him, but Brody couldn't answer her.

He was sorry that the kids had witnessed the argument. The last thing they needed was to be subjected to more hostility. There was a problem with Sammi's request, though.

He wasn't sure he was sorry for what he had said.

CHAPTER 11

Angels Bowling

Sleep was more elusive for Brody in the days following the confrontation with his mother. Or the latest confrontation, anyway, and he found that avoidance was the only way to keep it from happening again. Laura would have a field day when he finally got back in to see her. He'd promised to talk to his mother, per Laura's instructions, and it had gone horribly wrong every time.

He hadn't even mentioned that he knew his father's name, or that he knew they'd once been married.

When he closed his eyes, when he allowed himself to dream, they were full of rage. Sometimes Frank would be standing before him, his dream self would slam Frank into the door, tell him what a worthless piece of shit he was, pummel him over and over until he would wake up, wanting so badly to do the same in real life that he'd work out extra hard that day.

Now, that rage also included his mother.

How dare she lie to him for all of these years, making him believe that his father was a mere blip on the radar screen who had simply disappeared? Who was she to take away his right to know the man who made up one half of his DNA? Did she bend to Frank's will, or did she do it all on her own?

Sometimes, though… sometimes he would be screaming at his brother to wake up, get off the floor and clean up the mess he'd made his damn self. Or he would demand answers: what had he found out? Did he know which one of these three *Nikos Kostopoulos* profiles belonged to their father? Why had he turned a gun on himself instead of Frank?

That was the most common dream, the most common thought.

He leaned back against the shingles with a sigh. Another night on the roof, this one starless as the clouds moved in. It had been just before two when he had climbed up there, not even bothering with sleep, not wanting to wake up feeling like the countdown was nearing an end on his sanity. They'd been to see the meds doc the day before, with Brody's mother insisting he shouldn't need medication, just discipline.

Discipline.

The word Frank would throw around whenever he would use Brody as his personal punching bag.

The world around him was beginning to wake, and he didn't feel the least bit tired. He watched as neighbors' inside lights turned on, as some took their dogs out for the morning, as the older gentleman at the end of the next street left for work dressed in factory clothing.

His mother was already awake and had the television on the local news. Brody could hear the weatherman speak of cold fronts and extreme weather threats, the distant rumbling of thunder cutting off the rest of what was being said.

"What time is it?" Brody whispered as he pulled out his phone. "Fuck."

Six AM.

Another day of watching the kids ahead of him with no sleep in sight. Or maybe a little, if his mother didn't have the television going so loudly. He eased his way back into his room and shut the window, drowning out another low rumble of thunder. The bedroom door took an extra tug to get open, but once he did, he walked out to the living room to turn the TV down.

"You're up early." His mother emerged from her bedroom already dressed with part of her makeup done. "I was listening to the weather."

"Storms."

"No kidding. I only work until two, and I'll be back straight after. I know how scared Sammi gets when the weather is bad. You used to, too."

Brody grabbed a mug from the cupboard and poured the fresh coffee into it. His mother wanted to have a conversation, as if the last few hadn't blown up. He sighed as he sat at the small table and stared down into his cup. Was he even into being civil this early? Technically it was late for him, as he hadn't slept at all.

"So I am going to head out," his mother said as she emerged, purse on her shoulder. "Everything is in there for sandwiches for lunch."

"You're not scheduled until nine." He held up the paper that she'd left on the table.

"I have things to do."

He inhaled sharply, refraining from asking if she was going to see Frank. For all he knew, she was seeing someone else, someone who wasn't the monster who still haunted his every waking moment, and his dreams as well.

His gut told him otherwise as she left without a goodbye.

It wasn't until he heard her car drive away that it hit him how much he sounded like the monster he was sure his mother was on her way to see.

Sammi was curled up on the couch beside Brody, with her blanket and stuffed puppy. "Is it going to thunder all day?"

"I'm not sure. Probably."

"But puppy is scared."

Brody sighed and put his arm around his baby sister and placed a soft kiss on her forehead. "Puppy is going to be just fine."

"Hows come I don't understand any of the words on that page?"

"Because you're seven." Brody closed his laptop and set it aside. "And seven-year olds who say 'hows come' don't know every word that's in front of them."

"But those looked really weird, even the small ones."

That was because they'd been in another language, but Brody didn't want to tell her that and listen to her inquiries. He'd thought that searching for a producer with the same last name as his father would help him decide which of the profiles to look under, but he'd had no such luck. He hadn't understood the words on the page any more than Sammi could have.

"What was that?"

"Probably porn," Tyler piped up.

"Real smooth, kid." Brody stood and placed his laptop to the side amidst protests from Sammi, who wanted him to stay beside her.

"But what's porn?"

"See what you started?" Brody asked over his shoulder as he walked into the kitchen. "Sammi, you don't need to know. And Tyler, you don't need to tell her."

"This is why I need a dictionary," Sammi said matter-of-factly. "Come sit by me."

"I'll be back, I just need to get the trash out."

"He's sucking up to Mom."

"Are you my comic relief today?"

"Do I get paid?"

"No, Ty, you don't. And relax, Sammi; I'll only be out for a little bit. I need to do this while it's not raining."

"But thunder," she said, her eyes wide.

"I'll be fine, and I'll be right back." Brody stopped and shot a quick text to Catherine, as he tried to do whenever she crossed his mind. I miss you was all it said, but he'd learned the hard way not to wait to say whatever was on his mind.

The large garbage can was out back, freshly emptied during the previous day's pick up. Brody paid no mind to his other surroundings as he placed the bag in the can, only pausing when he heard a growl.

"The fuck?" He looked around, unsure of where the sound game from. He didn't see any animals lurking around, so he shook his head, laughing at what must have been an hallucination.

Brody paused before going back inside, just taking a moment to enjoy the smell of the rain. That was the part he'd liked most about rainy days, aside from the patter of the raindrops lulling him to sleep. There was a freshness about summer rains and the promise they brought with them. Ask him what his perfect day was, and he could say that it would be rainy, there would be hot coffee, a good book, and Catherine.

This rainy day just wasn't the same without her.

They had to follow the rules now, though, if they wanted any time together.

His phone buzzed once, and he pulled it out of his back pocket with a smile. Expecting to see a text from Catherine telling him how much she missed him, too, he frowned when there was only a message from his mother.

Turn on the news NOW

It was almost one in the afternoon, so the midday news was already over. Maybe she'd sent it earlier and it had just now gone through.

As he reached for the doorknob, he heard the growl again, this one louder, longer. He turned around, only this time his eyes were on the sky, watching as the clouds, dark as night, edged closer. Lightening was streaking through the oncoming system as the swirling mass let go another growl of thunder.

This storm was different.

He could feel it, every nerve tingling as it inched closer, the winds picking up ever so slightly.

Another buzz from his phone... another text from his mom.

NOW!

Brody threw the back door open, slamming it shut behind him. "Get out of the game," he said to Tyler. "You and Sammi go into the hall bathroom."

"I'm not in a good stopping,"

"Now." His voice was calm, but firm, and Tyler huffed as he stopped his game.

"Why are we going to the bathroom?" Sammi asked.

"I'll be in there in a little bit," he said without explanation. He already had the TV remote in his hand changing over to a local station, where a special weather report was being broadcast.

Severe thunderstorm warning.

Possible... no, *probable* tornadic activity.

He muttered a curse before turning up the television and going to the bathroom to wait out the storm. Sammi had tears in her eyes before Brody even told her and Tyler to get in the tub, just in case.

"But what about you?"

"I'm beside you." He sat on the floor, phone in hand which was only now showing the thunderstorm warning.

"Where's Mom?" Tyler asked. Brody noticed the thin sheen of sweat on his forehead, and he gently wiped it away.

"She's at work." Brody wasn't sure where this calm exterior had come from; it hadn't been present much at all lately, not since he hadn't needed to shield them from Frank's anger.

This was a different threat.

"It's okay," Brody added. "She's the one who told me to turn on the news. We're just in here as a precaution."

"What's a,"

"Just in case," Tyler answered Sammi before she could finish her question.

Sammi's lower lip was quivering as she looked at Brody. "But what about Daddy?"

It was an innocent question from a child who only saw the best in people. "I'm sure he's safe," Brody replied as he took her hand.

"He always said that the thunder was angels bowling in heaven, remember?" Tyler asked

"Maybe we should tell Brian to stop bowling."

If Brody hadn't heard the start of the sirens in the distance, maybe he would have laughed. Maybe he would have joined in when Tyler looked up at the ceiling yelling to quit bowling. Maybe he would have said a few words to Brian himself. Instead, he listened as the tornado warning was announced, and he sent another text with his shaking hands to Catherine telling her to be safe.

Just be safe.

The thunder was louder now, crashing and booming, shaking the windows of their small home. "Remember how they tell you to sit in school," he said to the kids. "Head down, okay?"

"Will you buy me a dictionary?" Sammi asked as Brody leaned over the tub, positioning her hands just so.

"I promise."

"And Harry Potter?"

"We have all the books," Tyler told her. "They're in our room."

"No, buy me Harry."

"You can't buy a person, silly."

Brody watched as Tyler took Sammi's hand in his as the storm barreled down, pelting the roof, possibly with the hail that was being talked about on the news, even as the lights dimmed once... twice...

"Hold on," he said to the kids as he crawled into the tub, laying over them, just in case everything caved down. All he wanted was for them to be safe; he'd wanted that for so long that all of his instincts kicked in whenever he was with them. It was why he would step in whenever Frank would be angry with one of them, or to lie and say he was responsible because he knew the consequences.

"I want Daddy." Sammi was crying, and Brody wanted to tell her that they were better off without him around.

Except in times like these.

Because Brody still remembered whenever a storm would come, one that crashed overhead, Frank would be calm, soothing, covering the children the way that Brody was now, protecting them just in case.

Just in case.

"It's okay, Brody. The angels are just bowling. See? Brian's not scared. It's okay... it's all okay."

Brody closed his eyes tightly, trying to will the memory away, telling himself those good moments didn't matter as he waited for the roar to come.

He could hear the tornado that the weather forecaster was warning everyone about. "Take shelter now," they said, and his face contorted as the tears threatened.

"Keep them safe."

Was his mind playing tricks on him, having those words in Frank's voice rolling around his head as he prayed for the same?

"Keep them safe. Please, keep them safe."

Once upon a time, Frank had been willing to sacrifice himself for them.

The way Brody was willing to now.

His arms shook as he held himself over the kids, not wanting to bear his weight on them as Tyler promised Sammi she would know all the words one day.

"And I'm going to write them," Sammi replied through her tears.

The roar... the growl of the storm began to subside, moving further away from them, but still they stayed huddled together.

Brody's entire body was tensed, sweat beading on his forehead, his brain preparing him for the worst even as the worst passed them by. It wasn't until he heard the words "all clear" stated on the television that he moved shakily, easing out of the tub and sitting on the bathroom floor, staring blankly at the wall even as the kids ran past him, wanting to see outside, Sammi happy that there was nothing more than a few branches down, Tyler disappointed that there wasn't more.

"Fuck," Brody muttered as he fisted his hands in his hair, pulling as hard as he could. All he wanted was his heart to stop racing, the feel of impending doom to subside the way the storm had. That wasn't too much to ask. The kids were already running around, talking about pictures and video that were on the television, Sammi saying it was Brian who kept them safe.

But Brian wasn't there.

And neither was Frank, who had distanced himself from the family after losing Brian, probably spending that time with his girlfriend that his mother must have known about.

Once Brian was gone, the whole family fell apart, and it was one upheaval after another.

"Brody?"

He heard Catherine's voice and pulled harder.

"Hey."

He jumped when he felt her touch, only then realizing that she was real, she was here beside him. He reached out, caressing her face to ease the worry he saw there. "You're okay."

She smiled. "Yeah. I made a quick trip over here because you weren't answering your phone. I need to be getting back home, though. Dad says it's family night."

"Thank you for stopping by." He took her hand in his. "I needed to see you."

"Is that so?" When she leaned in and lightly kissed his lips, he wrapped his arms around her, holding her to him. He teased her with soft, open kisses, nibbling just enough to make her sigh. "No fair," she whispered as he kissed along her jawline. "And your mom might see us."

Brody leaned back and narrowed his eyes. "My mom?"

"Yeah, she's the one that let me in."

"What time is it, Cat?"

"I got here after two."

After two... how long had he been sitting there? Had he lost that much time?

He smiled, masking the fear gripping his heart. "Just got lost in thought, I guess."

His thoughts were still racing as he walked hand-in-hand with Catherine to the front door. "We got lucky," she was saying. "Brentfield was hit hard. They say there were no fatalities."

He knew that Catherine was still talking, but he couldn't hear her.

Brentfield.

Sarah lived there.

Audrey lived there, too, as well as many other Valley High students.

"I have to go." Catherine stood on her toes, and Brody still had to lean slightly to give her a kiss goodbye. She was smiling as she waved while walking towards her father's car.

So carefree.

He knew these people, though. He'd grown up with them.

"What are you doing?"

He ignored his mother's question as he grabbed his backpack and unloaded its contents onto his bed. He still had a myriad of first aid bandages and such that he'd taken with him when they left the house on the hill simply because they'd been hidden among his belongings. He grabbed them now, stuffing them into his backpack, along with the camera that Catherine had given him.

"Brody, I asked you a question."

He brushed past her and walked to the door that led to the garage, which was full of unpacked belongings. "I have to go."

"No, you don't have to do anything. Brody!"

He found his old bike and brushed the cobwebs off of it before he opened the garage door.

"Young man! I don't know what you think you're doing, but,"

"I'll be back," he said as he climbed on his bike, standing on the pedals as he made his way as quickly as he could towards Brentfield.

CHAPTER 12

Too Quiet

It was quiet—too quiet—as Brody weaved his way around fallen limbs. The flags still out on some neighbors' lawns weren't moving. The leaves were still. The people in his town that were walking outside weren't speaking. Perhaps they were as stunned about what happened not far from their home as they were that their homes, their trees, their lives were untouched. No children were out playing, no dogs barking, no birds chirping.

It was unnerving.

Still, he pedaled on, cutting behind a row of houses with unfinished fences and back into the woods, the trail a perfect short cut to Brentfield. He knew if he followed roads, they would be blocked by emergency personnel telling him to go back home. He had friends that lived there, kids he'd grown up with, played baseball with, girls he had dated.

Catherine was going to give him tens kinds of hell, he was sure of it. He would make her understand, though. Maybe she'd already understand, agree that he should go there, make sure everyone was okay.

He had to make sure they were okay.

Beads of sweat broke out on his forehead despite the drop in temperature. Was it exertion from the bike ride? He couldn't tell. The further along he got on the trail, the more it was cluttered with limbs, displaced shingles from someone's roof, a stop sign bent around the trunk of a tree that was missing its bark. That sight distracted him long enough for him to hit a fallen tree with his bike, and he flipped over the handlebars, landing with a thud before skidding along the muddy path.

"Shit."

He wasn't hurt, thankfully, but was definitely a mess. He stood and brushed off what he could, then examined his bike, which didn't fare as well. The front tire was bent at an odd angle and flattened.

"Shit," he muttered again before pushing his bike out of the way. Only then did he check the contents of his backpack, letting out a sigh of relief when he saw they were unharmed. He didn't have cellphone service, but judging by the destruction he was surrounded by, he wasn't surprised. He took a few shots with his camera, focusing in on missing bark, on the huge oak tree he and his brother had marked as the halfway spot that was now split in half, the row of trees with their tops sheared off.

There was no way he was turning back despite his mangled bike, so he decided to walk to Brentfield instead. He made his way through broken limbs, over downed trees, his heart constricting as he saw the first glimpse of the town so close to theirs. He took a moment to just breathe, the disturbance of the earth leaving a heavy smell of dirt hanging in the air. His camera was still in his hand, and he began snapping photos, one after another, where the tornado drove straight down the middle of the neighborhood. Brody estimated the width to be at least a quarter of a mile wide.

"Shit... shit, fuck, oh god." He knelt to the ground, unable to stand at that moment as grief, shock, and a myriad of other emotions he just couldn't name took over him. When he wiped at his face, this time it was to brush away his tears.

It looked like a bomb had gone off, taking out most of a neighborhood close to home, that he, his brother, and their friends had frequented. Houses were just *gone*. Second floors to others were ripped away. Windows had been blown out, trees uprooted, debarked, stripped of leaves. Vehicles had been tossed around like they had weighed nothing, and they littered the area, windows broken. One had a plank of wood sticking out of its roof as if an arrow had been shot and made its mark.

This wasn't the place he'd played street hockey.

This was now a war zone.

He stood again and focused his camera, each shot taken with the same precision as when he'd shot the sunset from the same spot he stood now. Those shots would be compared side by side once he had them printed. When he was finished, he tucked his camera into his backpack and eased his way down the debris-laden hill into the neighborhood.

A crying child was the first sound he heard.

Brody absentmindedly touched his chest, where the child's cry was tearing at his heart. He turned his head towards a voice, loud and booming, calling out a woman's name. Sirens were further in the distance, although Brody could see first responders helping people from beneath rubble, tending to injured, marking standing buildings with a spray-painted X once they were done with them.

Victims... they were looking for victims. That realization hit Brody with a sickening jerk, urging him to walk faster, get two more blocks over. Audrey's home was in the affected area, there was no doubt about it now. He had to get there, see that she and her little sister were okay. Her parents would have been at work, like many of the kids in this neighborhood.

"We'll need your names to call them in," he heard a man's voice coming through a bullhorn. "To mark you safe," he added. "They are setting the high school up as a shelter. For anyone needing transportation there, please see me, or let any emergency personnel know. They will be bringing buses to Ash Street, which is just past the tornado zone. Please, head in that direction."

Brody fit in with the few people walking, most not carrying anything. Some would stop to hug neighbors, and Brody would stop, too, taking a few pictures along the way. There was a child crying beside a tree, her face hidden from him as he snapped the shot and began to walk up to her in case she was alone. Thankfully, she wasn't, but she cried harder as her mother told her she couldn't climb the tree to get her bear.

"I can do it," he said, interrupting their conversation, holding his camera out to the grateful woman to watch over as he scaled the barkless branches. The tattered bear was stuck in the tangled brush, but Brody maneuvered it free. He'd never felt better, stronger than when he handed that teddy bear back to the little girl who'd thought she had to leave it behind. As her mother knelt beside her, Brody aimed his camera, waiting until the woman nodded her approval.

Another picture. Another piece of this town that was torn apart, forever committed to memory.

He was so preoccupied with taking pictures, snapshots of the residents of Brentfield who had been home, that he hadn't heard the voice calling for him, yelling his name, and he was startled when a strong hand came down on his arm.

"Harris, what the fuck?" Max's strong hug was more of a shock than anything. "You asshole. You *asshole*. I saw your bike and it's all fucked up and I'm going to kick your ass for making me think I'd lost you, too."

"Too?" Brody panicked. "Who's gone?"

Max stepped back and shook his head. "Your brother."

Max's admission hit Brody with a wave of sadness and guilt. "I'm sorry, I didn't..." He shrugged when his voice trailed off, the silence between them filled with the footsteps of those walking past, the crunching of broken glass beneath their feet.

"Nah, man, I'm just glad you're okay."

One corner of Brody's mouth lifted. "Thanks. What are you doing here?"

"Sarah, but their house wasn't hit. C'mon, let's get out of here."

"Audrey,"

"She's fine. Their house is fucking gone, though, man. It's gone. Kaitlyn said hers is gone, too."

"I have to go there." Brody walked past Max, heading in the direction of the street that Audrey lived on. He was pretty sure that Kaitlyn lived on that street as well.

"You're fucking crazy, but I'm going with you so what does that make me?"

"An accomplice."

"Sweet."

Their walk was in somber silence permeating with cries of small children, soft spoken words from stunned residents, and the distant barking of a dog indicating to first responders that another person had been found. Brody took a few pictures along the way, mostly of people with dirty, tear-streaked faces. They turned at what was once Audrey's street, which looked like it had been hit hardest. Some houses were leveled to the ground, reduced to tossed bricks and broken studs of wood upon a slab.

"How did no one die?"

Brody pondered Max's question as they stood in front of the leveled two-story home that had housed Audrey and her family. "Enough warning," he finally said, remembering the text from his mother and the detailed forecast that had been blaring while he and the kids had huddled together in the small bathroom.

"They're not letting media outlets back here, you know."

"I didn't." Brody snapped another picture in the distance where a man was pulled from the rubble of his home by rescue workers, blood and torn clothing visible from down the street. "Maybe they're not sure about that zero casualties."

The distant buzz of a drone overhead was drowned out by a medic asking Brody if he was okay. He stared at the young woman for a moment and then nodded. "You two need to head towards Ash street. All residents," she added before they could protest. "For your safety."

Max didn't even pipe up that they weren't residents. He placed a hand on Brody's arm and told him they should go.

"Yeah," Brody agreed with a nod. "Let's go."

"We can go to Sarah's, catch a ride home."

"I'm heading this way." Brody motioned in the opposite direction. "I can walk, really."

"That's a long walk, dude."

Brody shrugged. "It clears my head. I'll see you later."

"I'll come by your house tomorrow."

"Yeah, okay, cool."

Brody walked alone towards Ash Street, as much in shock as those who lived there. The tornado had cut a clear path, and once he was out of that area, only branches and residual debris littered the ground. There were media trucks and school buses, the former having people wanting in the destruction, the latter taking residents out of it. He waved at Mr. Cooper, who had been his driver as a child, smiling as he knew that the man was volunteering his time to help others. He'd always been kind to Brody and Brian as they grew up, teasing them about how they could pass for one another anytime they chose to.

"Brody!" He heard Audrey before he saw her dirt-streaked face in the crowd. She was smiling... *smiling*. She ran to him and jumped into his arms.

"I was so afraid," he admitted as he hugged her.

"We're all alive." She stepped back, still smiling. "All of us. How amazing is that?"

Her happiness for life, for seeing the brightness in the midst of a tragedy, was infectious. Others around her began to smile, to hug one another, to promise help with clean up and rebuilding. Brody snapped one shot after another, his heart warming with each one.

"And look!" A small girl pointed to the distance where a double rainbow shown brightly. He snapped more pictures of this, of everyone's wonder.

"We're blessed," Audrey said, met with many "amen"s.

Another volunteer was ushering the residents onto the buses, and Brody shook his head. "I can walk home from here," he said, even though the school was closer to his house.

"Excuse me, sir." A young woman, smartly dressed with professional makeup accentuating her features. "You were in the tornado affected area?"

"I don't live there."

"No, I mean…" She gestured to his camera. "I would love to see your pictures, perhaps use a few of them. How did they let you in to take them?"

"They didn't." He shrugged. "I have friends here."

"The camera crews captured you with your girlfriend. That was so sweet."

"She's not my girlfriend."

"Well, if you have one, you may want to contact her soon," she said with a laugh, and she handed him a business card. "My email address and phone number are on there. I'm sure people would pay premium to publish them."

"Yeah, sure," he said as he put the business card in his pocket. "I need to get going."

"To explain things to your girlfriend, I'm sure." She laughed again. "You wouldn't happen to be a model, would you? Your features are striking."

Was this woman flirting with him? Unused to the attention of a stranger, he smiled his thanks before setting off on the long walk home. He knew that Catherine would understand, once he had cell service to reach her, and that probably wouldn't happen until he was past the place he'd discarded his wrecked bike.

He still had a soft smile on his face as he retrieved his bike and walked it the rest of the way home. It wasn't over a stranger's attention, or even over the business card he'd stuffed in his pocket with the potential of making money off of his pictures. It was over the sense of community he'd seen in Brentfield, with the survivors praising their respective deities, hugging one another, being amazed and inspired by the double rainbow. He even wondered how his pictures would turn out, more for his own memories than the prospect of money. His mother may be impressed by that, though, as Frank had told her over and over that photography was a waste of Brody's time. It brought him just as much joy as the rainbows had brought the residents of Brentfield.

He was still smiling as he parked his bike in the small garage and walked back around to the front of the house to get a shower, still smiling as he stopped to send a text to Catherine.

His smile fell as Frank Harris opened the front door.

CHAPTER 13

Behold my Rebel-ness

"What the fuck are you doing here?"

Brody's voice was loud, forceful as he felt the words more than he heard them. Frank was supposed to be locked up. It was just supposed to be a postponement. He shouldn't be there, where he would make Brody his personal punching bag again.

Frank had the nerve to smile at him. "Your mom called me. She said you took off in this mess, and she was worried about you. I'm glad your safe."

"Don't take another step towards me, asshole." Every nerve in Brody's body was on alert, waiting for this monster before him to lash out, grab him by the throat the way he used to.

"Don't speak to your father that way." His mother was outside now, her eyes angry and accusatory. How dare she look at him this way?

How dare she call this monster to come and find him?

"He's not my father. Or do I need to remind you of all the times you told me so?" He asked that question of Frank, who had the nerve to look apologetic. "A bastard. That's what you called me. Which was a lie."

"Brody,"

"Nikos Kostopoulos," Brody cut his mother off. "Your first husband. Remember him?" Even as she paled, he turned his attention back to the monster before him. "Leave."

"Brody,"

"Sandra, it's okay." Hell, Frank even had the balls to speak softly. "I'm organizing help with clean up and rebuilding, Brody, if you'd like to help out. How's Audrey?"

"Fuck you."

"Get inside," his mother said to him.

"Not if he's coming in."

"I said get inside."

"Sandra, he's just a bit surprised." Frank's voice was still calm, soothing, charming.

Brody pushed past him on his way indoors. He would take a shower and take off. There was no way he could talk to his mother, not now.

Not until he found a way to calm himself.

The door slammed, letting Brody know his mother had come in behind him. "You complain over and over of his treatment of you. What about your actions?"

Not now, Mom.... Not now.

"You're disrespectful, unruly, unmanageable without him here."

And he snapped.

"You bitch!" He was yelling as he turned towards her, his chest heaving. "You fucking *bitch*, you really think that him beating the shit out of me made me manageable? *He turned me into this!* Look at me! I can't sleep, I can't function, but I'm expected to be *respectful* and *obedient*. Tell me, mother, what if it was Tyler he held against the wall with his hand around their throat? No! Don't fucking walk away from me!"

"You need to calm down."

"Answer me! What if it was Sammi? Would it suddenly be a problem then? How can I be so expendable to you?"

"This right here is why your father needs to be here."

"Then tell me how to find him!" He pulled his phone out and tossed it at her. She stepped aside and let it fall to the floor. "Tell me which one is his profile. Tell me where he is. And then tell me why you weren't honest with me. Isn't that *disrespectful*?"

"I was completely honest with you."

"Omission is the same as lying, *Sandykins*."

"Brody, you're scaring me."

"How fucking scared do you think I am! Or is that okay with you? Is it?"

Sandra pulled out her own phone. "He needs to come back. He needs to be here."

"And I would rather die than live under the same roof as Frank fucking Harris!" Brody grabbed his backpack and threw the front door opened. His walk was brisk, picking up to a jog with the first call of his name, then into a dead run, as fast as he could.

Frank Harris. At his house. In his life.

He'd turn on him, show his true colors. Have all of them walking on eggshells afraid to set him off, and when he did, he'd take it out on Brody. Every punch, every kick, every choke hold, every vile name that man had called him screamed in his brain. His feet pounded against the pavement faster, faster, sweat ran down his face, his back as he ran. He didn't slow down until his feet took him exactly where he knew they would.

It was Coach who answered the door, his face pale as he took in Brody's appearance. "What happened?"

Brody hadn't realized he'd been crying until he tried to speak. Tried and failed.

And he collapsed in sobs into Coach's arms.

"Thanks for the clothes," Brody said to Coach. He was sitting on the couch with Catherine, who was uploading the pictures he'd taken earlier onto her laptop.

"Yeah, not a problem. I threw yours in with the laundry. You sure you're okay?"

No, he wasn't sure. In fact, he was quite sure of the opposite.

"Yeah, I'm good."

"Aside from your mom calling that asshole," Catherine muttered, her eyes on her laptop.

And your grandfather for getting him out of jail.

He didn't say the words, even though he felt them in his soul.

"I have summer school grading to do," Coach said with a sigh as he sat down at the table.

"We'll be super quiet." Catherine's smile she shown in her father's direction was tight, showing Brody that she was definitely still angry over the reporter's slip, along with his admission that he'd gone to look for his ex-girlfriend.

"This is the email account here." Brody put the card on the table.

"You don't just send the pictures. You watermark them, then you price them. Or were you not paying attention in class?"

"I was a little distracted, yeah."

She almost smiled. "So email her and ask her how she would like them sent, and tell her your terms."

"I don't have my phone, and what terms?"

Catherine glanced sideways at him. "What do you mean, you don't have your phone? I saw it in your pocket on television."

"I kinda… threw it. Not hard," he added.

"Please tell me it was at Frank."

It was Brody's turn to almost smile. "No, this was at my mother."

"And you're probably grounded, less than a week until the fireworks. Bravo."

"I don't know."

"I'm just saying if I was stupid enough to throw my phone at my dad,"

"You wouldn't have a phone," Coach finished for her.

"Not sure how I'm supposed to talk to you now."

"Cat, I've had a bad enough day. Can we please not?" He was tired, physically as well as emotionally, and didn't need any more thrown his way.

The look she shot in his direction began with venom that dissolved into sadness. "I hate this for you, all of you. How did the kids take it?"

Brody's eyes narrowed. "I don't remember seeing them." Had they been hiding in their rooms the whole time? Or had their mother sent them away?

"Well, be prepared to be pissed off."

"Fuck, what?" He sat back wearily and covered his face with his hands.

"I messaged all three profiles to see if any of them knew your mother. And there, email is sent to the news lady."

He took her hand in his. "Tiny and fierce."

"You're not mad?"

He shook his head slowly. "I'm ready to know him. Or at least hear his side about this bullshit." He jumped when Coach's phone rang, then muttered another curse. Even Catherine curling up beside him did little to calm him.

He wasn't safe anymore.

Not in his home, not walking around, not going back to Brentfield, where he wanted so badly to help. Frank was going to be everywhere, and not just in Brody's dreams, haunting him, taunting him with the acceptance he craved but had never gotten. He would most likely be staying there soon, taking away his right to feel safe and loved and secure.

And his mother was welcoming him with open arms.

"Brody." Coach walked into the living room. "That was your mother. I let her know that you're here. I also let her know that Frank Harris doesn't want to come anywhere near me. Hope you don't mind that part."

Brody shook his head and mustered a shaky smile. "Not at all. Thanks."

"Oh my god." Catherine's breathy words were followed by tears filling her eyes as she looked at the screen. "This is... it's awful."

"May I?" Coach asked, not quite meaning the question as he nudged his way between Catherine and Brody to sit on the couch. Brody's photos were beginning to come up as thumbnails, one by one, showing the sheer devastation to the town not far from them. "Jeezus," Coach whispered, and Brody nodded, his eyes on the screen.

"This doesn't even touch it, not really. It's a war zone, not a neighborhood I played in as a kid. See that? That's where Kaitlyn's house was."

"Kaitlyn... Kate Evans?" Catherine asked, and Brody nodded. "I keep forgetting how it is here."

"A community." Brody pulled up one of the crowd smiling up at the rainbow. "Even more so now."

"You captured it perfectly."

Those words came from Coach, who picked up the laptop and walked towards the kitchen as he scrolled.

"We were kinda busy here, Dad."

"Yeah, email that lady. Wait... let me draw up a proposal for you first, then email her with it."

Catherine handed her phone to Brody. "You know the passcode, if you want to do it on my phone. Or you can wait until Dad has a proposal ready and email her from my laptop. And trust me, Brody; Daddy knows how to wheel and deal."

The edges of Brody's mouth lifted in a partial smile. "We can do it from the laptop. You know my email stuff anyway."

"Yes, because I set you up with something better, because you're not plain and ordinary."

"Changed your perception of me, huh?" His grin widened as she curled up beside him and he wrapped his arms around her.

"Those are two words I can't use when it comes to you." Her fingertips traced his smile. "You, sir, are far from either."

This girl... she had a way of healing his heart, making him feel worthy of love that he'd grown to think wasn't meant for him, in any way. Hearing these words from her meant more than some local reporter asking if he was a model, more than praise for his photography, more than the promises of love from a mother who couldn't be bothered to protect him.

He placed a kiss on her forehead, wanting to convey exactly what was in his heart without saying the words that he'd once thought he knew the meaning to. She smiled up at him, scrunching up her nose in that adorable way that made his stomach dip. Perhaps it was a good thing that her father sat within watching distance, or he would have pushed her back onto this couch and kissed her fully.

"When do you have to be back?"

"Technically I wasn't allowed to leave, behold my rebel-ness."

She raised an eyebrow. "Is that even a word?"

"Doubt it, but I'll ask Sammi when I get her dictionary that I promised."

"What in the…"

Brody and Catherine separated at her father's exclamation, but he was looking outside as he walked towards the front door.

"What's going on?" Catherine asked.

"I'm about to find out." He opened his door and stepped outside, closing it behind him, but not before Brody heard him say, "Good evening, Officer. What can I do for you?"

"What the fuck?" Brody stood and looked out the front window, where one cruiser and an ambulance were, with their lights flashing.

"What do you think happened?" Catherine was beside him now, as curious as he was. He was about to tell her that he didn't know until a car pulled in behind the ambulance.

His mother's car.

No, no, no

What had she done?

His hands automatically fisted in his hair, pulling, pulling, but this wasn't a dream.

His mother had called the cops on him.

His mother... his mother had turned him in.

And an ambulance. What was the...

"Fuck, fuck, fuck." He repeated the words as he closed his eyes tightly, not hearing Catherine's questions over the whooshing of blood in his ears, rhythmic with the thrashing beat of his heart.

How could she?

How could she?

"Let me talk to him for a minute." Coach was inside now, his hand on Brody's arm. "It's okay, son," he whispered. "C'mon into the kitchen and we'll talk."

"We need to keep him in our line of sight," someone said, and Brody choked back a sob.

"I didn't do anything, I swear, Coach."

"Let's just go into the kitchen."

Brody followed blindly, not even aware of Catherine holding his hand. He couldn't even speak, only nodding or shaking his head to Coach's questions.

"Brody, they said you threatened suicide."

Brody's eyes grew wide. "But I didn't," he said, finding his voice.

"Your mother is the one you said it to."

"No, I..." Brody's eyes slid shut. "Fuck, that's not what I meant, Coach."

"They're going to take you to the hospital."

"They're fucking locking me up?"

"A hospital, Brody." Coach placed his hand on Brody's shoulder. "They're going to get everything straightened out, okay? I need you to do this, and do it willingly."

Catherine was crying softly, her arms wrapped around Brody. "It will be okay. It's just three days, and you'll be back, and… and then we can go to the fireworks, okay?"

"Cat, I swear I wouldn't. Not after Brian."

"I know." She smiled through her tears. "Please do this, for me."

His heart was still pounding in his chest as he looked down at Catherine. He knew the drill: 72 hour lockdown in a mental health facility. No phones. No visitors, or at least that's what Frank had said when he'd had his mother committed, first to the crisis care wing, and then into a long-term facility.

He didn't know if he could last that long, didn't know if his mother had already made the plans for him to go away.

"Brody, please."

He finally nodded. "For you."

For Catherine, he'd do anything.

CHAPTER 14

That's Rich

No pens.
No pencils.

No phones.

No cameras.

There was even a no shoelaces rule, which frustrated Brody the most and had him walking around in his socks.

They claimed this wasn't a jail, but he was locked in a facility with no way out and no contact with the outside world. The clothing his mother brought him had to be devoid of strings, so he didn't have any pajama bottoms, either. At least he was allowed to read, although his mother had packed up the book that Brody had been reading with Catherine.

He'd promised Catherine that he wouldn't read it without her. What would she think if he broke that promise? And if he did, what was to stop him from breaking another, and another, and another?

That's what Frank had done. He'd promised he wouldn't lose his temper again, and he did.

"Brody, I can't help you if you don't talk to me."

Brody's eyes lifted from the floor to see the male therapist—Christopher, that was his name. "I told you that this is a mistake. I didn't say I was going to kill myself."

"Your mother is concerned about your erratic behavior as well, your emotional outbursts, your temper."

"*My* temper?" Brody scoffed. "Oh, that's rich."

"So your mother has a temper?" Christopher paused, waiting for Brody to answer. When no answer came, he continued. "Is it your father?"

"Frank is not my father," Brody snapped. "I never met my father. Not yet."

"I see." Christopher was silent as he looked over the notes in front of him. "Frank Harris is listed as your father, Brody."

"What, do you think I'm lying to you?"

"No."

"So you're trying to make me angry, then."

"Something like that."

Brody was stunned by the admission, and his eyes narrowed as he looked at the therapist, who was reading over the notes still. "That's kinda shitty."

"That's kinda my job."

"To be shitty?"

"To see what's upsetting you. Tell me about your..." Christopher paused and looked up. "Frank. Tell me about Frank."

"I've been his personal punching bag since I was about six years old. There's not much else to tell."

"With a statement like that, I'd say there's lots to tell."

"Yeah, well, I told Laura." Brody shifted in his chair. "Can she come here? It would help if I didn't have to repeat myself."

"She's not on staff here, although we do work closely with the center. We've requested your records."

"Good. Wait for them."

"How have you been sleeping?"

Brody scoffed. "Sleep? What's that?" Aside from something he hadn't had nearly enough of for quite some time.

"I've got a call into the physician, and,"

"You're not going to drug me into submission." He'd fight them on that, no matter what. He hadn't had a say so in his admission, as he was a minor, but this? This he would find a way out of.

"That's not what we do here, Brody. If you have issues with the medication that you're currently on, we work to resolve that. I think you and I can both agree that sleep would help your mood tremendously."

"You're way too calm, you know that?" Brody wasn't sure why he'd said it out loud, other than it was what he had been thinking.

Christopher smiled. "It's because I get sleep. And we're going to help you get sleep tonight. I know you're not at home, and I'm guessing you're not used to sharing a room?"

Brody's eyes dropped to the floor as he thought of Brian, cold and lifeless.

"Let's go ahead and get you settled in, then. The nurse will bring you something to help you sleep. Relax, Brody. Okay, so that's a stupid thing to say when your life's in a bit of an upheaval, but try."

"This really is a mistake, you know. Me being here."

"Is it?"

Brody crossed his arms and scowled.

He wasn't sure he knew the answer.

The floor in the small room he was sharing was brown, speckled, square tile, similar to the tile in many of his classrooms at Valley High. His roommate was turned on his side with his back to the door, seemingly sleeping despite the light being turned on. He walked slowly to his bed and sat down with a silent sigh.

He was so tired.

He was tired of living in fear. Not that he was tired of living, because he had far too much to do of that. He was just... tired. The nurse had given him his evening medication along with a sleep aid that she'd sworn was mild. If it was, why was he ready to drop right then and there?

"It's my first night, too."

Brody jumped at the sound of his roommate's voice, even though it was soft spoken. "Hey. Sorry, I didn't mean to wake you."

"Wasn't asleep. I'm Matt."

"Brody." He stepped across the room and shook Matt's hand.

"Is it your first time here?"

Brody blinked a few times as he sat down on his bed. "Um, yeah."

"It's my second." Matt turned back around leaving Brody a bit stunned. He could tell by the bandage that he'd seen on Matt's arm exactly what he was in for. But... second time?

"Lights out in five minutes," came the call from the hallway.

"I'm good if you want to turn it off now," Matt said over his shoulder.

"Yeah, me, too."

"They'll bed check several times, in case you thought there may be some way out. There's not."

"Thought really hadn't occurred to me." Brody turned the light off and walked back over to his bed, using the light from the hallway as his guide. Actually, that had been a lie; he'd looked over as much as he could, wondering if there would be a way for him to get out of here, get back to Catherine.

But what then?

Then Frank would be able to convince his mother that he needed locked up in some long-term facility like he'd done to her. That was, if he hadn't convinced her already. Was he really crazy, though? He just didn't want to live like that again. He wouldn't fall for Frank's charm anymore. He wasn't vying for his attention, or even his love that never came without condition. He had Catherine. He had his friends.

And somewhere out there, he had his father.

Brody was still staring at the ceiling a few minutes later when they were checked on and the door pulled to, leaving only a sliver of light in the room. He wasn't sure he'd sleep even with the sedative; all he could see was Catherine's tear-streaked face as they wheeled him out on that stupid fucking unnecessary stretcher. He didn't bother to look at his mother; he had nothing to say to her, and definitely wasn't in the mood to see her. But he did see Coach as he draped his arm around Catherine's shoulder and let her cry into his chest.

For the briefest of moments, and for the first time ever, he was envious of what she had.

"Don't let them bullshit you into thinking it's 72 hours," Matt said to him. "We're minors. It will be four or five days. Probably just four."

"Great."

"We'll be out before the fourth. They'll clear us out so they don't have to pay as many employees holiday pay. Or so I've heard."

Brody sighed and placed a hand beneath his head. Four or five days of praying for Tyler and Sammi to be safe.

Could he do it?

"Families can come visit on Thursday nights. Most don't, but they can."

Would his mom come? Would she bring the kids?

Would she bring Frank?

"Most of our days are in group. We talk shit out, like anyone will actually listen."

"They don't?"

"No one's listened to me." Brody heard Matt's bed creaking and his covers rustle. "G'nite."

"Goodnight."

With no roof to climb on, Brody stared at the ceiling for what seemed like an eternity before finally drifting into an exhausted sleep.

The chairs were in a large circle, and Brody sat as far away from its facilitator as possible. He had no intentions of sharing anything. Like Matt had said... who would listen? He'd handed over evidence of Frank's physical abuse, and now they were turning it all on him, saying it was his fault.

Just like he'd been told since he was a first grader.

"Yeah, this is my third time," a girl was saying. "Oh, um... Cassie. Self-harmer. Runaway." She paused for a moment before adding, "Rape survivor."

"Is that why you ran?" a younger girl asked.

"Yeah." Cassie sat up and pushed her red hair back. "Mom's boyfriend. But I'm a whore, right? I won't go back there. They say if I don't then I can go to juvie, but for now, they've sent me here. I reported him. I did everything I was supposed to. I'm only in here now because I try to take my pain away by..." Her voice trailed off, and Brody noticed the healing cuts on her arms. "So, that's my story. And now someone else can talk, because I don't want to anymore."

"I feel you, girl," someone else spoke up. "Got marks like those on my legs, but that's not why I'm in here. I'm Emily, and I steal my mom's drugs and get high. Like I'm the bad person. I get them from her, so fuck it. I'm here. I'm unruly and shit."

"Do we have to do this every group? I've introduced myself, like, ten times."

"Only five, Craig," Emily said to him.

"Fine. I'm Craig, I tried to kill myself. The beam broke, so I'm here. Apparently I can't kill myself right on top of everything else I fail at. Next."

"Dude, don't talk like that."

"Fuck it. It's the truth. Next."

"I'm Matt, and this is my second time here." Brody's roommate sat up a little taller. "I'm here because I took every pill I could have, slit my wrists, and then they found me. Yes, I know I speak softer than everyone else, but that's mostly because of the tubes they shoved down my throat. My parents tell me that I'm an abomination. They've sent me to camps to try to 'deprogram' me." He used air quotes, then continued. "They even moved us to Brentfield thinking hey! We take him away from all his friends, maybe he won't be gay anymore. But guess what? I am. So…" His voice trailed off as he wiped away tears. "They say our house wasn't touched in the tornado, but I don't know."

"What street?" Brody asked, and Matt looked over at him.

"Norton Avenue."

Brody shook his head. "You're good. It's still there."

"Is it bad that I wish it had blown away and taken my parents with it? I don't know if I want to make it to 18 to get out or…" He held up his bandaged wrist. "You don't know."

"I do," Craig corrected him, then turned to Brody. "You were in the storm?"

"No, but I made it in there not long after. It's… it's like a bomb went off. There were wooden planks through people's cars, looking like they'd been shot from a canon or something. Glass and bricks and… and blood. But it smelled like dirt. It all smelled like fresh dirt. I took so many pictures."

"Dude."

"Can we see them?"

"They're on my girlfriend's laptop. Some reporter asked me about rights and publishing."

"No shit."

"Then why are you in here?" Emily asked, and Brody shrugged.

"Uh… I'm an unruly little shit?"

"Look at the newbie go," Emily laughed. Even Cassie, who seemed to hide behind her hair laughed

"Let's reel it back in," the facilitator said as he sat back with a smile. "Brody, what brings you here?"

"An ambulance. Kidding, sort of. Um…" He looked down at his hands, which were folded together. "My mom, she, uh…. She had her husband out looking for me. I didn't even know he was out of jail."

"What was he in jail for?" Emily asked.

"Beating the shit out of me. I don't know how he got out of… yes, I do. He got out of it because they're blaming it on me. And I lost my shit. I told her I'd rather die than live like that again, and here I am."

"How are they blaming that shit on you?" Craig asked.

"Well…" Brody's voice trailed off and he shrugged. "I guess he did catch me making out with his girlfriend's daughter."

The rest of the participants erupted in raucous laughter and applause.

CHAPTER 15

This Family

B rody picked at his food during that evening's dinner. It wasn't that the food tasted bad; it was that their last group had been about nutrition and Cassie had explained exactly why she was a vegan. Suddenly his burger didn't look so good.

"You too?" Emily sat beside him and placed her tray on the table.

"Yeah." Brody grinned. "I am hungry, though."

"Their salad is supposed to be good."

Brody picked up his burger. "Maybe tomorrow."

"So you're a Valley High kid." It was more of a statement than a question. "I'm from Easton."

"And you're sitting at the rival's table?"

"Well, you were alone, so..." Emily picked up her burger. "Cheers. If it makes you feel any better, I doubt these are real meat."

"Actually that kinda does." He grinned and took a bite.

"So I was wondering... when we get out of here... I mean, I know you have a girlfriend, that's not what I'm asking. Are you gonna act like none of this happened? I was thinking about it, but, I don't know. Maybe I'm learning a thing or two."

"I'm learning that those pills they hand me in the morning are gross."

"What the vitamin and fish oil? You know you don't have to take them, right?"

"I didn't know. Thanks," he added before taking another bite of his food.

"You're not really here because you're an unruly shit, are you?" Again, it sounded more like a statement, like Emily knew some secret about him. 'I've watched you when they talk about suicide. So, what, did you take pills to do it? Or to try, I should say?"

"I'm not here for that." He put his burger down. "I mean, kinda not here for that. I said some stupid shit to my mom."

"Like you were going to off yourself. Harsh."

"Not exactly, but yeah. Harsh." He frowned and began picking at his bun.

"Then what exactly did you say?"

"I'm sure there will be some point that I'll share it with the group." He stood and picked up his tray. "Massive headache," he mumbled as he walked away, not meaning to be rude, but at the same time not giving a damn if he had been.

No caffeine. That was another item on the 'forbidden' list. As if being here wasn't enough to put him in a bad mood, now he had a raging headache to make it even worse. He didn't feel like he had slept much the night before, he didn't have time alone, away.

He didn't have Catherine.

He missed his morning routine— not only his coffee, but his girl, who would call or text him every day. The mornings she called, when he could hear her voice after either a sleepless or a restless night, he knew the day would be a little bit better. He missed stopping by the dance studio to surprise her with a kiss. He missed playing a video game with Tyler and having her pop up online. He missed the way she would work with Sammi to make sure her gymnastics form was proper so that she didn't hurt herself. He missed...

"Brody."

Matt was gently shaking his shoulder, and it startled him enough to grab his roommate's arm. Where the hell was he?

"It's time for group."

Oh, right. His mother had him locked up, thinking he was a "danger to himself." What a joke.

"Yeah, okay," he mumbled as he stood to follow Matt. The group had changed only slightly, with Craig leaving and two more girls taking his place. Brody had found that this facility wasn't just for those who had attempted suicide, or threatened to; it was also for those whose parents felt their behavior made them a danger, as his mother had.

"Dude, you look like hell," Emily said to him, and he shrugged.

"I'm not on a vacation."

"I hear that."

The facilitator was the same, and his announcement of stress management almost made Brody laugh. He stifled it back as best he could, though judging by the look from the facilitator, it had been noticed. He straightened up and listened to the instructions, then waited for his turn as each of his inmates as he now thought of them responded.

"Well…" Cassie held out her arms, old scars and newer wounds, pink and healing to leave new scars behind.

"Thank you for being honest," the facilitator replied. "What could you do instead?"

"I journal, but it isn't always enough."

"But far healthier. Matt?"

"Thirty second dance party." His response was met with murmurs about how it was rather brilliant, along with requests to see it.

"Please tell me you do the Carlton," Emily piped up.

"No, but I could."

Brody remained silent but smiled as the other members of the group urged Matt on, and he got up to perform the Carlton to a round of applause and Emily calling for an encore. Nope, a thirty second dance party was not something Brody could see himself doing, any more than he could take a knife to his arms.

Each person was different, open, honest. When the facilitator called on him, he hesitated.

What did he do for stress relief?

"Um… I go up on my roof at night," he began. "Just to look at the sky the way I did with Brian."

"Who's Brian?" Matt asked, which made sense. He'd talked briefly about Tyler and Sammi, but hadn't mentioned his twin brother at all.

"My brother. He's dead," he added before he could be asked more about him. "Catherine. I go see Catherine. She always calms… almost always calms me."

"What is it about her?"

He ignored the lewd comment about sexual release, answering with, "She knows me, and knows everything. I can tell her all about what's in my head and my heart. And she saw firsthand the bullshit I was going through daily. I've watched her go from this spoiled rotten princess to this amazing, empathetic human being, and that transformation is..." His voice trailed off as a smile finally found its way through. "It's inspiring. She's beautiful, and funny, and brilliant, and she's... well, she's a gymnast and a dancer. She's graceful, every move she makes. And for some reason, this incredible girl sees me and says 'that's my person,' and I don't know how or why. With her, I can just *be*, and she gets it. She gets me. All I have to do is hold her hand or hear her voice, and my day is infinitely better."

"Oh, wow."

"See, Cassie?" Matt nudged her. "Good men still exist."

"So she's your drug of choice then," Emily commented.

"What?" Brody asked, instantly defensive.

"Your drug. You know, she's what you need to get through it. And no offense, but setting all of that on another's shoulders isn't too bright. Trust me," Emily added.

"I'm not using her, I," he stopped short and shook his head. "I really care about her, and she helps me."

"And what about when she lets you down?"

Irritated as he already was, her question sparked the anger, the rage that lived just beneath the surface. "What, like if I was so fucking happy then we wouldn't be together? Newsflash, Emily, having a happy-go-lucky personality doesn't mean a fucking thing. Brian was the happiest person I've ever been around, and I'm the one that walked into that fucking room and saw him laying there with a fucking bullet hole in his forehead, with his brains all over his side of our room, with the smell of shit and piss and metal. When I looked down at the one person who was happiest, when I saw *my* face, my *dead* face—yeah, he was my twin—do any of you know what that's like? Do you?" He stood up then, his hands fisted in his hair. "I've lost half of me forever. For fucking ever, and I don't even know *why*." He began to pace, not caring what anyone else was saying, not even hearing them. "So, yeah, I know what it's like to have the one person you thought would always be there just fucking up and bail on you, leaving you to clean their brains off your walls, leaving you to pack up their things, leaving people blaming you, leaving you blaming your fucking self. And now I'm stuck in here, and I don't know if my brother and sister are okay, and you know what? I shouldn't fucking be here! I would never fucking do that to them. And so fucking what if my girlfriend means that much to me, huh? *So fucking what?*"

Someone put their hand on his shoulder and he shrugged it off, pissed off at himself for revealing so much, enraged that there would be tears on his face when he raised his head for the rest of them to see.

"Brody?"

"Do you have any brothers or sisters, Matt?" Brody looked up and wiped his eyes. "Do you?"

"A brother. He doesn't like me very much, though. I don't think I really have a family."

Brody shook his head. "Yeah, you do." He held out his hand, which Matt shook. "You have another brother now. And I'll look out for you."

Matt's own eyes were shining. "I've got your back, too. Maybe turn a little less Hulk when you're angry though. Unless you want to turn that on my parents, because, hey." He held up his hands. "I'd be all for that shit."

There was a smattering of laughter along with the scraping of chair legs on the floor as one by one the members of the group hugged one another.

"I'm so sorry," Emily whispered in his ear. "I'm so fucking sorry."

"I'm sorry, too."

"You know what?" She squeezed one last time and stepped back. "Catherine's a lucky girl."

He wasn't so sure about that.

Even as he laid in his bed that night, calmer than he had been in some time but unable to sleep, he wondered if Catherine being saddled with a mental case for a boyfriend was what she deserved.

She'd been the one to calm him when he took a baseball bat to a set of lockers after he'd missed a pop-up ball, costing his team the game.

She'd been the one to calm him after he went off on a teammate for striking out.

She'd been the one to calm him in the basement of that house on the hill whenever Frank used him as a personal punching bag.

She *was* his drug.

She *was*.

And she deserved so much more than that, so much more than him.

It was Thursday night, and as Matt had predicted, his family didn't show. Brody was surprised that his mother hadn't, or perhaps he wasn't. He wasn't quite sure what to make of his mother anymore.

"Welcome to the losers table," Matt said as Brody sat across from him.

"Losers my ass." Emily joined them. "Look, over there. Cassie's sister came. She lives in another fucking state and she came. My ma's probably high as shit. What about yours?"

"I'm an abomination," Matt replied with a shrug.

"I'm not sure what I am," Brody admitted.

"Hey," Emily said to him, "we cool?"

"Yeah." He ate a couple of fries as Emily and Matt began to talk about when they should be leaving.

"Tomorrow afternoon for me," Emily said with a grin. "You bitches only get one more group with my smiling face."

"Saturday," Matt said. "I think. Brody?"

"Supposed to be Saturday," he said, expecting the anxiety to edge in, to tell him that his mother wouldn't show, to tell him that she was shipping him off somewhere else.

Instead, he felt a profound sadness.

"Maybe I'll look the two of you up. They keep telling me I need better friends and shit like that." Emily grinned. "You two can be my big brothers."

"Big brothers? How old are you?"

"Fourteen."

Brody choked on his water.

"You're how old?" Matt asked.

"Yeah, little sister, don't let me catch you getting thrown back in here. Fourteen? Fucking hell, Emily."

She shrugged. "You grow up quick when your only parent is a junkie. Or too wrapped up in grief." She looked at Brody then. "You're not like any seventeen-year-old I've ever met, but somehow you kinda are. Cut yourself some slack, okay? You're just a fucking kid, too. Just like the rest of us."

A kid was one thing he hadn't been able to be in far too long. He wished he could; he wished he was a normal carefree teenager with a beautiful girlfriend and amazing prospects for college, any college he wished instead of those he could get a scholarship to. He wished he didn't have warring emotions, feelings of inadequacy, uncontrollable rage.

He wished he could trust himself.

"Are you in there?" Matt asked.

"Hmm?"

"A toast. Lift your cup."

"A toast with water," Emily joked, but she was holding her cup up as well. Brody played along like he'd been listening and lifted his cup, waiting for Matt.

"To this little family right here."

Brody smiled as he touched each of their cups with his. "To this family."

CHAPTER 16

Goals

Nights in the facility were the worst for Brody. After family night, when his own family didn't show, he silently let his tears fall. If Catherine were permitted, he knew she would have been there, no questions asked.

He missed her.

Sleep had been elusive for him once more, and the disinfectant permeating the air told him the night shift was getting ready to leave and it would be time to wake up soon, or get out of bed as was his case. The shuffling of rubber soles against the tile passed by the door with no bed check this time, which was another indicator of the impending morning. One more day, he told himself. One more round of groups.

One more night in a strange bed with invasive thoughts and no reprieve.

He wrapped his arms around himself as he wondered what Catherine was doing right at that moment. She was probably with

Jen, or at the very least she was online, posting and commenting, being the early riser that she was. She'd seen a surge in popularity after JJ's party where Audrey had deemed her the Mary Sue because everyone loved her. He wondered in the silence if her popularity would wane should they get to know her sober, or if perhaps the Catherine of old may surface.

Nah, he thought. She wouldn't revert to her old self.

Or would she?

Frank went back and forth, depending on what suited him at the time. Would Catherine do the same?

Just as quickly as the thought entered his mind, he shook it off. There was no comparing the two, not anymore.

Catherine, like him, had seen too much, lived through the hell of abuse. He was sure of his answer. He'd watched as her compassion had been ignited, how her affection towards Tyler and Sammi had grown. She'd risked everything to ensure their safety. Granted, it was cunning, and she could have let him in on it, but the verification that his feelings had been reciprocated was worth the payoff.

Getting back to the town he'd grown up in, back to his friends—especially Max—was worth it.

Max... Brody wondered how he was doing. Max's reaction, his admission that he'd been afraid that he'd lost Brody, too, had shaken him. They hadn't really talked about Max's feelings over losing Brian; it was a conversation he'd most likely had with Sarah. The pure relief and joy had been relayed in the first hug Max had given him since...

Since he moved back home.

That first night, his mother had allowed him to go over to see Max, and his excited rambles about everything Brody had missed replayed in his mind. He'd even joked that the reason he and Sarah started dating was because Brody and JJ were gone.

JJ, who'd not only lost his best friend, but his older brother as well. It was time to tell JJ that he was sorry that he hadn't gone home. He was sorry that he'd wanted to be shitfaced instead of dealing with Frank. He understood where JJ's anger was coming from, because he blamed himself for Brian's death, too. That didn't make JJ an asshole just because he pointed out what was, to Brody, the truth.

"Rise and shine," a young aide said as he turned on the lights. "Breakfast will be ready soon. Get your showers in."

Brody rose slowly, pretending he'd slept to avoid his stay being prolonged. Matt, who actually had been asleep, groaned and covered his head.

"Yeah, probably not the thing to do." Brody pulled his covers back. "We're almost out of here."

"Yay and not yay." Matt sat up and rubbed the sleep from his eyes.

"Yes yay. I told you, you're not in this alone."

"Neither are you."

Brody managed half a smile and gestured with his head. "It's a long enough line as it is. Let's go."

The first in the showers were always the ones going home that day. That would be tomorrow for him and for Matt if they played their cards right. He couldn't wait to get out of here, to go home, to see Catherine and his friends.

He couldn't wait to see if anyone had responded to Catherine's inquiries.

He may finally know who his father was, and more than just a name. And if his father lived close enough, he could go to see him in person, find out what, if any, of his traits, his personality, his everything came from being a Kostopoulos.

Brody Kostopoulos didn't sound quite right, though.

Brody smiled as he remembered Catherine's response to him saying he was happy he hadn't had to spell it in kindergarten. Her eyes had sparkled with the laughter than rang from her, had warmed him in the way only she could. No matter what bonding occurred with the other kids here, he was still needing to see her. Be near her. Tell her about breaking down and admitting he blamed himself for Brian's death.

That thought took the smile from his face as he entered the small washroom to take his shower.

"I'm going to live with my sister."

Cassie's announcement before the official beginning of morning group was met with applause and congratulations. He was happy for her, and yet he couldn't help but wonder what was in store for him the next day. His chest tightened as he realized he didn't know if he was going home after all; he could easily be heading towards a long-term facility, or juvenile detention, as he didn't know what criteria really fit. Counting backwards wasn't working anymore, so he simply smiled through it, taking his seat when instructed to.

"We're going to talk about goals today," the facilitator— Richard, who was called 'Dick' more often than not—said. "Both short term and long term. Go around the room so that we aren't waiting forever for someone to begin. Cassie, let's hear yours."

"I'll be moving out of state, to Virginia. My sister works in D.C." Her smile lit up the room. "That was a long-term goal, but now it's short, so I suppose I need to think of what I want to do."

"Is there anything in particular that you like doing?" Richard asked.

The usually shy Cassie didn't miss a beat. "I'm good with my hands. I like building things. I may work with the drama club building sets or something like I used to before."

Drama club. Another thought of Brian flashed in Brody's mind, this one of him onstage performing. He could make an audience laugh or bring them to tears, each as effortlessly as the other. What was it his mother had said? Oh, right... Brian was a good actor.

He'd continued acting off stage, pretending nothing was wrong.

"I dunno, try not to die." It was Emily's turn now. "Hey, I'm being serious. Addiction is... well, it sucks, almost as much as detox. And when that's the environment I'm in, or going back into foster care... yeah. No thanks. So, try not to die. And if I survive, I like to do hair and makeup and shit like that. Not for theatre, though. No offense."

"Would foster care be so bad, though? Compared to living with your mother?"

"Well, Dick, I lived out of a brown paper bag while I got shipped from home to home that only wanted me around for the extra money from the state that was supposed to be used to take care of me but wasn't. At least I have my own room at Mom's, and I know everyone around there."

"What about your father?"

"Dead. Drugs, imagine that."

Brody looked at this young girl and felt the same pain in his heart that Catherine must have felt for him at one time. How could a parent not put their child first? How was it that drugs or money were more important?

How many other kids in here had gone through the same hell that he had?

"Short term, adjust. I have friends now... I think," Matt said.

"You do," Brody said, and Emily agreed. "But don't listen to her; she's from a rival school." He laughed as Emily flipped him off.

Matt seemed a little flustered, a little emotional as he continued. "That's a first. The friend thing, I mean. And, um... well, I love to dance, but where will that take me?"

"Ever heard of Broadway?" Emily asked him.

"There's a dance studio close to the high school," Brody spoke up. "I can show it to you."

"And how do you know about it, lover boy?" A new kid was obviously trying to impress someone, or at least attempt to.

"My girlfriend works there."

"Yeah, what's his name?"

Matt became flustered, folding into himself as Richard admonished the new kid, reminding him of the rules that some didn't want to adhere to. Brody, on the other hand, looked inquisitively at this new kid, through eyes of someone who'd acted tough when he was scared out of his fucking mind.

Maybe this kid was simply a great actor, like Brian had been.

Like he was being now.

Brody was so wrapped up in his own thoughts he hadn't realized it was his turn to go before he was nudged. "Hmm? Oh." Short-term goals. "I'm going to find my father, my real one. I have a lot of questions for him." Like why he would give him and his brother up like they'd never existed, and did he ever think of them, did he regret his decision.

"What kind of questions?"

"The kind that are private." Brody quickly regained his composure. "I'm sorry, but they just are."

"And long-term?"

He smiled. "I'm going to travel, take photographs, see everything the world has to offer. Get my passport, obviously, and just go. I'd thought it was just to see things and places, but… I don't know, I would like to capture humanity."

"Is there such a thing?" someone asked.

"I've seen it."

He'd seen it in the residents of Brentfield, in the volunteers that had shown up to help.

He'd seen it in Catherine.

"What does your girlfriend think about that?" Emily asked.

"She knows." Catherine also thought that Brody was going to wait until after college. He wasn't so sure that college was in the cards for him, even if he got a scholarship. She was already applying everywhere, and he hadn't even bothered to look.

"No, I mean, what does she think?"

She believed it's something to do on the side, but Brody didn't want to do photography as a hobby any more than Catherine wanted to dance or do gymnastics as a hobby. It was in his blood. It was what he was meant to do.

"She's supportive."

"Oh, that was said with conviction."

One corner of Brody's mouth lifted in a smile. "Give me coffee, Em, and I'll put all the emotions behind those words."

"It was tough seeing Em go, too. Her and Cassie both." Matt was lying on his back looking at the ceiling, same as Brody. "Do you think they'll really keep in touch?"

"Facebook is sometimes a wonderful thing."

"Did you really say wonderful? All I've seen is hate."

"It can be useful, I mean." Brody sighed and closed his eyes, picturing Catherine's face in his mind, remembering what she'd been through after her break up with Mitch. "But I've seen the hate, too."

"What do you get hated for? You're gorgeous, have a girlfriend,"

"I'm not gorgeous."

"I'm a gay kid, Brody, and I know gorgeous when I see it. I bet you're popular, too."

"Known, but not really popular." Except just after Brian had died, when everyone wanted closer to the tragedy, to fulfill some sick fascination with being a part of it. He hadn't really noticed; he'd been too busy immersing himself in school and his then-girlfriend, Audrey. Even she hadn't truly been interested in him as a person.

But Catherine was.

It didn't have anything to do with her seeing his head bashed into a mirror and helping to close the wound. It didn't have anything to do with seeing him in pain, seeing him tortured, seeing him want so badly to find some bit of normalcy.

No, Catherine wasn't like Audrey.

He was almost sure of it.

"What about you?" Matt's voice pulled Brody back to the present.

"What about me?"

"Are you going to keep in touch?"

"I told you, man, I got you." Brody smiled over at him. "No worries."

"No worries."

And despite repeating the words over and over in his head, the closer dawn crept in, the more worried he became.

CHAPTER 17

Nothing Shady

"You're quiet." Finally free of the confines of the facility, Brody was watching the passing scenery as his mother drove. He didn't have much to say to her. She'd still questioned his need for medication when the doctor had told her they were switching it, as well as including something for sleep. The drone of the car engine as they weaved their way around the back roads was almost making him sleepy.

"I suppose you're angry with me."

He shook his head. "I get it." He understood the fear those words he'd said would instill, especially after Brian's suicide.

"Do you?"

He was far too exhausted to argue with her. "Where are Ty and Sammi?" he asked instead, dreading the answer should they be with Frank.

"Oh, your Aunt Sheryl's in town."

Aunt Sheryl. She would have known his father personally. Suddenly awake, he said, "I'd like to see her."

"That's where we're going."

"Where?"

"The hotel. She wasn't on the list, so she couldn't get in on Thursday."

"Why didn't you come?"

His question was met with silence, and he continued watching the trees swaying. He could feel his anger, but knowing where he had ended up the last time he voiced his opinion about his mother's treatment of him, he kept it bottled down. His stomach ached in a familiar way, one that told him he had another sleepless night ahead.

"You know, your father is helping a lot with recovery and rebuilding in Brentfield."

"He's not my father, and I would appreciate it if you didn't bring him up right now."

"Well, I see your vacation did nothing for your mood."

She was testing him, he was sure about it. He wasn't going to play into her hands, and remained silent. Vacation... she should know better. She'd been placed in a facility herself. Had she seen that as a vacation? Dreading the answer, he left it unasked and the car was silent for the remainder of the ride to the hotel that Sheryl was staying in.

The upper scale hotel had a valet service. A year ago he may have been impressed; he'd lived in a grand, large house, though, and wealth had done nothing for its occupants' happiness. When his mother failed to tip the driver, Brody pulled out his wallet and handed what was left of his cash to the driver.

His mother's demeanor changed the moment she stepped into the high-ceilinged lobby, her shoes clicking on the marble floor as they walked up to the front desk. There was an air of superiority about her as she paused, almost looking bored. "Excuse me, sir. My sister is in the penthouse suite, and we need assistance getting to that floor."

He'd seen this behavior before, the one where service workers were looked down upon. His mother's face was slightly upturned as they followed the young hotel manager to the elevators, where he inserted a key card to get them to the top floor. Brody apologized for not being able to tip him right as Sheryl walked forward, money in hand.

His mother, despite her modest second-hand clothing, reminded him of Catherine's mother, Theresa.

Everyone was beneath her.

"We won't be staying long," Sandra said.

Just Sandra.

He couldn't find it in his heart to call this woman, this stranger his mother.

"Hi, sweetheart." Sheryl pulled Brody into her arms, her warmth enveloping him. He returned the hug, then stepped back, his eyes roaming the large room.

"Where are Ty and Sammi?" His tone was far less accusatory than it had been when he'd asked his mother.

"They went to get ice cream. Don't give me a lecture on how it's too early, Sandy. They're absolute angels."

"Well, Brody doesn't seem to think so."

"I never said that," he retorted with an edge of resentment.

"But you were complaining about watching them."

"I was complaining about you being gone all the time. Big difference. Huge."

"Okay, I'm going to step in here. I want to see my nephew, so..." Her voice trailed off as she put her arm around him. "I have something for you," she whispered. He followed her in silence, the plush white room so bright it hurt his eyes. Once out of earshot, he spoke softly.

"I want to talk to you about my father, Nikos."

"He goes by Nick," she whispered, then loudly said, "I'm sorry, but I really can't answer you." She turned to him, a baby book in hand. "Put this in your backpack," she whispered. As Sandra droned on about how she wanted to quit her job but couldn't afford to, Sheryl handed him another baby book, similar to the first.

Those must be his and Brian's.

And considering how Sheryl was hiding them from Sandra's sight, they were sure to hold answers that he was looking for.

Brody sunk down onto a couch, his eyes stinging with unshed tears. He signed 'thank you' to Sheryl, who only smiled and handed him some trinket from Chicago. "Cool, thanks," he said when he knew his mother's eyes were upon him.

"We do have to get going," Sandra said as she stood, her expression one of envy as she surveyed the posh high-end details of the room.

"Mom... Ty and Sammi."

"Oh, I'll bring them back, don't worry," Sheryl said with a laugh as she hugged him once more. "It's all in there," she whispered, and one lone tear escaped his eyes, trailing down his cheek.

The house was far too quiet without the kids there, and Brody walked around the new furniture, the new television, the new dining room table and chairs. They even smelled new, leaving the house scented of wood and leather. "This from Catherine's grandfather?" His question was another that was met with silence, this one he knew all too well.

The answer was yes.

"I imagine you want to go spend time with your friends." Her statement was unexpected, arousing his suspicion.

"As in, Frank's coming over and you don't want another confrontation."

"Something like that."

Brody inhaled sharply, telling himself not now, *not now, not now.* "Well, yeah. I... guess I'll see you later." He sent a quick text to Max, who told him to get his ass up to the pool with a quickness, followed by another.

Nothing shady. We just miss you and are tired of seeing Queen C mope around

His smile was genuine as he gathered his swim trunks and a towel, then feeling bold, he walked back out to the living room. "Can I borrow the car?"

"Keys are on the table. Do you see that? We have an actual dining room table. Isn't that wonderful?"

"Oh, it's great." It was hard to keep the sarcasm out of his voice, but his mother was so busy flipping through channels that she didn't seem to mind. "We have cable?"

"They were running a special."

Brody only nodded instead of asking her where this special came from. "Okay, well, I'm going to the pool."

"Yeah, yeah, okay."

Just like she'd always said.

He'd never paid attention to it before, as she rarely bothered to pay attention to him.

He picked the keys up and tossed them in the air once. "See ya," he said on his way out the door, and didn't pause for a response that wasn't going to come. He was grinning to himself as he sat behind the wheel of his mother's car and sent Catherine a message.

Tell me your wearing that white bikini

And he wasn't the least bit surprised when he arrived at the pool and she ran straight up to him and jumped in his arms.

"So I have to go tomorrow to pick a few things up at the house." It was break time when Catherine announced this to Brody, and he leaned in so that she could hear his question above the crowd poolside.

"What house?"

"My mother's."

"I thought you didn't want your things from there."

"I never said that."

"Yeah, Cat, you did."

"I'm doing donations for the storm victims." She grinned, seemingly choosing to ignore his comment. "I'd rather that then allow my mother to sell them the way she threatened to. Dad said I could use his car, since he obviously doesn't want to go."

Brody looked away for a moment, not wanting her to see the thought process that was sure to be in his eyes. Theresa went to the wedding. She must know something. Hell, if he really looked as much like his biological father as Frank used as an excuse, Theresa probably knew exactly who he was. "I could see if I can take Mom's, too."

She scrunched up her nose, which he promptly kissed the tip of. "I was kinda hoping you'd ride with me."

"To keep you from chickening out?"

"No, because I haven't seen you in days. Besides, that means we spend all day together, and we can go up to the park for the fireworks."

"I thought we were going anyway."

"Together." She nudged him. "Oh! Get this... so your ex called me the other day. Audrey, I mean. Seems that the girls want me on the cheerleading squad. I said no, but *still*."

"Why did you say no?"

She lifted one shoulder. "I have work and stuff. And Dad already had to take summer school work on. I didn't need to add another bill. Trust me; even though they're not a competitive squad like Davis, it's still not cheap."

He didn't quite know what to say to her, his mind a million miles away, wondering if Cassie was happy, if Emily was using again, if Matt would really make it up for the fireworks like he'd said he would. He wondered if he had to choose between a job and photography exactly what the answer would be. Of course his job was in a grocery store while Catherine's was working in a dance studio, and...

"Are you even listening to me?"

"I'm really fucking tired, Cat, and I can't even go home."

"Why not? Tell Frank to leave. Tell your mother you don't want him there."

"Because I haven't tried that before." There was no masking his sarcasm and annoyance, not necessarily at Catherine, but she was the one with him.

"Could you not? Please," she added, although her tone was clipped as well.

"I've tried to 'not' and look where I ended up."

"Yeah, my badass juvie boyfriend."

"Not juvie. A psych ward. Try saying that one with pride." He stood and walked away, towards the snack area, only then remembering he'd given all of his money to the valet his mother refused to tip. With a muttered curse, he turned back around, his hands fisted in his hair.

"I know that look." Max was beside him. "I'm fucking parched. Want a drink?"

"What look?"

"The one you'd always get before you did something stupid. Just don't, okay? We're in enough trouble here for fucking cursing and jumping in and throwing the kids around, even though they ask us to. I'd rather not get kicked out, because I wouldn't be able to see my hot girlfriend up in that chair with a whistle, which somehow is hotter than it sounds."

Brody frowned. "Why would you get kicked out if I did something stupid?"

"Because I've got your back, always. Unless you break up with Catherine, because I'm afraid we're gonna have to keep your girlfriend."

Brody forced a grin. "Yeah." He looked over at the girl he adored, the one he wanted happiness for above everything, and wondered if he was the right person for her.

CHAPTER 18

The Name He Was Given

There was an uneasy silence at the dinner table as Catherine set the food down while smiling at her father. "I tried to make it as good as Greta, but you know how she was a magician."

"It looks wonderful," Coach replied, his smile matching his daughter's.

"Did she make this while I was there?" Brody asked, also smiling at Catherine.

"Nope. Chicken Fettuccine Alfredo is Dad's favorite, not one of Theresa's."

"It was yours, too, if I recall correctly." Coach sampled his food and nodded. "Wonderful."

"You're quiet today," Catherine remarked to Brody, who shrugged.

"Last time I was here ended kinda awkwardly."

"But you understand, don't you?" Coach asked. "You understand why she did it."

Brody's eyes dropped to his plate, his stomach protesting food no matter how delicious it was. "Yeah, I get it." There was much more to the story, though… details he wasn't sure Catherine had shared with her father.

"It's nothing to be ashamed of. It was extreme, but not shameful considering everything you've been through."

Brody held back the urge to snap at Coach, tell him that compared to some, he had it easy. And it wasn't shameful no matter the circumstances, he was sure of that after meeting so many others who had been stopped in time. Hearing their stories, though, had him second-guessing the last few months of Brian's life, knowing now that Brian had been saying goodbye in his own way to everyone.

The realization hit him straight in the chest, constricting it.

"Well, the real reason for this dinner is for my daughter to apologize to you."

Brody's eyes snapped to Catherine. "For what?"

"Well, I kinda went ahead and did the online stuff for your pictures." Catherine shrugged. "Daddy set the asking price, though. And in my defense, they're really good, and they tell a story. If we'd waited until you got out, they may not have sold at all. They're national, Brody. National."

One corner of Brody's mouth tilted upwards. "I figured you'd see it through. I was counting on it, actually."

"See, Daddy?" Catherine's smile was triumphant. "I told you he'd be happy."

Happy.

What exactly was happy?

Was it elation over his dreams of nationally published photos becoming a reality? Was it this beautiful girl smiling at him as if he could conquer the world? Was it the look of pride in Coach's face, one that he'd wanted so long from his own mother, and even from Frank?

Was it pasting a smile on his face while going through the motions the way that Brian—the boy that everyone was convinced was happy—had done while he was planning his death?

Was it putting on a tough exterior and drowning himself in alcohol the way JJ did?

Max... Max probably knew the definition. Brody needed to ask him about it, what his secret to happiness was, because he was full of doubt on trepidation and a foreboding sense of doom. That most likely had to do with Frank being at his home, with his mother, doing who knows what.

His appetite vanished.

He picked at his food while he asked questions about the terms, and was humbled to find he would have a large check coming by the end of July. His chatter was the perfect excuse to eat very little, despite the fact that it really was good, and he even told Catherine that Greta would be proud.

"Plans for this evening?" Coach asked when the meal was done. Catherine shrugged.

"We were thinking about going to hang out with Jen."

"You mean you wanted to go to another party at Nan's." Coach looked over his shoulder as he walked into the kitchen carrying plates. "I was a teenager once, too."

"Actually," Brody interrupted Catherine's comeback, "I have a couple things I was wanting to go over with Catherine, if you don't mind."

"What things?"

He unzipped his backpack, revealing its contents. "Answers from my aunt Sheryl."

"How did you not tell me this before?" Catherine took one of the baby books from him and sat on the couch with a bounce. "This is amazing!"

"Wait, don't." Brody stopped her from opening it, his heart hammering.

"Oh, sorry, I forgot." She bounded past him into the kitchen while he walked over to the couch, sitting slowly as he took that first book into his hand. This one was blue with teddy bears on the cover, the corners worn. When Catherine returned to the living room, she had a cup of black coffee in her hand that she held out to him.

"You're an angel," he said with a warm smile.

"Who drinks coffee this late at night?" Coach asked as he passed them.

Brody took a sip and sighed. "Someone who hasn't had any in days."

"I'm going to give you two a little bit of privacy." He continued walking down the hall. "Stress on the word little."

Brody's smile was timid as he looked over at Catherine. She was ready to dive right in, absorb all of the information that she could. As much as he adored her and her enthusiasm, right at that moment he wished he'd been able to do this at home, in his room.

Alone.

The way Brian had been when he put a bullet through his brain.

"Okay, ready?"

"Not really," he admitted as he looked down at the blue book. Was this one his or Brian's?

"Here." Catherine held her hand out, and instinctively his fingers clasped the book a little harder. What if what was in there is what sent Brian over that edge? "Brody,"

"Give me a minute, okay?" He placed the book on the coffee table and took a sip of coffee. "Um... tomorrow,"

"Nope, not waiting until tomorrow." Her arms were crossed and her eyebrow raised. "Stop stalling. You wanted to know, and now you can. You're one of the bravest people that I know. Don't let a little thing like the truth get to you."

He sat back with a sigh and a grin. "One of? Really?"

"You're being defeated by a baby book, Harris. Oh, sorry... Kostopoulos."

"I'm still a Harris."

"You really want to keep Frank's name?"

"It was Brian's name, too."

Brody said the words without thinking, only then realizing that was half the battle—stop thinking so much.

Just keep moving forward.

He reached over and opened the cover of the book, and Catherine read aloud.

"Dante Mateo Kostopoulos."

Without her even saying that the time of birth was 1:57 in the morning that this was Brian's book. Brian Matthew Harris is who he'd become, who he'd died as.

"Is this one yours?" Catherine asked, and Brody shook his head. "Should we look at yours instead?"

Again Brody shook his head, this time as he turned the page to read Brian's firsts... first smile, first tooth, first word. The notes about how he was a sullen baby who cried often were what got to Brody, as he'd never known his brother to be anything but happy.

The book continued on, with monumental commemorations of birthdays, of Christmas, of the beginning of his toddler years before abruptly ending when he turned two.

Fitting, how his life had abruptly ended when he was 16.

"The only thing that's missing are pictures," Catherine said with wonder as she read, absorbed, took notes of his grandparents' names and places of birth. "So you're straight-up Greek," she'd pointed out when it listed his father's birthplace.

"Looks that way."

"And they met at a sorority party. Ooooo, that's right, we have those to look forward to soon. Where have you applied?"

"I haven't."

"You can't keep putting it off."

"Cat, we haven't even started our senior year of high school. We still have time."

"This summer is the best time to scout colleges, though, but that's later. For now…" Her voice trailed off as she reached into Brody's backpack. "There's this."

The green baby book.

The one that had to be his.

His heart hammered as his fingertips traced over the imagery and words on the front. Many of the questions he had would be answered right there in front of him. He noticed that this book had a couple of envelopes in the front. One had pictures, and he set it to the side, the fear he'd told Catherine wasn't present preventing him from looking. The other contained a letter with his name—his current name—on the front of it in Sandra's scripted writing.

"Do you want to read that first?"

Brody shook his head and removed it as well, placing it on top of the envelope of pictures.

It was 7:30 in the evening of that muggy July 3rd, with fans circulating the fixed air conditioning in the small house that Catherine shared with her father and the soft floral scent of her perfume lingering when Brody found out the name he was given at birth.

Dimitri Philip Kostopoulos.

CHAPTER 19

Or Himself

The world was slowly moving as Catherine turned towards Brody with an excited smile. Her exclamation, her joy had her father walking quickly down the hall, where he then congratulated Brody on finding what he was looking for.

Inside, Brody felt like a piece of him had died.

Who was he now? Was he still Brody Harris, the lone survivor of a set of twins who'd grown up far too quickly? Or was he Dimitri Kostopoulos, son of an apparent cinematographer, grandson of a producer...

Lone survivor of a set of twins.

Brian... he wanted so badly to reach out to Brian, tell him he was finding the answers to questions that he'd had for so long, questions that Brian had told him to stop asking because he had a family. An imperfect family, but a family all the same.

But this other family, the one foreign to him, was depicted in words and an envelope of photographs, along with a letter from his Aunt Sheryl that he'd had yet to read. Catherine was fascinated by the details of him that his mother had claimed to have little recollection of, including a trip to Greece to visit grandparents who hadn't been bothered to check on his welfare for years.

Or had they?

"Look at this," Catherine said as she held up a photograph of his parents on their wedding day. "You definitely favor your father's side."

That much was true; he and Brian were both the spitting image of their grandfather more so than their own father, though they looked much like him as well. Had Frank truly known about the resemblance, or had he merely guessed? That would be a question he would either have to pose to a woman who hadn't been honest with him his entire life or a man he'd rather never see again.

"Aren't you going to read that?" Catherine asked as he shoved Sheryl's letter down into his backpack.

"Not now," he mumbled, still staring at words written in his mother's writing across pages of firsts. He'd been the happy one, he found out, who was always smiling, always loving, always wanting to share with his brother.

When had their roles reversed?

Had it been at Frank's hands that morning he'd mistakenly woken him up, setting him off in a rage that had left him bruised for weeks?

Or had it been at the loss of a family, of his real father, who was always the one holding him in the pictures?

"You were named after your grandfather," Catherine pointed out, although he'd already seen the name *Philip Kostopoulos* written in that space when they'd been through Brian's—Dante's?—baby book.

What did this mean? Should he continue searching for the man who'd abandoned him to this life, or should he resign himself to having not one, but two fathers who couldn't seem to love him enough?

Brody stood, coffee forgotten, hands fisted in his hair as he took measured breaths to calm himself. He was seventeen and soon he'd be an adult, able to leave all of this behind him. But then again, he was only seventeen, and he longed to be loved and accepted as he was, faults and all.

He should never have to question whether or not said love came from his parents.

"Are you okay?"

"Hmm? Oh, yeah, I'm fine. I'm just tired, Cat."

"So you've said before."

Before, in the house on the hill, when life was getting to him there, too.

He leaned down and kissed her, soft and full of promise. "I just need some sleep. I'm going to head back, and we can just," he gestured with his hands, "go over all of this tomorrow on our long ass drive to your mother's."

"It's not that long."

He wrapped his arms around her and pulled her close. "It's never long enough with you."

"I'm worried about you, Brody."

He stepped back with a tight smile. "Don't be."

But he wasn't sure if he was trying to convince her or himself.

The BMW parked in Brody's driveway was the same car that Frank had been driving when they lived in the house on the hill the previous summer. He wasn't sure how Frank could afford it, unless he was still working for Catherine's grandfather. Perhaps it was for hush money, so that no harm would come to the Davis name.

At that moment, he couldn't bring himself to give a shit.

He hopped the fence so the noisy gate wouldn't give away his presence and walked across the lawn towards the large oak tree by his window. Backpack in hand, his silent climb was effortless, and he settled by his window, placing the backpack beside him.

"Fuck."

The curse was muttered as he laid back on the shingles and stared at the starless sky, his thoughts a proverbial jumble. Below him, within the walls of what should be his sanctuary, he could hear Frank's voice raising. He couldn't hear the words, and again couldn't bring himself to care, to feel sorry for his mother. She knew who Frank was; she'd spent years allowing Brody to be the buffer for everyone.

That realization brought another bout of his eyes stinging with unshed tears. Maybe that was why he'd understood Catherine's mother so well: his own mother had acted nearly the same, sans the alcohol. No, that was Frank's vice, one that doubled his anger at everything and everyone. His mother's indifference to his suffering, her silence whenever he tried to ask her what he'd done that was so wrong were all the more apparent now.

He sniffed back the threatening tears as he crossed his arms, hugging them around himself. He was no stranger to affection now that Catherine was in his life, but was nothing compared to the love and compassion that he needed from Sandra. That's who she was now, and judging by the late hour when the front door opened and closed followed by the BMW's engine as it drove away, it was who she would remain. He waited another few minutes before he retreated to his air conditioned room through the window. After a few blinks, his eyes adjusted to the darkness and saw new prescription bottles on his dresser. One was his new mood stabilizer, and the other was a sleep aid that he swore to the staff was working just to get out of there. With a shrug that no one was there to see, he opened the bottle and took out his pill, swallowing it without the aid of a glass of water before he took off his clothes and slid in between the sheets of his freshly made bed.

Sleep blissfully took over the moment his head hit the pillow.

Brody woke to the smell of fresh coffee, calling like a beacon for him. For a moment he wasn't sure where he was, then realizing that yes, it was his bed and no, he wasn't dreaming, he sat up and rubbed his eyes. Light from the rising sun was filtering through his curtains, dancing on the thin layer of dust on his dresser. He grabbed his second bottle of medication and walked down the short hallway, where his mother stood holding out a cup.

"Your father liked his black as well."

He hid the surprise from his expression as he took the cup from her, knowing she wasn't speaking of Frank, who despised it.

"I suppose you have a lot of questions."

"Just one," Brody mumbled as he walked slowly into the dining room and eased himself into a chair. "Where is he?"

"I don't know."

He nodded once, although he refused to believe her answer, then unlocked his phone and sent a text to Catherine letting her know that he was awake. "I'll be back some time today. Got stuff to do."

"I don't think so, Brody."

"Well, I do." He looked over at her, keeping his expression neutral. "I'm helping out tornado victims, then going to the fireworks with friends."

He didn't lie to her; he was going with Catherine to retrieve items to donate, and then they were going to meet Max, Sarah, Jen, and Jen's girlfriend, which Catherine was excited to do.

"Frank would be happy to pick you up, take you with him."

"No thanks." He kept his reply short to keep from asking her what the hell she was thinking, especially knowing where he'd end up if he did.

Just a few short months and he would be 18, and the closest thing to sending him away that she could do was kick him out of the house.

Somehow he had no doubt that she would.

"When are Tyler and Sammi coming back?"

"I'm not sure. Sheryl wanted to take them for a short vacation, and I thought it was best."

"Why?"

"Because they don't need to think that it's okay to act the way that you have been."

"You suddenly don't trust me with them?"

"I suddenly don't trust you at all."

He shrugged, the memory of their fight a blur. He knew his words had backed him into a corner before, one that he hadn't meant to be in. "That's fair," was all he said as he took a sip of his coffee.

"I don't want her here when I'm not home."

"Those are the rules, I know."

"Are you going to follow them?"

"I'm not even going to be here today."

"And I don't want you going to Nan's after the fireworks. I know what goes on there."

"A bunch of teenagers being a bunch of teenagers. You're right; that's scary. Maybe I shouldn't associate with any of my friends."

"I wasn't aware that JJ was even talking to you."

Brody shrugged. "He doesn't talk to half of the people that show up there." Which wasn't exactly true; JJ thrived in an environment where he was surrounded by people. "I go there every year after the fireworks."

"That was before your brother killed himself directly after one of them. I don't want you going."

Brody held his mug tighter. "You're the one with Brian's letter, Sandra, so I wouldn't know why."

"Brody,"

"Aren't you going to be late for work?"

Sandra glanced at the time on her phone. "I have to go. Remember,"

"She won't come in when she picks me up."

"Good."

He remained motionless as she walked over and kissed his temple before she gathered her things and left.

All she cared about was that no one else came in.

That Tyler and Sammi didn't fight back if they were treated unfairly.

She hadn't even corrected him when he called her by her name.

CHAPTER 20

You Just Are

Brody greeted Catherine at the door with a lush, full kiss that had her sighing in his arms. "What did I do to deserve that?"

"You just are," he murmured against her lips before kissing her again. "You ready for today?"

"Duh." The word was more full of sarcasm than confidence. She was fidgeting, running her fingers through her hair and pushing it behind her ears. He followed her out to her father's car, which had seen better days but was nicer than the car Brody's mother owned. She was pulling the keys out of her pocket, but she fumbled—something she never did—and they slipped from her fingertips.

Brody caught them and tossed them up in the air. "Would you feel better if I drove?"

"How much sleep did you get?"

He tilted her face up towards his with his fingertips and noticed, the dark circles showing beneath her eyes. "More than you, I would imagine."

"I don't want Theresa to be there." Catherine stomped her way over to the passenger side. "I just don't. There's nothing like hearing your own mother didn't want you."

"I think I kinda get that."

Her bottom lip stuck slightly out. "I don't want to see her, but then again, what if she isn't there? What if she really meant it when she said... oh, whatever her housekeeper's name is would be there?" She opened the door with a huff. "I don't want to see her, but what if she doesn't want to see me?"

"Then you have me."

Her smile was trembling as she slid into her seat without responding, leaving Brody standing beside the car, his lips turned downward in a frown. It had always been enough for her before, the way her mere presence made him feel as if he could conquer the world.

Maybe since seeing his darkness, it wasn't the same for her.

"C'mon, slowpoke," she called out before closing her door. As he got in, she asked, "Who are these friends of yours coming tonight?"

"Hopefully coming tonight." He turned the key and turned down the blaring radio. "Matt is from Brentfield, and Emily goes to Easton."

"Do I know Matt?"

"He just moved, doesn't know anyone else here. And Em's just a kid. Fuck, we all are, aren't we?"

"Not you."

He glanced sideways at her, then his eyes were back on the road. "What do you mean?"

"You're Mr. Responsibility Guy. That's how I've always known you, even when you had Greta to fall back on."

He nodded his agreement, unwilling to go down the path of how tired of responsibility he was. "You'll like them. I mean, Em's a little rough around the edges, but she's still a good kid."

"If she was a good kid, how did she end up in there? Sorry," she added quickly. "I didn't mean it that way."

"We're a lot like each other, all of us." He merged onto the highway with ease, most holiday travelers either sleeping or already at their destinations.

"And I'm not?"

"It would kill me to see that happen to you, Cat. Absolutely fucking kill me." His words were more raw and honest than he wanted to admit, but they were out now, lingering in the stilled conversation, floating with the music that played soft and low in the background. He inhaled sharply as her small hand rested atop his, and they remained that way for the rest of the drive.

The house on the hill no longer looked impressive to Brody. He'd lived through far too much within its walls, as well as the abandoned gym in the back. The pool was still sparkling, pristine as they walked past it towards Catherine's former private gym. "What's in here?" he asked as Catherine unlocked the door.

"A few weights, some dance shoes, some of my old gym stuff." The air was stagnant, the air conditioning unit not turned on as it wasn't going to be used. "I hear that she's getting it torn down. Or so she says, anyway, with the whole if-I-don't-move-back speech." She paused as she placed a box down, putting the remaining possessions in the gym within it.

Brody walked over to the opposite side, where a racket and tennis balls sat, and he remembered with a smile some of the only days he'd found tolerable. "Do you want these?"

"They're Theresa's. Unless you want them, then just put them in the box."

"Why did we come back here first, Cat?"

"Because there's so little to do." Her voice was high and tight, choked with emotion. This had been her place, her gym, her sanctuary for years where she honed what she loved best.

And Theresa was having it torn down.

"So let's get it done," she added before Brody could say any words of comfort. He knew this side of Catherine also; do whatever you have to.

Break down later.

The gym didn't have many items, only a single box's worth, and he carried it to the car with her behind him, their silence permeated by chirping birds and the occasional vehicle passing by on the street far from the front door. He watched as Catherine took a deep breath and steadied herself, calling in all of her composure, and he followed as she walked with purpose in her graceful steps towards the front door.

This time her key didn't work.

"Fuck it," she said, so unlike the Catherine of old, and she rang the doorbell. When she turned to him with one eyebrow raised, he smiled.

"You've got this, Cat."

Brody didn't recognize the woman who answered the door, the one dressed in the same type of uniform that Greta would wear daily. Catherine apparently did, and she smiled, although it didn't quite reach her eyes. "I'm here for my things."

"I was told you'd be coming." The woman also spoke perfect English, unlike Greta whose vocabulary was broken at times with Spanish.

"Thank you," was all Catherine said to her as she and Brody walked past and into the entry way. This was where Sammi had spilled her KoolAid onto Catherine's jeans and boots.

It was also where Frank confronted Brody on his birthday—the day of the lake party—and drug him by his hair through the house and to the gym, in front of Theresa who'd only turned up her nose and walked down the hallway.

"There are fresh boxes and tape so you don't have to drag anything in here," the housekeeper called after them.

"Oh, we wouldn't dream of it," Catherine said loudly, and a little too sweetly, making Brody laugh under his breath.

"Tiny and fierce," he whispered in her ear as he passed her, and he was rewarded with the first genuine smile from her in over an hour.

"Too over the top?"

He shook his head. "Not even close."

"Good. Could you put a couple boxes together? I'm just going to throw everything in them. If I can't use it, someone else can."

"Are you really the same girl who threw a fit over stained jeans?"

"And boots," she said. "Don't forget the boots. But... no. No, I don't think I am."

He smiled over his shoulder as he grabbed the first unmade box. "You've grown, Cat."

"I'll take that as a compliment. Now hurry up. We have all day together and I don't want to waste it in our former prison."

"Oh, harsh," he laughed, and together they began the swift packing of all things Catherine of old. Every piece of clothing from her walk-in closet as well as her dresser had designer labels on them, and all of them in pristine condition. Catherine even pulled out her formal dresses, adding them to the pile, stating she never knew who could use a donated dress, or if she may wear one of them to any of the dances they had coming up.

She began piling in the unpacked shopping bags full of lavish bath items and makeup, and then came the shoes.

"You bitched about... sorry, I'll shut up," he said quickly when she shot him a glance with one eyebrow raised.

"We need more boxes."

"Are all of these going to fit in your dad's car?"

"It's an SUV, and yes. We will make them fit."

"Sorry, it's an SUV, but... okay, okay, I'll make them fit." He held up his hands in defeat despite the smile on his face. "What, you're not taking your TV?"

"The one we watched *Star Wars* on? You bet your ass I am. Here." She pulled her comforter off her bed. "Wrap it up in this."

"Yes, Queen."

"You know me so well."

"That I do." He leaned over and kissed the tip of her nose. "TV wrapping, box slinging, me totally knows you."

"Could you two please keep it down?"

Theresa was in the doorway, glass in hand, looking down her nose at the pair of teenagers who were so clearly dressed for packing up Catherine's things.

"It's a little early for that, isn't it?" Catherine asked, her hands on her hips. "And don't worry; we're almost finished."

"The television is,"

"Mine," Catherine cut her off. "So is the DVD player. Everything in this room is mine."

"So you'll be taking the furniture as well?"

"We don't have room for it," Brody said as he finished wrapping up the television. "Cat?"

"I'm good," she said with a smile. "You can take what's done out and load it, if you would like." It wasn't as much a suggestion as it was a request, and Brody nodded. He wasn't comfortable leaving Catherine with her mother, remembering how his confrontation with Sandra had gone and where he'd ended up as a result. Despite his stomach being in knots, he grabbed the first two boxes and stacked them on top of each other. Lifting them with ease, he walked towards the door, and Theresa stepped back as her eyes looked him up and down.

His trepidation increased as Theresa stepped into the room and closed the door.

Telling himself repeatedly to breathe, he walked down the hall and descended the stairs to the entryway, pausing only to glance at the stairs leading down to the fully finished basement that had been his bedroom nearly a year before. As he heard Theresa and Catherine's muffled shouts, he was taken back in time where the monster stood before him, snarling his contempt.

"Fuck," he muttered as a wave of nausea hit, threatening to empty the contents of his stomach in that entryway. He barely made it outside before he was setting the boxes down with force and wretching into the bushes.

And he laughed.

His response was so inappropriate that he found himself laughing harder, doubled over where he'd thrown up in the pristine bushes in front of the house on the hill that so many students at Davis High had coveted.

"Maybe it does fit," he said to himself as he loaded the boxes into the back of the small SUV—the one he still considered a car.

This house, the people, everything without was a show, one that Brody had seen straight through the moment he'd walked in the door. He hadn't even considered Catherine merely a spoiled rich girl; he'd seen her as a little girl lost without guidance, without love, without compassion.

He'd wanted so badly to show her that they all existed.

And now he was, even as he took a swig out of his water bottle, swished it around his mouth, and spit it out onto the white concrete of the long circled driveway between Theresa's Cadillac and the BMW...

The BMW.

Frank was here.

CHAPTER 21

Surprises

Brody barely made it inside the front door before coming face to face with Frank as he emerged from the basement, box in hand. "Well, imagine seeing you here," he had the nerve to say.

"Like you didn't know. Either Theresa or San,"

"Are you calling her by her first name now? That's rather disrespectful of you. She's your mother."

"One of them told you, so you decided to show."

"I was asked." And now Frank even had the nerve to grin. "As you were."

"Yeah, I'm not falling for that shit. Catherine didn't ask for you to be here."

"What the hell, Mother?" Catherine's shriek permeated the air, but Brody was so focused on the monster before him that he didn't flinch.

Neither did Frank.

"You look good, kid," he said to Brody nonchalantly, as if they had the best relationship. "I hear you're working at Mack's, too."

"And?"

"And that's good for you, teach you some responsibility."

As if Brody hadn't had responsibility for years already, especially since losing Brian. A muscle in his jaw twitched as he kept his mouth shut, wanting so badly to go off on the man who'd treated him worse than shit on the bottom of his shoe.

"So, I take it you haven't heard the news."

"Not that I would be interested in it," Brody replied coolly.

"Oh, I think you would."

Brody heard Catherine's stomps along with the rustle of a box, and he saw her stop at the top of the steps. "You need to leave," she snapped.

"We both know your boyfriend is violent, Catherine." Theresa sounded bored rather than concerned as she walked up behind her daughter. "He's gathering your things from the basement, since the two of you can't be trusted down there."

"This house is the last place anything that special will happen."

"Are you wanting your trophies, Cat?" Brody asked as he looked at her writing on the side of the box that Frank was still holding.

"No, I don't." She huffed her way down the stairs to the entryway, carrying the box in her arms as if it were light as a feather. "Burn them for all I care."

Frank's smile dripped of sarcasm. "If that's what Lady Catherine wants, that's what Lady Catherine gets."

"Just put them in that gym that her grandfather wasted money on." Theresa smirked. "They can go with the rest of the garbage."

Brody could hear his blood swooshing in his ears, felt every muscle as they tensed up, balled his hands into fists to keep from reaching for his hair and pulling with all of his might. "Cat, are you ready to go?" His voice was low with an edge of an ominous tone, one that Frank scoffed at.

"You know," Catherine began, "I get that you don't want me, that you never did. But to think you'd be any better at raising this asshole's kid? What about when Frank decides to shove his head into a mirror?"

"Wait, what?"

"Oh, you didn't hear the news, then?" Frank walked past him and up the steps, box still in hand. "You're going to be a big brother again."

Brody felt the blood drain from his face as he thought of what that baby's future could possibly be.

"And they call us irresponsible," Catherine said to him, not seeing that he felt the urge to get sick all over again. "It's called birth control, Theresa. I get that you want to be in grandfather's good graces again, though. Way to use another child to do so. C'mon, Brody, let's go."

She didn't have to tell him that twice, and he was out the door before Frank could finish telling them how good it was to see them.

Lies.

All lies.

And now he was having another baby, one that Brody wouldn't be around to protect. One that would be related to Tyler and Sammi, one that was probably the reason he heard Frank and Sandra arguing the night before.

One that had Catherine break down sobbing over as soon as they were on the road.

"Sure, I lose my baby, and someone who hates kids is pregnant," she sniffled. "And she didn't want me. *She didn't want me*, but she wants this baby? She's having this baby knowing that she isn't going to marry Frank? That he's trying to get back with your mother?"

"I've already thrown up once today, Cat, let's not make it twice."

"You... why didn't you tell me?" Her hand was on his forehead at once. "You're not running a fever. Did you eat? You said you had to eat with your meds."

"Remember when you were wondering what kind of mother you would have made?" Brody pulled into the parking lot of a small diner. "That's the kind, the mother that would be concerned."

"I'm not trying to mother you."

"I know." He kissed her forehead. "And no, I didn't eat. I did get paid, though, so let's do this whole eating thing before we get back on the highway.

"I don't think I can." She pulled her visor down and flipped open the mirror. "Oh, wow. A drugstore mascara that actually is waterproof. Okay, then."

He laughed softly, its sound a stark contrast to his tumultuous emotions. He couldn't show how unnerved he was, how devastated to know that yes, Frank was wanting back with his mother. He'd hoped for one brief second that this new baby meant that Frank was going to be gone, but no... of course not.

Of course not.

"Do I look bad?"

"I think you're beautiful no matter what, so you may want to ask someone else that question."

She slipped her small hand in his. "Oh, you're smooth."

"Yeah, I'd like to think so."

"I'm glad you were with me. I don't think I could have... what the hell, is that Taylor driving my car?"

The pearl white car—which Brody could only see as pink— pulled into the parking lot of the diner with Taylor behind the wheel and Laura in the passenger seat, both of whom looked like they were stopping just to get Catherine's reaction.

"Well, I thought that was you. I see you're not trying to hide now."

"I see you like my hand-me-downs." Catherine gestured both to the car and the outfit Taylor was wearing.

"Well, you left the outfit at Chelsea's," Laura spoke up, but Taylor waved her off.

"The way you like Bethany's?"

Brody gave Catherine's hand a squeeze before he spoke up. "Don't start, kid," he said to Taylor, knowing that would anger her, and was awarded with her shocked expression.

"Chelsea's captain," Taylor called after Catherine when she and Brody continued walking towards the restaurant, as if Catherine wouldn't have guessed this already. "Turns out we didn't need you at all."

"We're stuck with last year's routine," he could hear Laura say, and obviously Catherine heard it as well as she grinned up at Brody.

"It must really suck, not even cheering anymore. Rumor has it you didn't even try out."

"Didn't have to," Catherine called over her shoulder with a smile. "I was asked."

"So you'll be at the fundraiser today with the rest of the Valley High squad."

Brody groaned inwardly, knowing what was next.

"It's a donation drive, and yes." Catherine stopped and turned towards Taylor, who was still following them. "And we haven't invited you to breakfast, so go on your merry way." After Taylor turned with a knowing grin, Catherine regained what little of her composure she had lost.

"Babe," Brody began quietly as they resumed their walk towards the diner entrance.

"I know, I know, I turned down the squad. And we weren't going to the donation drive today, but..."

Brody exhaled his resignation. "Fine, but you may want to give Audrey a heads up since you told her you weren't joining the squad."

"I'll just explain the sitch with her and see if she'll go along with it." Catherine pulled out her phone as soon as they were seated. "We don't have to eat here if you don't want to."

"I'm starving, and besides, their biscuits and gravy are to-die-for."

Catherine paused her text and glanced up at him. "You're starting to sound like me, you know."

He grinned. "Was hoping you'd notice. What exactly did your mother say?"

Catherine scowled. "Here? Now? Besides, I kinda laid it out when we were there, and... oh, shit."

Brody's pulse quickened. "Oh shit, what?"

Catherine blinked several times as she glanced down at her phone, then grinned sheepishly at him. "Looks like I joined the squad?"

The squad.

More time for them to be apart.

It's okay, Brody. This is what she wants, and you know it.

"You say it as though it's a question," he commented lightly as the waitress walked up. After they'd ordered and the waitress returned with Brody's coffee, Catherine finally answered.

"It kinda is. I mean, I still have to run it by my dad, and I have to try on their summer uniform and hope that one of those boxes contains my cheer sneakers. You know, the pure white ones."

"Did we grab the shoe box? Because that's what there was; an entire box of shoes. And boots, let's not forget those."

"And sandals and pumps. You act like my shoe obsession is new or something."

"What did you do with those boots? The ones that Sammi spilled KoolAid on."

"Oh, I threw them away," she said with a dismissive wave of her hand.

"Did you try to clean them? To salvage them?"

"Um, no. I threw away the jeans, too."

"Instead of cutting them off into shorts."

"Why would I do that? I have cutoff shorts."

"No, you have specific shorts that were bought that way. Cat, the people getting these clothes… hell, most of the people in the town that we live in, have one pair of shoes that have to make it for years. They can't just throw away things. They can't worry about a white pair of shoes so they can be in a uniform that they didn't want until someone else made a point about them not having it."

"We are not having this conversation in the middle of a diner," she whispered. "And besides, you know this about me. You've known all along who I am. Changing isn't that easy, and at least I give a shit about it now, about everything that I have. I'm not about to have a meltdown in front of my father and get locked up over something trivial."

He set his hand down with enough force to rattle his cup. "Frank fucking Harris is not something trivial."

Her eyes were wide as she looked down at his hand, then back up at him. "Really?"

"Jeeeezus." He sat back in his seat, his hands starting to go for his hair, but he stopped them. "Look, it's been a really bad day, and I've already thrown up in your mother's bushes, so… that's not supposed to be funny."

"It really is, though."

He almost smiled. "Yeah, okay, kind of, but I just need to eat."

"So you're hangry then."

His nod was short. "Must be." He let out a sigh. "And I don't want anymore surprises today."

But when they swung by his home so that he could change and brush his teeth, he had one more surprise waiting for him.

His key no longer worked.

CHAPTER 22

We Discuss

"Thanks so much for this," Brody said to Max when he was handed clothes to change into.

"Yeah, not a problem. See?" Max handed him a packaged toothbrush. "Always ready. And you didn't have to bug your mom at work, either."

Brody nodded, not letting Max know that his key didn't work, that his mother had placed a bar in his window so he couldn't get it open from the outside. He didn't tell Max of his meltdown, of his screaming obscenities, of the way Catherine had told him he was frightening her.

He didn't tell Max of the barrage of texts between him and his mother, the ones where she said she didn't trust him to be alone in the house, the ones where she told him that he would need to find things to do outside of the home while she was at work until that trust returned.

He didn't tell Max his fears that his mother had sent Tyler and Sammi away because she didn't trust him with them.

For all Max knew, Brody had simply forgotten to take his key with him, and since he'd thrown it as hard as he could, Max would be none the wiser.

Brody's shower was purposefully cool to ward off the heat of the morning. Lost in thought, in hurt, in confusion, he let his tears mingle with the water as he leaned against the wall and cried. What did he do that was so wrong to warrant his mother essentially telling him it was a place to sleep, but not to live? Was he truly that bad of a person? He was still her son, still a minor for a few months.

What then?

Was he going to have to pack his things and leave in the beginning of his senior year of high school?

What if she was already making plans to send him away?

With a shake of his head, he sniffed back the rest of his tears. They wouldn't serve any purpose, any more than the tears threatening over his fight with Catherine. Or those over a man who'd made him believe he could never do anything right.

He was barely done rinsing the shampoo out of his hair when there was a shout from the bathroom door. "Dude, you didn't tell me Frank knocked up Catherine's old lady! This is high level gossip here."

"Are we turning into our girlfriends?"

"You'll never be as cute as your girlfriend, Harris. Now hurry the fuck up. I have to piss."

"Whatever," Brody shot back. "Hold it."

"You suck!"

There was no holding back the barrage of questions as soon as Brody was done and dressed, Max shouting them from the bathroom as he took his belated piss. "Can't hear you, shithead."

He sat down on the couch with a sigh and laid his head back. There was no time for sleep, not with the donation drive, the fireworks, and JJ's party, which he still hadn't decided if he was going to.

"I said," Max's voice brought him back, "when did you know?"

"Today." Brody closed his eyes, damning the headache that was beginning to pound. "This morning, just after Cat found out. Fuck, do you have any aspirin?"

"Tylenol, coming right up. So when's the big day?"

"Can't be too far off, unless he was getting conjugal visits from her, and I suddenly feel so fucking sick."

Max handed a bottle of Tylenol to him. "So they're married?"

Brody shook his head before taking a couple of pills."He's still married to Mom."

"That dog."

"Are we really gossiping about this?"

"Chicks gossip. We discuss."

"Right, right. Oh, apparently he wants back with my mom."

Max was silent for a moment and Brody looked over to see him gazing off into the distance. "Are you okay with that?"

"No."

"I don't mean about how dirty he did your mom, I mean... you know." Max shrugged. "I know you don't talk about it; you never did. But I would've been fucking blind to not see how shitty he treated you. Brian was the golden boy, and you... fucking hell, he was such an asshole towards you, no matter what."

"It got worse." Brody's voice was quiet as he recalled how the abuse escalated after Brian's suicide. "And then we moved into that huge fucking house, and..." He began to pick at a thread in the shirt that Max had loaned him. "Mom didn't get rid of him. He left her, took us with him when she was checked into a hospital."

"No shit?"

A little more weight eased off of Brody's shoulders. "Yeah, no shit. And then he went to jail for beating the fuck out of me. I got a few good hits in there, too. I suppose that's how he got away with it."

"Tell me she's not taking him back, dude."

Brody glanced down at his cellphone, where Catherine had sent him a text of her all dolled up in her brand-new summer cheerleading outfit, and he sighed. He didn't want Sandra to take Frank back. He didn't want to live that hell again. He just wanted a normal senior year of high school with his friends and this beautiful girl that he'd scared the shit out of earlier.

"I don't know," he finally said.

"Sarah's almost here with her dad's pickup."

"Why do we need a pickup?"

"We need to swing by the high school and drop off some laundry that my mom was doing for the people there."

Brody smiled. "I hope you know how lucky you are."

"I'm grateful every day. Sarah's awesome."

"So are your parents."

"Maybe. But I need to act like they're not until I'm about 25 so they don't think I'm strange."

"But you are strange."

Max thought for a moment. "Yeah, I suppose I am. What does that make you?"

"Please don't say normal."

"I hate to break it to ya, Harris; you're the most normal one of us."

"We're fucked, then."

Max grinned. "So fucked."

The donation drive was in full swing by the time Brody, Max, and Sarah arrived. JJ was in the parking lot, hair freshly bleached and a cigarette in hand as he stood beside his beat up Jeep. As he waved them over, Brody noticed that despite JJ's smaller stature, his presence was larger than life itself. He was directing others on where to take their donations, from kitchen needs to clothing.

"JJ, my man." Max greeted him with a high five. "You coming to the fireworks tonight?"

"Wouldn't miss it. Kate will be there, too. She's staying with us until her parents can rebuild."

"I have a couple of girls staying with me, too," Sarah said with a smile. "Brody?"

He only shook his head, unwilling to tell them that he was barely in his home himself. He couldn't see Sandra opening her doors to someone else.

"No one's at our place, either," Max said. "That might change, though. Mom said something about Christopher needing a place."

Christopher, who was one of Brody's teammates, who hadn't asked him. Why would he? Brody had been the biggest dick during the season.

During this day, when he needed Catherine, and had only proceeded to lose his shit despite his source of comfort being there.

"Oh, hey!" Max was suddenly excited. "I found our signs."

Brody and JJ both groaned, but Sarah was ecstatic. "You didn't! Tell me you're bringing them tonight."

"I did, and duh." Max threw his arm around his girlfriend. "We need to unload these boxes. Oh, and cameras."

"I have mine," Brody said, "but I can help with the boxes."

"Clothes are over to the right, which is where your girlfriend is," JJ said, the first words he'd spoken to Brody without contempt in his voice in quite some time. "And Kate is in charge of kitchen things, to the left. They have other stuff here, but those are the two that I know of."

"So you're in charge of directing people?" Brody asked him, and he shook his head as he took another drag off of his cigarette.

"It just kinda happened."

Max and Sarah had already gone to retrieve boxes, leaving Brody and JJ alone. "Got a minute?" Brody asked him, and JJ inhaled sharply.

"You coming to the party?" JJ asked, and Brody nodded. "Cool. I'll see you there." He dropped his cigarette into a half-empty water bottle, replaced the lid, then tossed it through an open window into his Jeep before walking away.

He wasn't ready to talk, apparently, but Brody felt the first glimmer of hope for their friendship that he'd had since losing Brian.

"Here." Max handed him a box. "Clothing. Go see your girlfriend before she sends another text telling Sarah you're not answering your texts and that she's sure you're not coming."

"Phone's dead. I left it in the car."

"Speak up sometimes, dick. I have a charger in there. Sarah!" She paused and turned towards them. "Can you unlock it so I can put this asshole's phone on the charger?"

"I already did," she called back, then blew a kiss before taking her box towards the kitchen donations.

"Isn't she the best?" Max asked with a grin. "Okay, following her. Get your ass over there, Harris."

"I was going anyway." Brody shifted the heavy box then began the walk among the many people in the stands of the football stadium. The marching band was on the field for entertainment, and as Brody looked around he saw that the concession stands were open, all proceeds from sales going to a fund for the tornado victims. There were bands from other schools in uniform milling around, waiting for their turn. A few feet from the entrance to the field was the large setup for clothing donations, with Valley High's cheerleaders in their black and red uniforms with bright white shoes, and each girl had their hair in a French braid.

Solidarity.

Unity.

Even the coach had her hair up in a French braid, and she was by her girls helping to sort the clothing. Catherine stood in the front, greeting each person with a smile that beamed and shown in her eyes, which were a bright green that beautifully warm day. Brody stood in the line, which reached back to the fence and was forming behind him as well. A local newscaster was broadcasting from the donation group, its camera focused on Catherine as she accepted another box and asked the donor if they wanted a slip for tax purposes. Most said no, and even more of them asked what else they could do for help.

"What we've heard is that the tornado victims need gift cards for gas and food, since most of the food donations they receive are non-perishable items," Catherine replied to the reporter when asked. "Those donations, or purchase of cards supplied by Valley High Marching Band, can be done over at the table by concession stand one, or the home side for those unfamiliar with our school."

One would never have guessed that she'd only lived there for a few months, or that she'd just joined the squad. Catherine had a natural leadership quality about her, which was another aspect of her that Brody adored. When he was with her, he felt the same, as her energy radiated rather than depleting others. She had exactly what it takes to be a true leader, and...

Co-captain.

He could see the title sewn into the shirt, along with her name above it.

One corner of his mouth lifted in a grin. She did it; she made her way to the top of Valley High in a matter of minutes at JJ's.

"You made it!" Her elation at seeing him there calmed his frayed nerves, telling him they were fine.

Just fine.

Catherine wasn't going to leave him when he needed her the most.

"You should have seen her!" Audrey exclaimed. "We did our thing with our pyramid, and this little spitfire puts on a crowd-raising display of gymnastics before landing *in the splits*, dead center in front of us."

"It hurt like hell," Catherine said with a laugh.

"I wish I'd been there."

She shrugged. "You've seen me cheer before. Don't act like you never watched us back at the house."

"It's different."

"We have a coach! A real coach, not one that lays it all on my shoulders. She used to go to school here, so she knows the basics of the standard routines, and,"

"Red and black suits you," Brody said, interrupting her, making her blush.

"It really does."

"Oh, you missed it, really," Audrey continued. "Davis High was here, stress on the was. It was so much fun."

"You'll tell me all about it, I'm sure," Brody said to Catherine who giggled.

"It was so awesome," she said. "The girls and I have a lot of catching me up to do, though, so, um… fireworks? Later?"

Don't be angry, Brody. This is what she wants. What she's always wanted.

"Yeah, sure."

"I have to…" She gestured to the other people in line, and he nodded curtly. "Hey,"

"No, it's good. It's a great thing you're doing," he said, when in truth he wanted to blurt out that the only reason she was doing this was because of Taylor's comments earlier. He wanted to tell her what he saw from her right at that moment, even though the other side of him—the one that could see the happiness in her eyes—kept telling him to stop.

Stop thinking this was who Catherine was becoming.

All about appearances.

The Catherine of old.

CHAPTER 23

Nowhere Else

O*n our way*

It was nearly 9 PM when Brody received that text from Catherine as he, Max, and Sarah kicked back on the lawn area of the neighborhood park. It was still fairly light outside, and the crowd was continuing to grow. Children were laughing and running around holding sparklers in their hands, reminding Brody that Tyler and Sammi should be with him, making him all the more agitated.

He didn't bother sending a text back; the drive was short, and he'd only told her three times where he could be found.

"You're going to JJ's, right?" Max asked him after looking at his phone.

"Yeah." Brody's answers had been shorter and shorter as the day wore on. One chance meeting with a member of her former squad, one snarky remark, and here he was alone on the day they were supposed to spend together. Okay, so he was with Max and Sarah, but this hadn't been his plan.

At all.

"We found you!"

Hearing Matt's voice outside of the facility grabbed Brody's attention, and he smiled his greeting as Matt and Emily walked up to him. "You made it."

"I told you that I would. This kid was a surprise, though," Matt added with a gesture towards Emily, who scowled.

"Would you two quit? I'm not a kid." She was still Emily, still clean and sober, though her dark hair was brushed out and swept up into a ponytail, making her look closer to her fourteen years.

"Guys, this is Matt and Emily."

"Hi, I'm Max. And our names are too similar, so Matthew it is."

"I'm Sarah, and that's just because he doesn't want to be called Maximillian."

"Hey, it's a family name."

"Have a seat," Brody said, patting the round.

"Where's the infamous Catherine?" Emily asked.

"She's on her way." Brody did his best to keep his tone light, wanting them to like Catherine for a reason unclear to him. "Cheerleading stuff today."

"Thought she was a former cheerleader," Emily commented, keeping the conversation going with him as Matt and Max were hitting it off.

"It was an abrupt change," Brody admitted.

"And you're not okay with it."

"Of course I am," he replied, a bit too defensively.

"Ease up, lover boy, I was just making an observation."

"Hi, I'm his girlfriend," Catherine announced as she made her grand entrance by straddling him and giving Emily a look that would have most girls shaking in their boots.

Not Emily.

"The infamous Catherine," she said with a grin. "Wow, way to go, Brody. She is gorgeous."

"Told ya so," Brody replied, fighting against the surge of blood through his body as Catherine began leaving wet kisses on his neck, no doubt staking her claim.

He should be angry that she was doing this in reaction to an overheard comment.

Instead, he turned his face towards her, kissing her fully as he wrapped his arms around her, pulling her flush against him. "Hello to you, too," he whispered in her ear, her resulting shiver scorching him. Catherine was never this overly affectionate around others, and he knew it was out of jealousy, but he drank it in all the same. His heart sang, wildly beating in his chest as the realization hit him that they were fine.

She was fine.

She'd seen a spiral—more than one—and here she was, wrapped in his arms, kissing him with sweetness and an edge of passion.

He could feel it rolling off of her in waves.

He was safe.

A loud snap startled them apart, and Max stood over them, grinning. "If you would come up for air, you could see all the goodies I brought."

"It only took him five tries to get one of those to work on this ground," Sarah commented with a laugh.

"Yeah, where's the concrete when you need it? Anyhow, lovebirds," he held out two unlit sparklers, and as Catherine took hers, she slid off Brody's lap to sit beside him. "JJ has the lighter, as per always."

"You really shouldn't smoke," Jen said to her cousin, who merely flipped her off before handing his lighter to her. "It could affect your voice."

"What, make me sound less like I'm twelve?"

"And stop bleaching your hair."

"Are you going to be my manager?"

Jen shook her head. "Never work with family." She lit her sparkler and the lighter began to make its rounds, even as Max tried feebly to get more of his snaps to go off.

Brody took the lighter in his hand and lit Catherine's sparkler, and then his own. Dusk was beginning to settle in, and he drank it all in—the anticipation, the laughter of his friends as they got to know one another, the beauty radiating off the girl beside him, the one whose smile was for him alone.

"Sarah, the signs."

"We have another thirty minutes until fireworks," she reminded him.

The rest of their conversation was lost in the mingling voices of the crowd, but for Brody, he and Catherine were their own little world. The sparklers burned down as he gazed into her eyes, knowing there was nowhere else on earth he would rather be. His calm had returned with Catherine's presence, his earlier worries dissipating with every passing moment.

"What do we do with these when they burn down?" Brody heard Emily ask, and JJ mentioned something about taking care of them. Emily collected the spent sparklers from everyone, and Brody handed his to her without breaking eye contact with Catherine.

"I told my dad I'm staying at Jen's," she said softly. "Except..."

"Except what?"

She moved in closer, and when she whispered in his ear that she'd rather spend it with him, chills covered his body.

"We'll make it happen," he whispered back. Maybe he'd send his mother a text that he was staying with Max; maybe he wouldn't.

But if Catherine wanted to spend the night with him…

Yeah. He'd make it happen, no matter the cost.

He teased her lips with his, their soft kisses slowly building until Max hit Brody atop his head with a thin piece of poster board.

"You're 'Ah' this year."

Catherine nearly snorted with her giggle. "He's what?"

"Pay attention, Queen C, and you'll know all about it. Matthew, my man, you are 'Wow.' JJ is 'Oh.' And…"

"What the fuck is all this?" Even Emily was giggling.

"You pay attention, too. You're too young to be ogling our resident musician, and now that you're obviously embarrassed, my work there is done."

"Asshole," Emily muttered, still grinning.

"Which leaves 'Oooo,' which is me." Max held up his sign. "Call dibs on which fireworks are yours."

"The big booming ones are mine," JJ said promptly, as Brody knew he would.

"Oh! I want the ones that sound like they have their own applause," Matt spoke up, and Brody noted his happy expression.

"Brody?" Max asked.

"The biggest ones that light up the sky," Catherine answered for him, catching on.

"And I shall be whatever I choose at the moment, and no arguing since they're my rules anyway and Sarah won't let me set off the firecrackers."

While JJ inquired why Sarah was taking the fun out of the holiday, Catherine turned to Brody with a smile. "Are these signs what I think they are?"

"Painted in glow in the dark colors and held up for the crowd." He held his up for her inspection as she threw her head back in laughter that warmed his soul.

"Only Max."

"Brian," Brody said, his voice soft. "It was actually Brian's idea. I gave the signs to Max since he made up the rest of the rules. We didn't do them last year."

Catherine brushed his hair back, and her touch burned in the best way. "I'm glad we get to this year."

He kissed the tip of her nose. "So am I."

"One more round of sparklers before showtime," Max announced as they were passed around, along with JJ's lighter.

Loved.

Brody felt loved that moment when Catherine lit their sparklers and shifted between his legs, settling with her back against his chest. They moved their sparklers together in time, watching as the light made patterns beneath the darkening sky, and the rest of the world faded away.

The show began promptly at 10 PM, it's first few pops having Max lift up his sign, the people behind them shouting a resounding "Oooooo" that had Catherine giggling.

"See?" Brody whispered in her ear. "It's genius."

"Which makes sense that your other half came up with it," was her whispered reply.

Brody looked up at the night sky, wondering if Brian could see it, too. Look, he wanted to say. *The signs still work. And my girl? She thinks they're ingenious.*

He remained silent, though, his eyes now on Catherine as one of the biggest fireworks popped in the sky, the purple color glinting off her soft green eyes. She held his sign up for him so that his arms remained where they were, around her, holding her close.

He loved this girl.

He loved this girl...

The realization hit him like a sucker punch to his gut, taking his breath away. He pulled her in closer, inhaling her floral scent, and let out a contented sigh rather than blurting it out right there. With her eyes on the sky, he was able to keep his on her face, watching as her eyes lit up, as her face filled with wonder.

He loved this girl.

For every time she stood up for herself, for him, for others that she cared about.

For her tenacity, her resilience, her heart.

For her sacrificing her own safety to make sure that he, Tyler, and Sammi would be okay.

For the way she looked at him as she was now, like he could do no wrong despite the many times he'd shown her that he could.

For all the times he had turned to her for comfort, for joy, for a sense of peace in his unraveling world.

He loved this girl.

She had seen his darkness, and so far she was staying, helping him weave his way through years of torment towards the light, and...

No... oh, no...

She was his drug.

She was his drug.

She was the only person, the only thing in his world that pulled him back, and he knew he couldn't put that on her tiny shoulders, no matter how fierce she was.

But he loved this girl.

He couldn't pull away from her, not now, not even if he wanted to.

Pulling away... that would have him spiraling, have his mother locking him up again away from her, away from his friends, away from life.

She turned her face towards his and he masked his feelings, choosing instead to kiss her there beneath the fireworks going overhead and in his heart.

He couldn't think about this, not right now, not with her there in his arms.

And by the time she held up his sign again, the thought was pushed aside.

He loved this girl.

All he had to do was convince himself that was enough.

CHAPTER 24

Seriously

"So here comes the squad, right?" Catherine was saying excitedly as she and the girls from her new squad gathered in JJ's back yard. "And they're being so smug and acting haughty."

"I see where you got it from," Audrey joked, and much to Brody's surprise, Catherine laughed.

"No, see, they got it from me. They got their moves, their routine, their attitude, all of it from me. So, anyway... Brody, are you paying attention?"

He smiled and took a long drink from his beer. "Hanging on every word."

"Smartass. Anyway, so they come up acting like they're all hot shit."

"Who is that bitch of a captain they have? The one that can't lead?" Audrey asked, and again Catherine laughed.

"Chelsea. And you got her good."

"Enlighten, please." Max was now there, sitting on the bench that had been taken from Randall's house at the last party.

"She can't even keep her girls in line, and I told her so." Audrey shrugged. "I may have added that it took all of five minutes and no tryout for us to get our new co-captain."

"Taylor was being mouthy, Laura was being weird, and… hell, I forget who the others were," Catherine said with a dismissive wave of her hand. "But loud, rude, not listening to Chelsea after they'd been warned, which I could have let the coach know would happen."

"And there's our girl," Audrey added, "all smiles, all 'thank you for helping' while I'm handing back torn and stained clothing letting them know those aren't donatable, right? Then… what's her face?"

"Taylor," Catherine said with a roll of her eyes.

"Taylor said it's all they deserved. Bam! Asked to leave. Them and their band and that creepy dude who was eyeballing you."

Brody's smile fell. "That asshole was there?"

"And I said nothing to him." Catherine flipped her hair back with another laugh, but Brody knew this one was just for show. After everything Mitch had done to her, for him to show up where he knew Catherine would be was a real dick move.

One that Brody wasn't going to tolerate.

"Where is he?" He finished his beer and tossed the bottle aside.

"Easy on the testosterone," Audrey quipped.

But it wasn't testosterone driven. It was full-on rage towards the asshole who had hurt Catherine, who had made her uneasy, who had disregarded her when she was pregnant saying the baby wasn't his, who had so publicly treated her like shit.

Most of all for that night in the woods, where he ignored her protests, leaving her with a memory that haunted her still.

And Mitch had the nerve to show up at Valley High knowing damn well that Catherine would be there. No, that didn't take nerve… that took gall, and Brody wasn't having any of it. He wouldn't get away with it… no, Brody would show Mitch once again that he had no business messing with Catherine, only this time, he would use his own two hands instead of a fucking baseball, and…

"Hey." Catherine was in front of him now, her hands up on his shoulders. With little effort, she hoisted herself up and wrapped her legs around his waist. "Not tonight," she whispered against his lips.

"Not what tonight?" He teased her lips open, his flash of anger dissipating as quickly as it came as their kiss deepened. His anger could be saved for another time, a time when Mitch was directly in front of him.

And he would make sure that the time came.

"Oh, would you two just get a room?" Max quipped. "Oh! Almost forgot. Jen's here with her girlfriend. I didn't even know she was,"

Brody didn't get a chance to hear what else Max had to say as Catherine had her feet on the ground and was pulling Brody along. "I have waited far too long to meet this girl," she said excitedly. Jen had spent plenty of time talking up her 'hottie,' as Catherine had referred to her as, and Brody was probably as excited as he was curious. Jen was actually coming out, when she'd sworn she wouldn't until she was out of high school, away from her parents, away from the judgmental high school crowd.

Yet, there she was, in the middle of this party, holding hands with…

"Bethany?!"

Catherine's near shriek of the name matched the one in Brody's head. Not so much about his ex-girlfriend being more attracted to women than men; he'd known that early on. But the fact that Bethany, someone who also thrived on appearances, was here, dating someone she had to know was Catherine's best friend.

This was not going to end well.

"Hello, Catherine."

And it wasn't just because Bethany was Brody's ex. Bethany had participated in Catherine's downfall at Davis High, providing information to Mitch, and ultimately ending up within the crowd, reveling in watching the school's queen fall from grace.

"Don't 'hello Catherine' me."

The crowd hushed and all eyes turned to watch the drama, as high school students tended to do. This crowd included a few parents, and the sheriff as well, and they were all turned with curious expressions, perhaps reliving their own high school years.

"And seriously? You're dating my best friend. Like you didn't know. That's what this is all about, isn't it? It's to get to me."

The Valley High cheerleaders were walking in from outside, all eyeing Jen and Bethany.

"Could you possibly contemplate getting over yourself for one second?"

"Okay, that's enough," Jen interrupted. "Everyone, this is my girlfriend, Bethany. Bethany, these are all the people that I told you would have a problem with this."

"I don't," Matt spoke up from the couch, his hand raised.

"Neither do I," another person added.

"You know I don't," Brody said softly, and Catherine turned to him.

"Really? And don't play like *you* didn't know. You and Bethany still talk."

"We're friends, Cat, and no, I didn't know they were dating."

"Oh, bullshit," she snapped, then stormed her way outside, the majority of the cheerleading squad joining her.

"Hi," Audrey said as she stepped forward. "I'm Audrey. Nice to meet you."

Brody motioned towards the back door. "I need to go diffuse this."

Jen stood there, tears in her eyes. "Should I come?"

"Give me a minute."

Slowly the rest of the crowd turned to each other, resuming their earlier conversations, some cheering to turn the music up as the next song came on as Brody made his way through the crowd and out the back door. The rising noise from the party muffled as he closed the door behind him. He looked over his shoulder as the sound rose again only to see Max coming out, his hand extended with a fresh beer in it.

"Figured you may want this."

"Yeah, thanks," Brody said. He peered out into the darkness, not seeing the cheerleaders around. "Shit."

"Yeah, no worries. Sarah says they're all out front waiting for Randall to come back with his second bench. What was up with that shit in there with Jen and that chick she brought with her?"

"Old Davis High bullshit," Brody replied before taking a long drink of his beer. "Thanks for this."

"Yeah, no worries. C'mon, dude. Spill so I can spill to Sarah."

"I don't,"

"Yeah, we don't gossip. We discuss. How many times must I remind you of this?"

Brody let out a short laugh. "Bethany's my ex."

"Wait, what?"

"And she was there when Catherine and that asshole she'd been dating broke up, which wasn't pretty, and no, I don't want to get into details."

"And she thinks that Bethany is dating Jen to get back at her."

"Yeah, but..." Brody's voice trailed off as he looked down at his beer, which was suddenly unappealing. "I don't think that's what it is."

"Said with so much conviction."

"Are they still here? Or did they leave?"

"If they left, they're all out front where your very pissed off girlfriend is."

"Fuck." Brody sighed as he looked down at his beer, and then chugged the rest of it. "I'm going in."

"Out front?"

"In, Max." He threw his arm around his best friend's shoulder. "Please for the love of whatever deity you worship, tell me you know the difference between in and out."

"Do you think Sarah would still be dating me if I didn't?"

Brody's laughter echoed off the back of the house before he opened the back door, the sounds of the resumed party rolling out from its enclosed space. It seemed that even more of the neighborhood kids were there, many of those who would have found something to do in Brentfield deciding to enjoy their evening at JJ's. The sheriff was there also, doing shots with Nan in the kitchen as Brody and Max walked by.

"Brody," Nan called out to him, "be a doll and get your girlfriend back in here. I need to reclaim my beer pong title."

"Anything for you, Nan," he called out over his shoulder as he pushed his way through the crowd. Jen was talking animatedly with Sarah, but Bethany was nowhere to be seen.

This could mean a world of trouble.

He felt as hand on his arm and looked down, relieved to see Bethany beside him and not in a screaming match with his girlfriend. "Hey, stranger," she said with a grin, and he reached down to hug her.

"This damn well better not be to get back at Catherine."

"It's not." Bethany stepped back and smiled. "I met her at an LBGTQ event, and just… bam, right in the gut." She smiled over at Jen and Sarah. "She's amazing."

"I could have told you that."

"Then why didn't you?"

"Aside from not playing matchmaker? She's Cat's best friend. I wouldn't do that to her, not with your history."

"Yeah, well, the history began with Catherine being herself. It isn't my fault she didn't like it reciprocated."

"I told you that two wrongs don't make a right, Beth." Brody took a sip of his beer as JJ slid past him, guitar in hand. "Be the bigger person and walk away. But no, you had to add all the fuel to it. And now you're dating Cat's best friend."

"Catherine doesn't know how to be a friend. Who Jen dates isn't her business, quite honestly."

"That's not what this is about."

"Yes, Brody, it is. It's all Catherine, all the time. You've been dating her for… how long? You should know this already."

"You don't know her, Beth. None of you really did."

"And suddenly after a few months you think you do?"

The stereo cut as JJ took his place on the couch and the majority of the girls in the party, as well as a few of the guys, gathered around. Brody took that as his cue to motion to Bethany that he was going outside to talk to Catherine.

"Do you want me to explain it to her that you didn't know?"

"I'm pretty capable of telling her myself," he muttered, shaking Bethany's hand off his arm. "You could have warned me, then I could have warned her."

"It's none of your business, either."

"Tell me who doesn't know how to be a friend again, Beth." Without waiting for a reply, he was out the door, walking towards the cheerleaders who were still out front, lamenting that it didn't look like Randall was bringing his other bench back. Catherine spotted Brody and one eyebrow shot in the air, letting him know the issue was far from resolved in her mind. It didn't help, of course, that Bethany followed close behind him, calling out for him.

"Brody, wait,"

"How about you not talk to my boyfriend, okay?" Catherine snapped, but Bethany ignored her.

"Let me apologize, okay? I'm sorry I didn't tell you."

"Like you said, Beth, it's not my business," Brody said without turning around. "Randall! Jeezus, how fucked up are you?" he called out to the young man stumbling down the road with the bench. "Just... I'll come get it."

He used the opportunity to get away from the chatter, from the showdown that was sure to be taking place despite the lack of yelling. It wasn't until he had almost reached Randall that he noticed Catherine beside him, her legs working twice as hard to keep up the pace.

"You scared the hell out of me, Cat."

"So you didn't know."

"I didn't hear you sneak up on me, no."

"About Jen and Bethany."

"I already told you that I didn't." They'd reached the spot where Randall had given up his quest and had sat on the side of the road, the bench beside him. "I've got this," Brody told him, hoisting the bench upside down and balanced it on one shoulder.

"I just thought that you and Bethany were friends, like I thought Jen was my friend."

"Just because she's dating someone that you don't like doesn't mean she's not your friend, Cat."

"But you didn't... did you know that Bethany..."

"Yes, but that wasn't my story to tell." He paused before they got closer to the other girls, who were talking animatedly amongst themselves. "Did you tell anyone about Jen?"

"No," Catherine said softly. "Okay, so you have me there."

"Don't I have you everywhere?"

Catherine stood on her toes, still having to look up into Brody's eyes. "Soon," she said, then she took off in a sprint she shouldn't have been able to run leaving him with his mouth hung open before he finally began to smile.

CHAPTER 25

Yes

The trees overhead were devoid of leaves at the top, some were even missing bark, giving the small clearing an eerie, haunted feel. The sound of their feet shuffling through the earth below was muffled in this space that seemed a million miles away from the rest of the surrounding towns.

Away from the chaos that had become Brody's life.

This spot, though… this spot was special. Nostalgic. His place of sanctuary when he was younger, when he could slip away unnoticed before he and Brian were always charged with looking after Tyler and Sammi. He and Brian had found it accidentally when they'd intentionally veered off the path to avoid being seen with the bottle of whiskey they'd found hidden beneath the kitchen sink.

"What if it's not really whiskey?" Brody had asked.

"Trust me, it is." Brian smiled back at him. *"I made sure."*

They'd been 12 years old, not even teenagers, the first time they'd gotten drunk, and they'd done it together.

Here.

Eventually they'd included JJ and Max, and the four of them had made this the place they gathered, mostly when one of them had procured something to drink, or in Brody's case, just needed away from Frank.

Tonight, though, he laid a blanket down and smiled across it at Catherine, who smiled shyly in return.

"Are you sure?" he asked, and she nodded as she kneeled onto the blanket and took her shoes off.

"I'm positive."

Her smile was now beguiling, calling to him, telling him that he was safe here, with her.

He sat beside her and laid back, resting his head on her legs while he looked up at the few stars dotting the cloudy sky. He held back his contented sigh as he felt her fingers running through his hair, though he wanted to show her the adoration—the love— he had for her.

And he would.

He knew he would.

"Do you ever talk to him?" Catherine asked, and he shook his head slightly, knowing she meant Brian. "Why not?"

"He's not here, Cat," he replied, his voice heavy with emotion. "This... this was the place we found to get away, you know?"

"This is the hideout?"

He smiled through his threatening tears. "Yeah. I didn't come here that night, because it was too far for me to stumble. I just fell asleep in the park. It was close enough to home, I could get there if I had to. But my phone was dead. I..." One lone tear escaped as he frowned up at the sky. "I went home, and I found him. And I think JJ... I think he may be right." He inhaled sharply. "I've never told anyone this, ever. I..." He allowed her to brush away his fresh tears. "When I charged my phone, when I turned it on, there was a text from him, and a voicemail, asking where I was. And I couldn't answer him because he was dead. He was dead and it's my fault."

Catherine urged him with her hands to sit up, and once he did, she pulled him close, one hand through his hair as she cradled his head into her shoulder.

And he cried.

Just as he had in that house on the hill, the day his mother had come for them.

He cried for his brother, half of his soul, left to die alone on Christmas day because Brody hadn't bothered to charge his phone.

He cried for Brian's warmth, his laughter, his smartass reply to nearly everything said, beating Max by a mile with his comebacks.

He cried for JJ, who had lost his best friend, and now had lost his brother as well.

He cried for Max, who'd had to go months without any of his best friends around.

He cried for Sarah, who had loved Brian as if he were her own brother.

He cried for Audrey, of all people, who had loved Brian so desperately that she'd turned to Brody when he was gone.

He cried for Tyler, who understood death at too young of an age.

He cried for his Sammi, that little girl who had seen Brian's body as Brody was laid across him, screaming and screaming.

He cried for his mother, who had fallen to the floor in grief.

And Frank...

Frank, who had pulled Brody off of his brother, who had held him the way Catherine was holding him now.

Frank who had told him it wasn't his fault.

Frank who had been a father to him, who loved him at times, who hated him at others, who was the only one who, even for a brief time, had comforted Brody on that day.

He cried for the upcoming senior year, when he didn't know if he was going to be there. And that was all he wanted.

To be with *her*.

And he didn't have his brother to turn to.

But he had Catherine.

His Catherine.

"I'm so sorry," he murmured against her neck before pulling back. "This... this isn't what tonight's about. This isn't what's supposed to be..." His voice trailed off as she brushed away his tears with a feather light touch of her fingertips.

"You've been holding that inside of you, Brody. Don't apologize for this, not ever." She cradled his face in her hands. "How many times have you done this for me?" He lifted one shoulder in response. "Too many for me to count. And you... you don't have to worry about my reaction or think that I'm going to pull away from you. Nothing is too much. Do you hear me? *Nothing is too much.*"

He pulled further away, studying her expression.

She had no idea how far down he could go, even with what she'd seen.

And it suddenly hit him... the woods. The blanket. Surrounded by trees.

"Does it bother you, being here?" he asked with a sniffle.

Catherine looked around them, up at the night sky, at the tops of the trees stripped barren by the tornado that devastated their community. "It's kinda like a horror movie, isn't it? Without the fog."

"That's not what I meant."

"I know." She smiled at him. "I know. It is really dark here, just like you said it would be."

Their fingers intertwined as Brody contemplated her answer. "Yeah, kinda. I brought… hold on." He pulled away and reached for his backpack that he pulled a small, battery-powered lantern from. The light cast of a bluish hue, adding to the ambience of perhaps meeting their fate to a serial killer. When Catherine's eyes met his, the laughter there let him know she felt the same way.

Oh, but she was beautiful.

Her laughter was a melody that called to his soul, moved him to do whatever he could to hear it again, to see her so full of joy that she couldn't hold it in any longer.

Her smile was his full heart on display for the world to see, and she didn't even know that about herself. Every smile was a part of him. Every one.

She moved, but he put his hand out, motioning for her to stop.

"Let me photograph you."

"Like this?" she asked, her hands reaching up to her hair, and he stopped her again.

"Exactly like this."

He pulled his camera out of his backpack and turned to her, his tears drying as he drank in the sight of her, her presence, the pure essence of her.

She was his drug.

Again, he pushed those feelings aside as he snapped each low-lit picture of her, some with her eyes downcast, some with her looking at him, some with her glancing off into the trees, an expression on her face that to most would be unreadable, but not to him.

He knew what Mitch had done.

He knew where he had done it.

"Are you okay?" he asked, setting his camera aside.

"Hmm? Oh, yeah, yeah, I'm good."

"Cat,"

"You're not Mitch," she said as she uncrossed her arms and leaned back onto them. "And this isn't *that* place, but mostly I'm okay because you're you."

Her words were a straight shot to his heart and the side of him that longed to show her exactly what she meant to him. His kiss, tentative upon her lips, asked the question for him, and her responding sigh was his answer.

Yes.

His heart soared and his stomach took a dive as he moved, slowly laying her back on the blanket, their lips and tongues speaking to each other. He swallowed her soft moan as his weight was fully on hers, and his kisses began to trail down to her neck with an urgency that he tried to reel in.

"You deserve so much more," he murmured between kisses—one on her shoulder, one on her collarbone, another where her own pulse hammered in rhythm with his. "You deserve a soft bed and a pillow. You deserve wine and roses and orchestral music playing, the kind I want to watch you dance to."

"We are dancing," was her breathless reply.

Not yet, he thought.

Not yet.

"You." He pulled her up and effortlessly removed her tank top before removing his shirt. "You deserve the best, Cat. Not this... this blanket on the ground in the middle of..."

His voice trailed off as she removed her bra.

His girl was beautiful.

So beautiful.

"You deserve," he continued, stopping her forward movement. "Cat..." He brushed her hair out of her face, concentrating more on her than the confines of his shorts. "You deserve to know how much I love you."

Her eyes widened in surprise, the flickering light from the dying lantern capturing the tears within. He pulled back then, her silence frightening him more than any word she could say.

"No, don't." She placed her hand on his arm, and her face turned upwards to look him in the eye. "That's what this is, Brody. It's love... you and me... *this is love.* And I love you with... with everything I have, and,"

He silenced her with a kiss, one that he poured his heart into, one that she shared her heart with as well.

This was love.

The urgent hands, seeking and finding places longing to be touched.

The sigh of skin on skin.

The turning beneath the stars as tongues touched and hands explored, lingering, heightening responses.

The tear of the condom packet.

The stranglehold on his heart as she nodded, letting him know it was time.

It was time.

Her gasp of pleasure as their bodies began the dance their souls had longed for.

Her short nails digging into his hips as she studied his movements and matched them with her own.

The whispered words of love, of adoration, growing to a heated crescendo as they sought release.

The tears of joy as she whispered that this is what it was supposed to be like.

His tears in return as he realized the gift he'd given her while they rose above the wave, crashing into bliss one after the other.

"I love you," she whispered breathlessly as their hearts beat in time.

"I love you, Catherine," he said in return. "And I will show you every day. You'll never have to wonder, I promise."

As they laid together on the blanket beneath the stars, kissing well into the dawn, Brody wondered if his words were what she needed, or if he was speaking for himself.

CHAPTER 26

Something Was Up

"Ssssh," Catherine giggled to Brody as he helped her sneak back up to Jen's house just before sunrise. "We don't need Jen's parents seeing this, me, bringing back her blanket that's in desperate need of washing. Oh, wait." She paused by the garbage bins and discarded the bag that held the trash from their night in the woods.

"You're the one being loud," he whispered in her ear, his arms pinning her back to his torso. "I could hold you right here, you know."

"Only if I let you. I'll have you know I've taken my share of self-defense classes in the past few months."

"I know all about them." One kiss to her temple and he released her, waving at Jen who was motioning for Catherine to hurry. He smiled his thanks, especially after the argument Jen and Catherine had at JJ's party a few short hours before. Jen nodded her acknowledgment, and Brody placed one more kiss on Catherine's lips. "I love you."

"And I love you, and I will see you... um... sometime. I think I have cheerleading stuff today."

"Then you better get some sleep." He stepped back into the shadows, watching his girl who was smiling so contentedly ascend the steps to Jen's back porch. Once she was securely inside, he stealthily made his way back to the sidewalk, unable to suppress his own smile. He shifted his backpack, made a running start, and jumped to hit some leaves on an overhanging tree branch before taking off in a jog towards home.

Sandra was due to go to work, and Brody made it back to the house with only minutes to spare before she left. "Where have you been?"

Brody ignored her question and headed for the kitchen, where there was just enough coffee in the pot to fill a mug. He sat at the table, carefully positioning his backpack on the floor. "I'm staying here today."

Sandra placed a hand on her hip. "We've discussed this."

"No, *you* discussed it. Now for some clarification: do I live here?"

Her mouth hung open for a moment before she answered. "Of course."

"Good. Then I'm drinking my coffee, taking a shower, and getting some sleep before I go to work. And I'm going to do it here, in my home."

"Brody,"

"She's busy, and besides, I know how to follow rules."

"You're breaking one in less than five minutes."

"Kick me out, then." He shrugged and took a sip of his coffee, knowing she wouldn't take the time to do so right before a shift at work. Instead, she grabbed her purse and her cellphone, then went out the door without saying another word.

Brody didn't mind.

The past 24 hours had been such a whirlwind of activity, of surprises, of everything he'd wanted with Catherine, he just didn't have it in him to deal with another change.

Satisfied that he'd made the right decision, he finished his coffee, took his shower, and fell into a deep and dreamless sleep.

The phone call came from Mack's late in the afternoon that his evening shift had been canceled. Brody should have been happy over the news, just to have some time to himself, but his brain was still on overdrive, processing everything that had happened in the past 24 hours.

Catherine loved him.

Frank was having a child with Theresa.

Catherine loved him.

Mitch showed up, and Brody was convinced it was to get to Catherine.

Catherine loved him.

She'd joined the cheerleading squad even after swearing it wasn't something she wanted to do.

But *Catherine loved him*.

The knob on the front door rattled, the sound of keys letting him know his mother had made it home from her shift. She walked in the house with a sigh of relief with the air conditioning being a welcome reprieve from her hot car. Brody watched as she set her purse down and removed first one shoe, then the other, and he didn't flinch when she shrieked with fright at the sight of him.

"I didn't think you'd be here."

"Work told me not to come in."

"Oh." She blinked several times as she walked past him towards the hallway. "I suppose you have plans for this evening then." It was a statement rather than a question.

"Nope, not really. Just catching up on some reading."

"Oh," she said again as she entered her bedroom.

She had plans for this evening, he was sure of it. Said plans involved Brody working late into the evening, not here to thwart them. For that reason alone, he erased the text he was sending to Catherine.

Something was up, and he was going to find out what.

Brody hadn't finished the chapter he was on with the first text from his Aunt Sheryl came. *Are you home* it read, piquing his interest immediately. When he replied that he was, she answered quickly with *Don't go anywhere.*

He knew before the knock on the front door came that his aunt was in town with his brother and sister, and that his mother had hidden it from him.

"Brody!" Sammi's squeal of delight filled the house as she ran down the hallway and jumped into his arms. Her tight squeeze around his neck matched his own as he held his baby sister.

"I've missed you, kiddo," he said softly.

"I missed you, too."

"Hey." Tyler was beside him, his arms wrapped around Brody's waist.

"Hey to you, too." Brody messed his brother's hair up, then walked down the hall with Sammi in his arms. "Look at this. Isn't it a surprise?"

Sandra's look was blank, and Brody knew he'd caught her in exactly what she had planned to do. She was having Sheryl and the kids over for dinner and hadn't expected him to be there. He wasn't sure of her motives, and he knew he had to play it cool. There was no going back to that facility for him. Even though he'd found friends in Matt and Emily, it wasn't a place he wanted to be.

"Are you making lasagna?" Ty happily ran into the kitchen where their mother was pulling out the ingredients from the cupboard. Brody sat Sammi down, and she promptly joined them.

"Did you read the letter?" Sheryl asked softly, and Brody shook his head. "Please do. And promise me you'll be on your best behavior tonight."

"You're here. Of course I will," he replied.

"We're not the only ones coming."

Frank.

Sheryl was talking about Frank.

Frank, who was invited to this family dinner when Sandra hadn't wanted Brody there.

Despite the anger taking hold beneath the surface, Brody smiled. "Fine," was his reply. He wondered if Sheryl knew about Frank having another baby on the way, a fact that he kept to himself at that moment. Why not join in on the family conversation? He'd learned enough tricks from his girlfriend on how to bring up subjects best left unsaid.

He was going to use those tricks at dinner.

Sheryl's hand was on his arm. "How are you?"

"Oh, I'm good." He was still smiling, this time his mind wandering to Catherine. "Very."

"I know that look," Sheryl said with a laugh as she sat down on the couch. "Well, this is nice."

"Frank's making good money in construction," Sandra called from the kitchen, and Brody stiffened, still sure the money was coming from Catherine's grandfather. He didn't expect Frank to divulge that bit of information to Sandra when he was obviously trying so hard to impress her.

"Good," was all Sheryl said in return. Her short answer let Brody know that Sheryl was less than impressed. "Have a seat, Brody. I'd love to catch up with you."

With a smile of his own, he eased himself into the beanbag chair. "Sounds like a plan."

Frank Harris was as smooth as ever. His smile was warm, his banter witty, his charm magnetic. Brody wasn't about to fall for any of it, even when Frank placed a hand on his shoulder. It took much of his energy to keep from flinching, but to show weakness was kindling to a fire. Frank would feed on it, press his buttons as he had so many times before to get him to break. Instead he stood there for a moment, that grin on his face.

"You look good, kid. Strong."

"Yeah, I've kept up with my workouts," Brody replied without emotion.

If Frank ever came for him again, Brody would be ready.

He'd make sure Frank regretted it.

"Dinner smells delicious," Frank said as he made his way to the dining room where Sandra was telling the kids to set the table. She actually blushed as Frank gave her a kiss on the cheek, making Brody nauseated.

How could she fall for his bullshit again?

Brody's phone vibrated in his pocket, and when he checked, it was a text from Catherine.

I miss you and I love you and what are you doing? Can you get away for a bit?

With a smile, he walked down the hall, phone in hand.

Family dinner. Sheryl and the kids are here. So is Frank.

Catherine's face lit up his screen as she called him immediately upon reading his text. "No, Brody. I know what you want to do, just don't."

"I don't know what you're talking about," he replied, feigning innocence as he stretched out on his bed.

"Mom said that your mom knows."

He grinned. "I know."

"Don't start anything. Please," she added, her voice a little softer. "Your mom tends to take what you say too literally anyway."

Brody was silent for a moment. "What if Brian did say something, Cat? I mean, they were gone. What if he said something to them before?" The thought alone sent a shiver through him. He'd never asked; he'd just assumed that Brian had said nothing the way that he hadn't mentioned his thoughts to Brody.

"Be careful," was all she said about it, knowing that he'd ask regardless of the consequences. "I have to get back to practice. I thought this would come right to me, and it isn't."

"That's not the word that's going around. Audrey is staying with Sarah, who loves to tell everything to Max."

"I can't believe you two gossip."

"We discuss, Cat. We discuss. I love you."

"I love you, too."

Her words were enough courage, and he stood to face the tension filled living room with ease.

"This is scrump... scrupdilly..."

"Scrupdelicious?" Sheryl asked Sammi when she was stumped for a word.

"That's not in your dictionary," Tyler quipped.

The new dining room table had just enough room to pull up two extra chairs so that everyone could sit around it. Brody sat at one end, his eyes on a far-too smug Frank at the other.

"Theresa and I are discussing co-parenting," Frank announced before Brody could bring up the subject. "I'm sure you've been filled in, Sheryl."

"Of course," Sheryl replied, much to Sandra's surprise. Sandra's eyes were then on Brody, who smiled sweetly at her.

Oh, Catherine had taught him well.

"So will the baby be a Davis or a Harris?" Brody asked nonchalantly.

"She will be both."

"Yeah, I'm finally having a sister," Sammi spoke up. Brody's first thought was of Catherine, of how cold Theresa's demeanor would be towards her own daughter.

Would she be any different with Catherine's sister?

"Is there something else on your mind, son?" Frank asked him.

"I'm Nikos's son," Brody reminded him, still smiling, much to his mother's chagrin.

"Frank raised you," Sandra reminded him.

"And what a fine job you've done," Brody added quickly. "But yes, I do have something on my mind."

"And what would that be?" Frank asked coolly.

"Brian."

Silence fell over the dining room at Brody's mention of his brother's name. The subject hadn't been broached like this, even though he'd been gone for over a year.

"What about Brian?" Frank asked, his eyes now on his plate.

"Well, all of you were gone. You must have told him that you were leaving. What did he say?"

"Nothing," Sandra replied, a little too quickly.

"Try again." Brody couldn't stop himself this time, even though he kept his expression neutral.

"He said he didn't want to go. Are you satisfied now?" Sandra snapped. "You've made your sister cry."

"He didn't make me cry," Sammi protested through her tears. "I miss my Bri is all." Instead of going to her mother, she went straight to Brody's arms. Instead of staying at the table, Brody walked her down the hallway to his room.

"I miss him, too," he said as he dried her tears. "I will always miss him, and it's okay to."

"But we... we heard a..." Her tears began in earnest again as she threw her arms around Brody's neck.

They'd heard it.

They'd heard the shot.

And they left Brian there for Brody to find.

CHAPTER 27

Meet Me On The Roof

"Baby girl... what did you say?"

He couldn't have heard her right.

He couldn't have.

"Mommy said I can't tell you." She cried harder, and he brushed her tears away.

But she had, and he couldn't turn back, pretend he didn't know.

He had to get out of there.

He ignored Sammi calling for him, ignored his mother asking where he thought he was going.

And he ran.

He couldn't run fast enough, hard enough.

Sweat rolled off him in waves as he ran through town, around the park, past the school, winding around and heading back again.

But he couldn't go home.

They'd left Brian for him to find.

They'd left Brian for him to find.

He passed his street wondering what kind of monster could do that to a kid, but he was sure he already knew the answer.

Frank.

How many times had Frank told him he would wind up dead? And Brody hadn't been a bad kid; he made good grades, had friends, excelled in baseball. Having fun, blowing off steam wouldn't make someone wind up dead.

But a fucking gun in a fucking house with a bunch of fucking kids did.

He kept running, turning back around and going through town, thinking maybe the track at the school would be open and he could just run it off there.

The pain... it wouldn't stop.

It wouldn't fucking stop.

He finally paused, out of breath as he kneeled down in front of the dance studio. He took his shirt off and wiped his face with it before he stood again.

The lights were on.

Catherine had said they were letting the cheerleaders work there after hours.

The door was just a few steps away, one turn of the knob would let him inside, bring him to Catherine who could soothe him back into his existence where he could feel and laugh and love.

But she couldn't take this away.

She couldn't turn back the clock, make Sandra and Frank call the squad before leaving his twin alone, lifeless on his bedroom floor.

She couldn't stop Brian from putting that gun to his head in the first place.

He turned again and began walking briskly towards his home, the walk turning into a jog, and then he was running again.

He wanted answers.

This time he was going to get them.

Only Sandra was there when Brody returned, shirt in his hand. He was almost surprised the front door was unlocked; he'd expected to knock, to wait for his mother, to ask her when she was going to bother telling him before he even entered. Walking into the bliss of air conditioning shook things up, had him bending over with his hands on his knees.

"Where did you go?"

"For a run," he replied as he rose. "Had to clear my head."

"You shouldn't run right after you eat; it can make you sick."

Now she wants to mother me.

He didn't bother with telling her that he'd already been sick in the park, throwing up what little he had eaten after only a short distance. Instead, he looked her up and down, refraining from screaming at her, and walked down the hallway to take his second shower of the day.

He needed to talk to Catherine.

He needed comfort from her to calm down, prepare himself for the questions he needed to ask his mother.

His text to her remained unanswered when he'd gotten in the shower, vigorously washing away the grit and grime of the day as well as his run. He'd had so much thrown at him the past 24 hours, he just didn't know if he was up to hearing anymore. He stood beneath the water, letting it pelt his skin, his eyes closed as he began counting backwards.

10, 9, 8

The ping from his phone let him know that Catherine had returned his text, and he felt himself relax beneath the shower spray. He had that text waiting for him, that buffer before he confronted his mother.

How could she?

How could she leave her own son dead on the floor, leave him for his twin to find?

Would that text from Catherine be enough to hold him over, keep him from saying something rash and stupid? But what could he say that would equal the wrong she had done him?

None. That was the answer he came up with as he turned the water off and stepped onto the mat beside the tub. There was nothing he could say that would equal what she had placed on his shoulders, and he'd been just a kid, more so than he was now.

He vigorously dried himself off, then wrapped the towel around him to walk to his room. "Ma?" He walked the short distance to his bedroom. "We really need to have a discussion, tonight," he called out, unsurprised when he heard no response. Of course, she wouldn't respond. She'd been silent for well over a year, why change that now?

Hell, she'd been silent for longer than that.

"Ma," he said as he stepped out of his room, fully dressed. Still, no answer. She wasn't in her bedroom, so he continued on down the hallway.

"Mom."

Not in the living room.

Or in the kitchen.

And when he checked out the front window, he saw that her car was gone.

"Fuck!" He began to pace, his hands in his hair pulling on the damp strands. "Fuck... fuck... fucking... shit!"

She was avoiding him, when he needed her the most. Why not? She'd walked out on Brian when he needed her most, too. What was the difference now?

He picked up a half-full glass of water from the dining room table, its contents sloshing as he prepared to throw it with all of his might at the wall.

Then his phone rang.

Catherine.

He placed the cup down slowly, never taking his eyes off of it or his unsteady hand. A trickle of sweat made its way down his forehead, traveling farther still to his chin.

Still his phone rang.

Once silent, it didn't stay so long enough for her to leave a message. She was calling again, and this time, after taking a deep, calming breath, Brody answered.

"Are you okay?"

"I'm not dead if that's what your asking." His voice had little emotion behind it, which she instantly picked up on.

"What's wrong? Where are you? What can I do?" She fired the questions off too quickly for him to answer until she'd asked all three.

"I'm at home."

"That bad, huh?"

"Can you come over?"

"Ah, so your mom's there, got it."

"No, actually, she isn't."

"Brody, that isn't funny. You know I can't be in there when your mom isn't home."

"I'm being serious." He glanced down the hallway towards his bedroom door. "Meet me on the roof."

"Will you tell me what's wrong?"

"All of it, I promise."

As he hung up the phone, he felt a bit of the weight leaving his shoulders.

Catherine was coming over.

He was going to be okay.

"I'm sorry, what did you say?" Catherine sat up suddenly, slipping a little on the rooftop, and Brody grabbed onto her to keep her from falling.

"For starters, be careful. You fall off the roof you may end up with more than just the stitches I had."

"I know, I know, but my reaction? Called for." She huffed a piece of hair out of her face. "You just told me that your mother and Frank were there when Brian shot himself. That they all were, and they left."

"Trust me, I know how fucked up it is." The bitterness in Brody's voice couldn't be masked even if he tried. He laid back down and opened his arms up to her and smiled as she curled up beside him once more.

"So what did she say about it? What did Frank say about it?"

"I'm not asking Frank. He'd lie. I know he would." Brody's jaw was set, and he was grateful that Catherine had her head laid on his chest so that she couldn't see his face. "And Sandra has left the building."

"Just like that, she just left."

"Hmm? Oh, she left before I could even ask her." He placed a kiss atop Catherine's head. "I'm so glad you're here. I was losing my shit."

"Define that, please, because ew."

His laughter was true as he held her closer. "Metaphorical shit, I promise."

He could feel her frown through his shirt. "You've been doing that a lot lately. And stop tensing up; you know it's the truth."

"I'm not tense… okay, I'm a little tense."

She lifted her head and raised an eyebrow at him.

"Okay, fine, a lot, but why shouldn't I be? I mean, isn't everything I've done a normal reaction to some fucked up shit? What about what they've done to me?"

"Hey." She brought her hand up and cradled his face, as he had so often done for her. "I'm not saying it isn't warranted, I'm saying it's a lot. And I'm worried, Brody."

"About me? Fuck, I've lived through so much worse." He looked away then to hide his expression, the one full of sorrow. "But he hadn't. And I still don't know why he killed himself." His heartbeat sped ever so slightly as she laid back into his arms.

"You may never know."

But he wanted to.

Didn't he?

Wouldn't that make things easier for him? Make him stop questioning himself to find out either yes or no if the reason was him.

"I know you're not going to want to hear me say this,"

"Then don't say it," he cut her off as he ran his fingers through her hair, the silky strands pouring through his fingers.

"Maybe Frank is the one you should ask. He seems all confessiony now. It's kinda weird."

"He's always been weird, and he always has some sort of confession to turn those tables."

"Oh." She drew out the word and shifted in his arms. "He seems rather happy about the baby."

"Sammi's kinda happy she's having a sister, but,"

"They're having a girl?"

Catherine hadn't known.

"Cat,"

"Do you know what she's going to go through? She's going to be raised by a nanny with a mother who sees her as a meal ticket with my grandfather. And either she's going to turn out to be a snooty bitch, or worse... like me."

"Wait a fucking minute here." Brody lifted her chin with his fingertips. "You are amazing, and if your sister turns out like you, this world will be a better place. This world needs more of you, Cat; much more than you'll ever know."

"What if she hates it there? What if she ends up with Frank?"

Brody was silent for a moment, his brow furrowed. "Cat," he finally said, "Frank wasn't always a monster. And... and I'm not just saying this because I think you want to hear it. Sometimes..." He blinked back threatening tears. "Sometimes he was a really great dad. Especially to Sammi," he added.

"That must have been terrible for you, watching him be so good to all of them and not you."

"No, he was with me, too. Sometimes, that is." He turned his eyes back towards the dotting of stars. "That was the hardest part. And it still is."

"Is he trying to be a good dad again to you?"

"I don't know." He held her a little closer and rested his head on hers. "I don't know."

"You seem to be handling this well," Laura commented as she peered at him during their session the following day.

"Yeah, well…" Brody stared at the art on the wall, then back down at the hole in his jeans that he was picking at. He didn't want to tell his therapist he was simply a good actor. He'd been playing the role his entire life. Sandra thought Brian was a good actor? He had nothing on his younger twin.

Or had he, and that's why everyone was so shocked?

"Yeah well what?"

"I talked it out with Catherine last night." He shrugged. "She calms me." Nurtures him.

Loves him.

"Have the two of you been intimate yet?"

"We've been more intimate than most people who have sex, Laura. Our definition of intimate isn't the same."

"Handling it well, but still snapping when someone asks a question. Maybe you're just pretending to be okay."

Had she read his mind? Brody shook his head to clear his thoughts. "I didn't sl… get to talk to my mom."

"Sleep. You were about to say you didn't sleep."

"Yeah, well, I forgot to take the meds."

"Hasn't your mother been reminding you?"

"She didn't come home last night." He hadn't meant the venom to be so present in his voice, but it was too late to take it back. "I think she spent the night with Frank. Which means I left the door opened because I don't have a key." He'd also thrown away the piece of pipe that she'd had lodged into his bedroom window, just in case.

"Brody, I need you to promise me that you'll do everything you can to remain calm when you speak to her."

He scoffed. "Yeah, sure. Maybe I'll just have Catherine with me. She keeps me in check."

"But are you relying a bit much on her for that? Your keeping in check should be on you, not your girlfriend."

"I don't rely too much on her." When Laura's expression failed to change, he added, "I don't, I swear."

But even he was beginning to question it as he stepped out of the building and put his earbuds in.

Instead of taking the bus, he ran the entire way home.

CHAPTER 28

Alliteration

Brody's alarm was screaming at an early hour, and he reached over with a groan to hit the snooze button. The last thing he wanted before caffeination was confrontation, and he almost laughed at the thought. *Alliteration.* He was already on a roll. He could hear his mother readying herself for her day at work, so he knew that putting it off would only mean more anger, more anxiety for him.

He reached for his phone, expecting his first text to be Catherine's good morning to him.

It was from JJ.

Can you swing by here today

It was the first text he'd received from him since that Christmas Day.

What's a good time he sent in return, surprised when JJ answered almost immediately.

Whenever

He knew JJ's schedule, so he probably hadn't even slept yet. That was the second hard conversation he was going to have today. JJ needed to know the truth about the day that Brian died, or at least as much of the truth as Brody was privy to.

Until he was able to get the truth from Sandra.

His walk was more of a stagger, his legs protesting his recent running, and he stopped to stretch out at the end of the hallway.

"Excuse me," he heard Sandra say from behind him, and he moved to let her through. "Coffee is in the kitchen."

"Good," he mumbled to her before walking with a bit of a limp towards the kitchen.

"What happened?"

"Hmm? Oh, the limp. Running," he answered.

"You seem to be doing that a lot lately."

"Keeps me in shape. Clears my head," he added.

"Good. You need that."

"What I need to know," he said as he lifted his eyes to her, "is why you left your son lying on the floor with a bullet in his head."

"I didn't."

"Sorry, let me rephrase." He took a sip of his coffee. "With a bullet that went through his head and killed him. Why? And don't, okay?"

"Why would you ask such a thing?"

"Sammi told me about hearing the bang." Sandra's skin paled at Brody's words, and he nodded. "Point is, I know. And now I want to know why."

"I'm going to be late for work. We will talk tonight."

"Are you going to leave me a key, or do I need to leave the house open when I go to JJ's?"

"Lock up and I will let you know when I'm home," she said, and he felt his anger begin to rise within, battling for control over his calm exterior.

"Sure thing," he replied through clenched teeth, and wasn't surprised when she merely walked out the door without saying goodbye.

Nan had already left for work by the time that Brody walked up to JJ's door. "It's open," he heard JJ call out after the strumming of his guitar had stopped. Brody wasn't surprised to see the house immaculate, the way it always was when the neighborhood wasn't stopping by to blow off some steam.

"Hey," Brody said to JJ, who motioned for him to sit.

"Want something to drink?"

"Not this early."

JJ rolled his eyes. "I wasn't talking about alcohol. For you, that is."

"Water, then." When JJ walked to the kitchen, Brody added, "Is this what we are now? Acquaintances who play nice like they're talking to strangers?"

"You are a stranger. I don't know you anymore."

Not by my choices. Brody refrained from making the snide remark, instead agreeing. "You're right. I don't know you, either. Thanks," he added as he took the cold bottle of water from JJ, its condensation a stark contrast to the sweat forming at his brow. It's just JJ.

JJ thinks you're the reason your brother is dead.

"I, um… got his things together." JJ motioned towards the box. "He kept giving me shit, you know? Like he didn't want it anymore." He pulled out Brian's favorite Guns n Roses t-shirt. "Like this. Who gives their favorite shit away?"

"Someone who feels they won't need it anymore." Brody's heart was heavy as he took the t-shirt in his hands, remembering how Brian wouldn't let him touch it. *"No way, dick. You have your own clothes."*

But Brody's clothes mostly came from hand-me-downs and the thrift store in town.

Brian's had been chosen from a department store, paid for by Frank who'd always played favorites with him.

But if Brian was his favorite, why did he just leave him there?

"You know," JJ continued, "I watched my brother fight for every minute that he was spared life. He wanted so badly to live, to follow his dreams, marry his girl, become a father. Brian had all of that ahead of him." JJ took a long drink of his beer. "I don't think I'll ever forgive him for throwing it away."

Brody was silent as he looked around the living room, memories cascading from every corner.

Fifth grade, when the four best friends were insisting they would rule middle school the next year.

"I don't care if they're older," Brian said. "They're not us."

"And we fucking rule," Max agreed.

"Language, children," Nan called out from her bedroom down the hall where she was catching up on her soap operas.

"Who do you think we learned it from, Gram?" JJ replied.

"Jason John Capisani, I told you not to call me that!"

"All three names," Brody and Brian said in unison.

"You two are fucking creepy," JJ laughed.

"We really don't know what he was going through," Brody finally said.

"Don't we? I know about Frank. I know what he was doing to you. And I know that Brian tried everything he could to keep your ass out of trouble. And where did that get him?"

Stunned silent with this news, Brody could only stare at the shirt in his hands.

Brian had tried to protect him?

"Yeah, I know most of the shit we did was Brian's idea, but I watched him, man. I even watched him try to take the beating for that whole bike-off-the-roof thing, but Frank wasn't having it."

The way that Brody took the beating for Tyler when he broke the window in Catherine's gym.

"I didn't know that." Brody's tone was soft, contemplative. He was more like his twin than he'd originally thought.

"Oh, come on, you lived there."

"I tried to stay scarce, JJ. I was at Max's most of the time when I wasn't here until,"

"Until they fired the babysitter that Frank was fucking, and you and Bri were babysitting, always."

Brody stifled a laugh. "Fuck, what a mess that was."

JJ's face still held anger, but the threatening smile was beginning to show. "I thought she would get rid of him then."

"But she didn't. And life was more hell, even though he was trying to be on his best behavior."

Frank had been a doting father then, when he wasn't at work. He'd stopped drinking, stopped going out, and didn't have the babysitter to take back to the room to discuss her pay, so Sandra was happier.

Much happier.

Brody shuddered at the thought that he didn't want crossing his mind.

They'd walked out on their son, the golden boy, as his blood pooled out onto the bedroom floor.

"He wasn't as good to Brian as you think he was. He put a lot of pressure on him."

"And then he cracked, and they left him there. Just… left him there." Brody was staring at the carpet now, remembering how many times the four of them had played there, from matchbox cars to fake wrestling matches.

"What are you talking about?"

Brody looked at Jase then, his anger overriding his tears. "They were there when he shot himself, and they left him. They just fucking left him." He stood and began to pace, his hands running through his hair. "And it took Sammi slipping that she'd heard it for me to know. All this time…" He took in a shuddering breath. "All this time I thought I was the one who found him. And I guess I did, but… but I shouldn't have. They should have called for an ambulance, for something, but they didn't."

JJ's expression changed from sadness to rage, just as Brody's had when he first found out. He mumbled his excuses before he walked out back, and as Brody sat down, he could hear the smashing of the glass beer bottle that had been in JJ's hand. Brody wasn't sure how much time had passed before JJ walked back in, his eyes a telltale red, the way they always got whenever JJ had cried. He'd never been one to hold his emotions back, not the way that Brody did. JJ grabbed another beer and came back out to the living room, popping the cap as he sat down.

"What did your mom have to say about it?"

"She didn't."

"She sure told enough people at the funeral that you're the one who found him."

"She did?" Brody asked, and JJ nodded before he downed half of his beer.

"Sure you don't want one?"

"Positive." Brody picked at a thread in his jeans as he tried to recall Brian's funeral.

None of it would come to him.

"He was looking for you, you know." JJ sat back in his chair, his expression far away. "That night he had us all out looking for you."

"I was at the park, passed out under a tree."

"I guess he never found you, then." JJ finished his beer and stood. "I'm about to get fucking shitfaced, just to forewarn you."

"You always warn us," Brody said with the slightest smile. "But we always knew anyway."

"Us... us kinda died with Brian. Then us died again with Michael, except with Kaitlyn and Jack."

"Who's Jack?"

JJ rolled his eyes. "Jason, Michael's best friend. He and Kaitlyn are a thing now."

"Isn't he a little old for her?"

"Four years." JJ shrugged. "Kaitlyn has always acted older, you know?"

"Yeah, trust me, I know. I thought she was staying here."

"She is. She's with Audrey today."

"Don't they have cheerleading stuff?"

"Yeah, but your girl canceled. Said she was too tired." JJ grinned slightly. "Dog."

"Hey, asshole, we were just talking." Brody leaned back into the chair and sighed, his eyes on the box again. "I can't believe he left all of this to you."

"Some of it was probably for you, but you left." JJ shrugged. "I kept a few things, some books. Gave one of them to a girl in Indianapolis, though."

"She must have been some girl."

"She was."

"Are we good, JJ?" Brody asked suddenly. It took some time, but JJ nodded. "At least we're all together for our senior year, except Brian."

"I quit."

"You what?"

JJ sighed. "I quit school. I was never into it anyway. I'm just going to focus on music, and putting a band together, and just really put everything I have into it. There's nothing holding me back now."

"What does Nan think?"

"That I'm crazy."

"Aren't you?"

JJ opened his mouth, possibly to protest, then he cracked half a smile. "Yeah, I am the crazy one. And... and I don't know what 'good' is anymore. You love someone, and they leave. Everyone leaves. Now it's my turn. I'm changing my middle name to Michael, I'm taking Nan's last name, I'm leaving all this shit behind me, and I'm never looking back."

"So I don't get to say I knew you when?" Brody grinned.

"Yeah, asshole, you can say it."

"You have the presence, you know."

"If that's a 'short' joke, I'm fucking decking you."

"Where, in the stomach?" Brody laughed as JJ snapped his bottle cap at him. "No, seriously, you have a large presence. You can do this, you know?"

"All five foot eight of me." JJ sat back with a satisfied grin. "You think I can make it?"

"Yeah. Yeah I think so."

"I'm thinking about New York."

"City?"

"When I turn 18, yeah. All of this when I turn 18. Nan's going to help with the name change, but the rest of it's on me."

"What the hell will we call you then?"

"Jase," he said. "Just like Michael used to call me."

"So from JJ Capisani to Jase Warner." Brody grinned at him.

JJ smiled sadly. "I miss it, how it was."

Brody looked around him at the living room, the last place he saw Brian alive. "Yeah, so do I."

It was over by the front door where Brian had stopped him, asked him to stay.

"Nah, man, I'm out."

"You're wasted, Brody. Don't go. Just… stay, please."

"I'll see ya later, don't get all weepy."

Brian pulled him into a 'bro hug.' "I'll always look over you."

Over you.

Not after you.

Brian had asked him to spend his last night with him, had told him he wouldn't be with him anymore.

Brody stood and wiped his palms on his jeans. "I… I gotta go. I'll catch you later."

He didn't wait for JJ's reply before he left, leaving the box of Brian's things still sitting on the living room floor.

CHAPTER 29

Travesty

"So your mom's not home yet?"

"Nope." Brody sat in the beanbag chair with his headset on chatting with Catherine as they played their game online. "Watch your back."

"You watch it for me. You're the one that got me sick."

He cringed despite her not being able to see him. "Sorry. I really thought it was nerves or some shit like that."

"Do you two mind?" Another player was growing increasingly annoyed at their chatter, so Catherine shot at him.

"Mind your business," she said to him, and Brody stifled a laugh. "Anyway, I thought so, too. I mean, hello! What fucking bombshells the past few days, one after another, and hey! Don't shoot at me, asshole!"

"You shot at me first."

"Children, can we just play the game?" Brody asked as he took out an opponent.

"I don't feel much up to it," Catherine replied. "Phone time?"

Brody closed out the game. "Phone time it is."

When he picked up his phone, he noticed a message from his mother letting him know she was going out for the evening. At least she'd asked if he needed in the house for anything, but he still enjoyed sending that text telling her that's where he was. Before he'd hit send, Catherine was calling him.

"Hello, beautiful," he answered.

"I'd swoon, but I might throw up afterwards. How could you function feeling like this?"

He was used to feeling that way: nauseated, anxious, feeling like he needed to crawl in bed and sleep the day away. "I have superpowers, Cat, you know this," he said, and was rewarded with her soft laughter.

"It's like I'm hungry, but food is... no, thank you. Dad's out at his other job, and I don't want to get up and fix anything."

Brody was already in his kitchen trying to figure out his own dinner. "Maybe you should just rest," he suggested as he found what he was looking for in the cupboard and tossed it into the air, catching it with ease.

"Is it feed a fever, starve a cold? Or is it the opposite?"

"You have a fever?"

"No. I don't think so anyway. I wish you were here."

He smiled down at the contents in his hand. Coach would understand, maybe even commend him for a job well done. "As you wish," was all he said before hanging up the phone.

To Brody, Catherine looked every bit as adorable as always when she answered the door in cutoff sweats and a crop top, her hair in a messy bun, and no makeup on her unnaturally pale face. Still, she smiled at him as he kissed her forehead softly.

"You're right, no fever," he said as he entered and slung his backpack off his shoulder.

"You shouldn't be here."

"I'm here for you to kick my ass for making you sick." He turned around. "If that would make you feel better." He laughed when she lightly touched his backside with her foot. "I've seen how much power you have; you must be feeling like shit."

"Brody, look at me. I have dark circles under my eyes. Me! This is a travesty."

He brushed away a few strands of hair, his fingertips grazing her skin. "You're the most beautiful girl I've ever seen."

Her smile was tired. "You're just looking for brownie points."

He kissed the tip of her nose. "I'm just being honest. Now go lay back on the couch, and that's an order."

"I'd argue that you're not the boss of me, but I have no strength." She nudged him again. "Your fault."

"But you love me."

"Yes, and you're lucky," she mumbled as she shuffled her way to the couch. Brody carried his backpack to the dining room table, unloading a few of its contents there. "What are you doing?"

"What I came over here to do. I'm no Max, but..." He held up two cans. "Chicken noodle soup."

"Is that supposed to make me feel better?" Her question was genuine, he could tell from her tone, and he smiled at her.

"It's what I was given whenever I felt like shit."

"I'm past shit, Brody. So past it."

He watched her curl up on the couch and his heart soared at the sight of her. Even with her pale face, the darkened streaks beneath her eyes, and her hair up haphazardly in a messy bun, she was the most beautiful girl he'd ever seen. Her wrinkled, baggy clothing was an unusual sight, only adding to how adorable she was to him.

"You're staring," she muttered as she closed her eyes.

"Can't help it."

"You're so weird."

"It's one of my redeeming qualities." His smile still in place, he picked up the cans, reading the directions on the back. Add water, heat up. That seemed easy enough. He found a pot big enough for both cans of soup and began to prepare it for her.

"Did you bring crackers?"

"Shit," he said as he cringed. "Sorry, no, I didn't."

"That's okay," she mumbled. "I think we have some."

He knew she was asleep before the soup finished heating. He tasted it and oddly enough felt like patting himself on the back. Such a simple task, but he hadn't trusted himself to do it before.

His mother hadn't trusted him to do it.

He paused with that realization, then shook it off. She was avoiding him, and he didn't want to waste his time with Catherine thinking about his mother. His search for bowls was brief, and soon he was carrying Catherine's out to the coffee table.

"Babe." His touch to her shoulder was light. "Where do you keep the crackers?"

"Some cabinet in there." She gestured with her hand without opening her eyes. He placed a kiss on her forehead, noting it's warmth before he began to search for the crackers. Once found, he brought them, along with his bowl, back out to the living room.

Catherine slept on as he lowered himself into the chair and began to eat. Max would be so proud of him, he thought with a stifled laugh. He managed to heat up chicken noodle soup without burning Catherine's home down.

She didn't stir when he asked her if she was going to eat, and he left the bowl before her in case she woke up and wanted it. Once finished with his, he rinsed his bowl out and placed it in the dishwasher. He wasn't about to leave her, not with her feeling this badly and her father being at work, so despite the fact that Coach could be angry with him should he be caught, he stayed.

She needed him.

He wasn't about to let her down.

"What chapter are we on again?"

"Twenty, since we read ahead."

"Some was over the phone."

His smile was soft. "Yes it was." He sat beside her on the couch, offering his side to her. She cuddled against him and leaned her head against his chest.

"Go on."

His mind was miles away as he read to her, although he could consider it close—it was all about Catherine. Her closeness magnified the affect she had on him, leaving him calm, ready to face whatever storm was going to be facing him when he finally confronted Sandra. But this... having his girl in his arms, the soft floral scent of her surrounding him, the silky strands of her hair against his unshaven cheek... all of this had him feeling ready to take on the world.

All he needed was Catherine.

He paused reading as another thought crossed his mind. "Are you sure your dad won't be pissed when he gets home?"

"He's on a date, and I already told him you were here."

"You did?"

"Yep. Sent him a text that said if you weren't here, I would need him to come home. Whoever she is must be special."

"Does that bother you?"

He felt her smile even before she lifted her face to him. "He's so happy. How could I deny him that?"

Brody kissed the tip of her nose. "One of the million reasons I adore you."

"He's even being responsible and not introducing us until he knows for sure."

"What then?"

"Then I meet my potential new step-mother. Wait... you don't think it's your mom, do you?"

Brody laughed. "No, I'm positive it's not."

"How so?"

"Frank."

"Oh, right. This time I'll be happy about that." She snuggled back in place. "We have an Honors English book to finish."

Brody spotted the clock, showing that it was nearly midnight. As much as he hated to do so, he closed the book with a sigh. "Not tonight. You need your sleep."

"I slept half the time you've been here. Thank you for the soup."

He kissed the top of her head. "You're welcome." Her arms tightened around her, and he held her a little tighter. "Cat?"

"Hmm?"

"This means I have to leave."

"I know." Still, she stayed where she was.

"As much as I would love to spend the night, I don't think it's wise."

"You sure?"

"Positive."

"Just a little bit longer?"

He pulled her closer and breathed her in, reveling in the moment. "Just a little bit."

It was nearly one in the morning when he finally made it home, prepared to climb into his bedroom window. Instead, his mother was pulling up in the driveway, parking crookedly as if seeing him startled her. He inhaled slowly, knowing this was the time.

He wanted answers.

Considering her slight stumble when she exited her vehicle, she'd had no business driving in the first place. As she fumbled with her keys, Brody approached her and held out her hand. "I've got it," he said, and she mumbled her thanks.

Her guard was down.

"You ready to talk?" Brody looked over his shoulder as he unlocked the door, pocketing the keys without her noticing.

"Not really."

"You promised." He opened the door and stood to the side as she walked past.

"I'm just tired."

She wasn't just tired; she was a least a little buzzed, and definitely avoiding. With her defenses down, though, Brody was sure to get the answers he was looking for.

"I know he was dead before you left, you know." He kept his tone light, conversational. "Sammi told me about the bang, about you leaving quickly."

"Kids." She sunk down into the couch with a sigh and laid her head back. "You know how they make things up."

"Mom." Brody sat beside her and took her hand in his despite the overwhelming urge to scream. "You told everyone that I found Brian, but I didn't."

"You did."

"I didn't."

"It didn't make any sense, you know?" She was staring straight ahead, where a picture of all four kids was displayed on the wall. "His note didn't even make sense. It was all rambling and disconnected."

"But he killed himself."

"Yes." Her expression was forlorn, her voice wavering. "He put that gun to his head and pulled the trigger, and I don't know why."

"And then you left him."

One tear ran down her cheek. "I didn't know what else to do. I... I panicked, and I didn't want the kids to see him, but they did anyway."

He squeezed her hand and controlled his voice as he continued, all the while urging his own tears to stay away. "You left him for me to find."

"I was looking for you." She squeezed his hand back. "I never thought you'd see him like that, Brody. And then you did, and it was so... I'll never forget your screams, and I thought that's what it must have been like for him, inside his head. So much screaming, and there was no turning back. I didn't even know he had the gun." She sniffled a little, her tears flowing in earnest now. "But he did, and it was so fast, and…"

Brody pulled his hand back abruptly. "You were in the room." It was a statement, one he knew to be true even before she nodded.

"He just raised it and shot, and,"

His heart sank, the guilt over not being there, over feeling this anger when she saw her own son die.

She saw him die.

"You could have called 911." He straightened up, resisting the side of him that wanted to hold her while she cried.

She watched her son die.

"He was gone, Brody."

"But what if he wasn't?"

"He was *gone*."

Brody stood and fisted his trembling hands. Brian had been their favorite, who could do know wrong, while to them Brody could do no right. "Mom, did you… did you ever wish it was me? Is that why… why it's like I don't exist sometimes?"

"I never," she sniffled, "never wished it was you. I wouldn't wish any of my children dead."

"But to you he was so good, everything about him, and I was always trouble."

"No."

"Why did you leave him?" His voice was beginning to raise, a defense against his threatening tears. "Why?"

"I told you, I panicked." She grabbed a tissue from the box on the brand-new coffee table, the one that Brody considered paid with blood money.

His brother's blood.

That's when everything had fallen apart, and she was there.

"You watched him put a bullet in his brain,"

"Through, it went through. He was gone."

He swallowed back the bile that crept up into his throat.

So much made sense, in many ways. Her break down, her hospitalization. But still…

"And you left his body."

"For the last time, *yes*. I panicked, and I went looking for you."

"And Frank left his golden boy to,"

"Frank didn't know." She wiped her eyes. "When I finally told him, he turned the car around, and… and he never forgave me." She sobbed into her tissue. "He never forgave me."

"Is that your biggest problem? That the asshole who beat me in front of you never forgave you for leaving his favorite?"

"You resented your brother, and I get that."

Something inside Brody snapped.

"I never resented Brian! I resented the asshole who called me a bastard when I wasn't one, and I resented *you* for letting him treat me that way." His hands fisted in his hair and he began to pace the living room floor. "All you've ever done is lie to me, one lie after another, one lie to everyone after another. You had a place to go, to take us when you left him, didn't you? You could have gone to your parents."

"But they're dead to me."

"And I was just guessing they weren't, so thank you for confirming."

"I am your mother; you don't get to speak to me this way."

"You're… you're just trying to make me feel sorry, and… stop, okay? Stop, please. I am your son, and all I've been is a buffer to keep Frank from taking his bullshit out on you. I'm right about that one too, aren't I?"

She hesitated for a moment before she spoke. "Your accusations are just garbage, Brody. If you have no sympathy for a mother who watched their child kill themselves, then you're not the same boy I've known all along. Maybe your girl has changed you, I don't know. I'm going to bed."

"You do that."

He didn't wait for her reply and wasn't sure if she'd said one before he walked down the short hallway and slammed his door shut, this time locking it despite the fact that it would stick. For the briefest of moments, he feared that he'd woke up the kids, then remembered that Tyler and Sammi were in Chicago with their aunt.

And his mother obviously didn't want him anywhere near them.

This... this whole new revelation was killing him inside. Should he be angry? Should he be devastated for her? He had no idea what to think, what was wrong or right anymore.

He shot a quick text to Catherine, wishing she would respond, but not surprised when she didn't. It was late, plus she still hadn't been feeling well when he left. Guilty for asking if she was still up, he shot another text to her saying he hoped she was feeling better, which was the truth. But damn, did he ever need to talk to her, need her comfort.

When he heard his mother's door shut with the telling *click* of her lock, he eased his bedroom window open and crawled out onto the closet branch. Deciding against the rooftop, he eased his way down the tree, careful not to make any noise, and began walking.

Anywhere else was better.

CHAPTER 30

You're Kidding, Right?

Despite the late hour, there were still people milling about JJ's home. Much to Brody's surprise, Emily was one of them. She sat alone in the front lawn, her eyes on the dark sky above her. Her expression was more of wonder than boredom, and she was aware enough of her surroundings that she knew Brody was the one who walked up and sat beside her.

"I'm surprised your mother let you out this late," she said.

"She doesn't know I left. Yours?"

Emily shrugged. "Probably high as a kite. I got placed with a foster family not far from here. Supposed to be for my own good, and yet, here I am, a fourteen-year-old at a party."

"Drinking?"

She glanced sideways at him for a brief moment before returning her attention to the stars. "No. My foster sisters are. And fawning all over the resident rockstar," she added.

"Does that bother you?"

"I'm used to being around drinking."

"Them fawning all over your crush."

"He's everyone's crush. Aside from your girl, that is. Anyway, I said I was used to being around drinking. That doesn't mean I want to be drooling all over someone who could probably drink my mother under the table."

Brody nodded, knowing JJ's penchant for drinking abundantly and often. "I get it."

"You're in a shit mood, and don't try to play like you're not."

He stretched out, his hands behind his head as he laid back. "How astute of you."

"Nerd."

"You knew that about me."

"So, what gives?"

What a loaded question that was for him. The guilt, compassion, and anger were warring inside, eating away at his resolve, each screaming for release. He didn't know if he should cry for his mother or go back and scream at her.

How could she?

Was she okay? Would she ever be okay?

How could she?

Why didn't he go straight home? Hell, why hadn't he stayed when Brian begged him to?

How could she?

"Okay, so you don't want to tell me." Emily stretched out beside him. "Things any better at home?"

"I don't know."

He didn't know if the confession his mother had made would make things better or worse. How would he react to her the next time he saw her? His first instinct would be to comfort her, he was sure of it.

But could he?

"I'd wanted some closure," he admitted. "I wanted to have Brian's death make some sort of sense, have it tied up with a bow so there were no more questions."

"I take it that didn't happen."

"Not even close."

"And now?"

"Now Catherine's asleep and I can't... I can't deal with this without her."

Emily was silent as she sat up, her expression hidden in the shadows that cast across her face. "You're kidding, right?"

Brody sat up as well. "Not even close. And why would I kid about something like that? He was... he's still my brother, even though he's six feet underground."

"That's not what I'm talking about."

"Catherine? She's my comfort. She... when I'm with her, everything just falls into place."

"Yo, asshole." Emily punched his arm hard.

"Ow."

"Did that get your attention? You don't need Catherine to get you through this. You have got to do this on your own. It isn't her place to fix you."

"I didn't say that."

"Yeah, you did. You need to get your own shit together, not put all of this on another human. It isn't right, and it isn't fair to her, either."

"What the fuck would you know? You're just a kid."

"Yeah, I'm a kid who's been taking care of myself since I learned how to pour cereal into a bowl. I was also my mother's crutch when she needed someone to lean on. Don't you think about what that does to her? How much pressure that puts on her?"

"She's not under any pressure."

"You're relying on her to keep you from losing your shit. If that's not putting someone under too much pressure, then what is?"

Emily stood and left him before he had a chance to answer, and he watched her walk swiftly away from JJ's house.

"Em, wait."

"I'm fine," she yelled over her shoulder before opening a door to a home across the street. "See? They even know where I was."

Despite the other people milling about on JJ's lawn, Brody had never felt more alone in his life. He'd thought his illness had been stress until Catherine came down with it... but what if it *was* caused by stress?

Had he put Catherine under so much pressure that she was starting to give?

She'd had her own fair share of bullshit to deal with. She'd come face to face with her rapist, with her tormenters, with her mother. She'd found out that her mother was having a baby, another girl no less, and all the while she'd been worried about him.

That had to be what it was.

"Brody, my man!" Max called out as he and Sarah walked outside. "What the fuck you doing? Get in, have a beer."

"I really do have to go," Sarah said, and Max gave her a soft kiss.

"I'll see you tomorrow," he said to her, motioning that he was coming over to talk to his best friend.

"Is Catherine here?" Brody asked the question already knowing the answer.

"Haven't seen her. Audrey said she was sick, though. Dude... are you okay?" Max offered a hand to help Brody up, which he accepted.

"Yeah, yeah," he lied. "I'm great." He glanced at the doorway. "Not really in the mood for a party."

"Let's walk." Max began walking in the direction of his home without waiting for Brody's reply. Brody followed him, and soon they were on the sidewalk, making the trek they'd walked so many times over their short lives.

"Emily said that JJ was rather inebriated," Brody commented.

"Always." They stopped at the corner, looking both ways before crossing the street. "But he also said I needed to talk to you. Want to tell me what it's about?"

Brody paused a moment, and Max stopped with him. One lone tear escaped Brody's eyes before he spoke. "Sandra—my mom, she was in the room when Brian shot himself."

Max's eyes slid shut as he muttered a curse, his head hanging low. "Fuck, man, are you okay?"

Brody shrugged and they began walking again. He really didn't know how to answer the question. No, he wasn't ever going to be okay. Half of him was gone. It was senseless, it was heart wrenching, it was infuriating.

"I take that as a no."

"I just need to talk to Catherine. No offense."

"None taken, as long as you tell me why."

"She brings out the best in me."

"Like?"

"She makes me human. Compassionate. Maybe I won't feel like going back and screaming at my mom."

Max let out a short laugh. "Newsflash for you, bro, you've always been the most compassionate person I know. You've always had the biggest heart, been the protector. Always, dude. Catherine hasn't changed you. So if you're not okay, the answer really is in you." They began walking again. "I get that you're angry, but you don't want to scream at her, dude. That's not you."

Brody was silent as they turned onto Max's street, disagreeing with him in his mind. Max didn't know; he couldn't see. Catherine was his calm, his center, his world. She brought out the best in him. Max just didn't know. How could he? They hadn't spent as much time together now that their girlfriends were in their lives. And his mom...

Brody couldn't even think about her right now without feeling blind rage and an even more blinding sense of guilt over it.

"I suppose now's not the time to let you know that her ex has been hanging around Brentfield, working with Frank's crew."

Brody inhaled sharply and shoved his hands into his pockets. *Sonofabitch.* "Is that so?"

"And he's been asking around about your girl. Audrey has your back, though. She told him that Catherine leveled up. Did you turn Audrey into a gamer?"

"I don't think she's ever played. Cat is a gamer at heart, though." Brody's words seemed to flow out of him, despite the fact that his mind was elsewhere.

Mitch.

Fucking *Mitch*.

"Back to your mom and this..." Max sighed. "I always knew something was up. It was sketchy the way she was telling everyone that you found him."

"I don't know what to think," Brody admitted. "I just don't fucking know."

"I know what will help." They paused outside of Max's house with its immaculate lawn, drastically different from the others surrounding it. "Star Wars and cold pizza. You up to it?"

Brody felt his mother's keys in his pocket weighing him down. He didn't want to go home.

"Yeah," he said with a half grin. "Sounds good."

Mack's opened at 7:30 sharp, as it did every morning. Brody was one of the first to enter despite the fact that he wasn't due in until later in the day. He took his mother's set of keys back to the small hardware section and handed the housekey over to the staff member there, paying the $3 charge in change. Unsure of his mother's motives for keeping him locked out when she wasn't there, he knew that keeping the key a secret was essential. Her morning shift didn't start until 9, and he had plenty of time to return home and place her keys in a spot she would believe she'd chosen herself.

Volunteers as well as construction workers were beginning to fill the aisles, gathering water bottles and other items for the Brentfield residents, many of whom were returning to their homes for the first time. Their chatter was low, keeping the store eerily quiet before the overhead music began to play. As Brody turned towards the entrance, he stopped cold.

Frank was walking in.

And Mitch was following close behind.

Perhaps Mitch was Frank's new golden boy, although Brody could think of a myriad of reasons that Mitch would never compare to Brian.

Thinking that they'd passed to the point where they wouldn't see him, Brody began making his way towards the exit of the store, receipt and key shoved down into his pocket. With a combination of lack of sleep along with the revelations he was still reeling from, the last thing he wanted was…

"Good morning, Brody."

…Frank Harris to acknowledge him.

He kept walking, pretending that he didn't hear him, but soon an icy grip held his heart as he felt a hand on his arm.

"Aren't you going to say good morning?" Of course Frank would be his charming self; he had an audience, after all.

"Wasn't planning on it, no."

"Well, I was hoping you were planning on volunteering over in Brentfield. Hey, better yet, the company I work for is hiring temporary help. Our fine boy, Mitch, is one of our best employees."

Brody needed to get out of that store, and fast.

"I gotta go."

"Say, your mother is missing her keys. You wouldn't know anything about that, would you?"

"No," he lied, thankful for his shirt covering his pockets.

"Mitch, why don't you go get what we were looking for?" Frank handed him a wad of money. "I'll meet you out front. My son and I need to talk."

Brody shook Frank's hand off his arm. "No, we don't."

Somehow he wasn't surprised when Frank followed him outside. "I know you and Mitch have a past, but it's just me now."

Brody scoffed. "I don't want to talk to you, either."

"Listen,"

"Don't call me your son, and don't ask me to act like everything is okay. You left my brother to die."

Frank's expression darkened. "That wasn't me."

"So Sandra says, too. Just don't, okay?" he added quickly before Frank could speak again. "I don't believe either one of you anymore."

"At least I have Mitch to work with me." Frank smiled again. "He sure misses Catherine."

"And you're going to see to it that he stays the fuck away from her."

"That's not my place."

"No, but it's mine."

"Mitch is a fine young,"

"He's a fucking rapist, Frank," Brody said through clenched teeth, not thinking through the consequences of his words. "That fine boy that you want to brag about raped her. Choosing him as your new golden boy shows exactly the kind of asshole that you are."

"What did you just say about me?"

Mitch was behind him now, trying to look intimidating, yet failing in Brody's eyes.

"You heard exactly what I said."

"You're just pissed she slept with me first."

Brody's fist landed straight on Mitch's jaw, stunning the large boy. "You don't speak about her anymore. You lost that chance when you forced yourself on her."

He waited for Mitch to fight back.

Instead he just smiled as the manager of the store—Brody's boss—walked up and told him to leave.

"I'm gone," Brody said as he threw his hands up, knowing his actions had just cost him his job.

He didn't care.

"Still think he's such a fine boy?" Brody asked Frank, and without waiting for Frank's reply, he turned and began walking briskly, knowing he had to get the keys back to his mother.

Knowing this would get back to Catherine.

And knowing she would never forgive him.

Brody's phone was being bombarded with message after message as he made his way home. Word always spread quickly in this community, and he was sure that Catherine had already been told long before he'd sent her the message that he needed to talk to her. He already had messages from Max, Sarah, a couple of his baseball teammates, but the one that stuck out in his mind was from his mother.

Get home with my keys now

His plan hadn't worked, obviously. He wondered for a moment if Frank had needed anything from the store, or if his mother had sent him up there.

"Fuck," he muttered, running a hand through his hair as he rounded the corner, his house in view.

His curse had nothing to do with being caught.

His curse was knowing he had to face his mother with his overwhelmingly conflicted feelings.

There was no time to waste, as she needed to leave for work and the keys to her car were now in his hand. As he came closer, she exited the home, her hand outstretched. He noticed she wasn't looking him in the eye as he placed the keys in her hand, and as she turned away, he called out to her.

"What?" she snapped as she turned around, then let out a gasp of surprise as Brody pulled her into a hug.

"I'm so sorry," he said, his voice choked with emotion. He wasn't so much sorry about ensuring he had a house key; no, that part he was satisfied with. It was the rest.

The argument with Frank.

Getting fired from his job.

But mostly for her losing her oldest son as she watched, helpless.

She returned his hug and patted his back the way she used to. "We'll talk when I get home," was all she said as she pulled away and got into her car.

"I love you, too," he muttered while she drove away.

The door was still opened, and he made his way inside, noticing right away that the picture of the four of them—him, Brian, Tyler, and Sammi—had been replaced with fancy artwork.

Perhaps he wasn't sorry after all.

CHAPTER 31

Righteous Indignation

Brody glanced at his phone for the tenth time. The only calls and messages had been from his friends wanting to hear his side.

Max.

Sarah.

Randall.

Audrey.

Even JJ.

Nothing from Catherine.

He was sure Catherine had heard what he had said by now.

He had been pacing the floor so long, the carpet was starting to show traces of his foot prints. His hands fisted in his hair as glanced at his phone again.

He should call her again, leave another message. She should hear it from him. The silence of the house was so unnerving he couldn't take it anymore. He had to talk to her. Brody grabbed the house key that he'd had made that morning, that had started this chain reaction, and yanked the door open, determined to find her and tell her first.

The slap that greeted Brody as he opened the door shattered the silence. Catherine stood before him with a red, tear-streaked face full of sadness and anger. The mark on Brody's face stung as he stepped back, allowing her to stomp her way in.

He deserved this.

He *deserved* all of it.

Everything he knew she was about to throw at him.

"How dare you?" she seethed, wiping at her tears. "You... you with all your righteous indignation, you with your moral compass. You couldn't tell me anything about your ex being gay because it wasn't *your* story to tell, oh *no!* It was Bethany's. But me? *Me!* Someone you claim to love. You blurt out *my* story in the middle of a goddamn grocery store as if you're talking about the latest movie you have seen."

His face paled as his heart raced. "I do love you."

"No! You don't get to talk right now. I am not through."

His head dropped and he nodded, each word from her tearing his soul apart.

"I trusted you."

"I know you did."

"Hey! Look at me and pay attention, Brody. *I trusted you.* There were two people that I spoke to, my therapist and you. I never in a million years thought that you would betray me like this."

He tried pouring his heart into his words, tried to make her see. "I swear I didn't mean to. I was just so fucking pissed it slipped out. It wasn't a betrayal."

"Wasn't... are you fucking kidding me right now? You purposefully told Frank, in front of people that we go to school with, what happened to me. Without my permission. And you think that's not a fucking betrayal? They call it betraying someone's trust *for a reason.*"

Sweat broke out across his brow. It never occurred to him that anyone else could have overheard them.

He hadn't even thought twice when he'd uttered the words to Frank, only wanting him to know what a piece of shit Mitch was.

"I have given you so much grace over the past few months, Brody. I have covered for you, cried for you, cried *with* you. I made excuses for you, mostly to myself. Every time you lose your shit, I always justify it. Always. But there is absolutely no justification for what you did to me today. And don't," she cut him off, "use Mitch as an excuse. You played right into his hands; you know that? You think I didn't know that he has been asking around about me? You're the one who told me what a great community it is that we're a part of. And it is great but, it also has small-town syndrome where everyone knows everyone else's business, and I don't play into that."

"Which makes it no different from Davis. And I thought you were past giving a fuck what everyone else thinks, Cat."

"I *am* past it, but this isn't even about that now. I am being called a liar, Brody! Or do I need to remind you that the word 'no' never left my lips, even though it should have?"

His eyes slid shut.

He knew this. He'd held her as she'd cried so many times over this.

"This is Mitch and his uppity family we're talking about here. My mother says they're already talking about a defamation lawsuit."

"You really think he wants to take this to court, Catherine?"

"No, I think he wants the money, and he wants to make me suffer for talking to anyone. And guess what? You played right into his greedy little hands. What are you going to do if he presses charges?"

Fuck. He hadn't been thinking about that, either. "Cat, I'm sorry, okay? I just... I don't care what happens to me, I care that he hurt you."

"Don't you get it Brody? *You* hurt me. Way more than anyone else could."

Unshed tears stung his eyes. "I didn't mean to," he stated, his voice barely above a whisper.

"It doesn't matter whether you meant to or not, you still did it. You really need to get your shit together, Brody, pay more attention to the things going on around you and start giving a damn. You need to quit just *saying* things that hurt others. I'm sorry that you lost your brother. I'm sorry that you had a shitty childhood. This downward spiral that you're on? You need to get off of it. I thought that therapy might help you, but it hasn't. I won't be dragged down with you; do you hear me? I will *not* let that happen."

"I'm sorry that my shit life has ruined your reputation," he shot back.

"Oh, it's not ruined, not by a long shot. I have come too far, and I won't let you do that to me."

"What the fuck does that mean?"

Catherine stared at him for what seemed like an eternity. Her beautiful green eyes piercing deep into his soul. She glanced away as Brody's lower lip began to quiver, his anxiety growing.

"Cat? What does that mean?" he asked again.

Because she wouldn't.

She *couldn't*.

When she finally looked at him, the love that had been so easy to see in those eyes was gone. What he saw staring back at him was nothing. No warmth. No love. Just.... cold.

It wasn't his Cat anymore.

Lady Cath-er-ine stood before him, stoic, emotionless.

"It means I am fucking done Brody."

"Done? Done with what?"

"With you."

No.

No, no, no, *no*.

"I am done with you and this downward fucking spiral that you are on. You're on a path I can't and *won't* follow."

Her words hit him with such a force he stumbled back, his unshed tears now spilling from his eyes.

"Cat, please... You're my absolute everything. I can't lose you. I need you." He choked back a sob, trying to get his own emotions under control, the way she so obviously had.

"You should have fucking thought of that before you betrayed me. What you did was... it was just as bad as what Mitch did." She shook her head when he tried to take a step towards her. "Actually, it was worse because *you* were the one person who was never going to hurt me. I trusted you with everything in me."

Brody's vision blurred as her words were swirling in his head.

This couldn't be happening.

She couldn't leave him.

This had to be a fucking nightmare.

That's what this had to be, this whole short morning.

Brody reached for her, having to touch her.

Catherine shook her head no and backed up. Her eyes still cold, still piercing deep into his soul. Without another word, she gave him one last scathing look, turned on her heel and walked out the door.

Out of his life.

His entire body jarred with the slam of the door, yet he stayed still, staring at it.

Willing her back in.

Willing her to listen to his side, to not leave him when she was his everything.

The sound of her father's car driving away took the last of his wishing away.

Catherine was gone.

Gone.

Gone.

No more comfort, no love.

No home.

His breathing sped up as the walls began closing around him, suffocating him.

He was unsure if he closed the door behind him as he ran as fast as he could, away.

Away.

He wasn't sure how long he stood there staring at the sign to the cemetery. He hadn't remembered taking the route, and yet there he was.

So close.

He knew which roads to follow, which plot his brother's stone resided, his body decaying six feet below. He'd never taken them, not since the funeral. His breathing had slowed, though his heart was too heavy for him to carry.

He could shut it off, all of it. Isn't that what others always did? Shut down. Shut it off.

Catherine certainly had.

He tried her number again, knowing he was blocked when it went to voicemail far too quickly.

Blocked.

She was hurt. He understood hurt, understood pain. He lived with it daily, dealing with it fine on some days.

But not today.

He could call his therapist; she'd told him in time of crisis to give her a call.

What would that get him, though?

Crisis care.

Back to the center.

There was no way he was going back.

A young woman stopped on her way in, rolling her window down to ask if he was okay.

"Fine," he lied.

His voice sounded strange to him, strangled.

But he'd cried, his tears still falling as he stood at the cemetery entrance.

Tears were expected here, weren't they?

"Are you sure?"

His world had fallen apart in a matter of hours.

In a matter of minutes.

In a matter of seconds.

"Positive," he said as he turned from her, hiding his face, his shame.

It was all his fault.

His phone began buzzing as the car drove away, and he pulled it out, hoping it was Catherine. Instead, he saw his aunt's name.

Sheryl, who had Tyler and Sammi.

Fearing something had happened to one of them, he answered immediately.

"Brody, what happened?" she asked.

"No, you… you called. Are they okay?"

"They're fine, hon. What happened to you? Don't tell me you're not crying."

He stared at the cemetery sign over his shoulder, then began walking the opposite direction, back towards home. "Doesn't matter."

"They're looking for you, and you haven't answered any calls or texts."

"Didn't want to talk to anyone." Except Catherine, who had decided their love meant nothing.

"Where are you?"

"On my way home."

"Good." She sounded relieved, but she didn't know.

She couldn't know.

Home wasn't home anymore.

At least he had…

"I wanted to let you know that… well, hon, Tyler and Sammi will be staying with me. Indefinitely, that is."

He stopped walking, trying to take in breaths that his lungs didn't want.

"Brody?"

"Are they safe?" he asked, tears threatening again.

"Of course they are."

She was trying to soothe him, comfort him, but he couldn't feel it.

She was taking Tyler and Sammi from him.

Yes, she was removing them from Frank's reach, but...

But what about him?

Was he so unlovable that no one wanted him?

"You didn't read the letter, did you?"

"No."

"Baby, please... read it."

"Sheryl,"

"You can come see them whenever you want."

But he couldn't stay with her. She didn't have to say it; he could hear it in her voice.

"I have to go," he said, hanging up before she could attempt to comfort him any further. It wouldn't work; he'd lost everything. He'd lost Tyler and Sammi.

He'd lost Catherine.

And his mother... what was she going to do with him now? Would she bring Frank back, force Brody to live in the same hell he'd escaped?

He began running then, slowly at first, then picking up speed and not slowing again until he rounded the corner and noticed his mother's car in the driveway.

And Frank's BMW parked on the road.

He could keep running, but nothing would change if he did.

And when he entered his house, his mother telling him to sit down, he knew what was coming.

He had officially lost everything.

CHAPTER 32

Away

She was sending him away.

She was sending him to some long term care facility.

He would be gone three months.

Three months.

"Your anger is entirely out of control. And now your violence has spread from objects to human beings."

She didn't care who or why, no more than she cared that this was what he'd learned.

Brody's eyes turned to Frank then, despite the fact that it was his mother speaking. His glare said it all; he was acting the same as he'd seen. Brody had been taught from a very young age that taking rage out on another was possible, even though he knew he shouldn't.

And he wasn't sorry.

Mitch had deserved it.

"Brody, look at me," Sandra said, and he returned his eyes to her.

She was no better.

She'd allowed it to happen.

"This is a three-month program, and the facility is one of the best." She'd already said that to him, but it didn't matter.

His mother didn't want him, either.

First Nikos, then Frank... Brian didn't want to stick around for him, and he was his mirror.

Catherine didn't want him.

Catherine wouldn't be waiting for him to get home.

"Are you listening to me?"

"Not really," Brody answered, and he was slapped across the face for the second time that day.

This time by his mother.

"This is what I'm talking about! No respect. None."

"Beating it into someone doesn't work, Sandra," Brody replied, his voice emotionless. "Ask Frank. He tried for years."

Brody tuned out what else was being said as he stood, walking robotically towards his room.

No one wanted him around.

"Young man, your mother is talking to you." Frank's voice was loud, angry.

"I suck, she's sending me away, got it," Brody replied. "Think I should pack now."

"Well, this program will be good for you," he heard Sandra say before he shut the door to his room just enough to where it would stick.

Of course it would be.

It would get him out of her way.

Tyler and Sammi were with Sheryl. And now, Sandra was about to be childless for the first time since college.

Brody imagined she felt relief.

Elated.

While he couldn't feel anything.

Would it matter what he packed? No, wait, of course it would. He would need clothing and his shoes, all two pairs of them, one of which had belonged to Brian. He would need his books, the ones he had all sorted on his shelves by author and order of reading. He would need his shaving things, which were in the bathroom just down the hall. Should he make a list, or just start?

Would Catherine care?

Pieces of her were everywhere in his room—photos, favorite books, pressed flowers that she'd left behind.

Memories.

Memories everywhere.

The scuff on the wall where he'd helped her climb through his window.

Her favorite pillow.

Her being curled against him while he would read to her.

Would he need to finish the book? He wouldn't be starting his senior year here. Perhaps when he came back...

But would he?

His phone buzzed, a message from Max letting Brody know that word of his and Cat's break up was beginning to spread. Small-town syndrome, she'd called it. He called it being teenagers, constantly comparing their lives to others, to do or say something that would make them feel better about themselves.

Wait until they heard about Brody being sent away.

His hands were shaking when he sent a text back to Max.

Packing. Mom's sending me to some program for 3 months

He wasn't surprised when he got the text back from Max telling him that he was coming over. He was going to demand entry, he'd said.

They'd let him in anyway.

That was Sandra and Frank, always putting on the happy face so no one would know the hell behind closed doors and shuttered blinds.

Or was that changing, now that Sandra was apparently done being a mother?

Brody sent another text back, asking if Max had a suitcase he could borrow.

One he didn't know if he would return.

Excellent idea was what Max sent back to him. Brody stared at the text, confused, then it sunk in that Max thought Brody had come up with a plan.

Brody couldn't come up with anything at the moment.

He stared at the shirt hanging in his closet—the one that Catherine had bought for him at the mall almost a year before— and let the only tear that had surfaced fall.

He had to get out of there.

Had to get out of that house.

Without a second thought, he threw his door open and walked swiftly toward the front door.

"If you run, I swear you'll go to juvenile detention."

Wasn't that essentially what she was already doing?

"I'll be back," was all he said before throwing the front door open and taking off in a full run before they could stop him.

He knew exactly where he was going.

Exactly who he needed to talk to.

"I don't know what to do." Brody brushed his sweat and tears back as he paced. "They're sending me away. Not that it matters, because what do I have here? Catherine is done with me. My friends... they're all drifting away, they all have their own lives, their own dreams, their own girlfriends. They don't have time for my bullshit. And that's what Catherine says it is, you know? Bullshit."

He sat on the ground before the stone that he'd never seen before today.

Brian Harris

Beloved son and brother

The dates between the dashes, the life that ended on Christmas Day far too soon, cutting off the boy that should have lived.

The one who had the future.

"I'm lost without you." Brody's fingertips traced the etchings, so simple, so little for someone who'd lived so large. "I... I took care of Ty and Sammi best I could, but Mom, she doesn't think I should be around them. I still can't cook for shit. You always could, though. You and Max, even though you were always with JJ. Yeah, you were Max on steroids, and I miss you every fucking day."

Another sob broke free as Brody rested his forehead on the stone. "I don't know how to forgive you. And I... I don't know how to live, how to not be another Frank. I... I had this girl, and she was everything."

Everything.

And now she was gone, too.

"I had this band of brothers who always had each others' backs, was always there for one another."

Until Brian put a bullet in his brain.

No, through his brain. Through.

Their mother kept reiterating that.

"I know our father's name. And you... you were Dante Kostopoulos. But you'll always be Brian to me."

But who was *he?*

Was he Brody Harris, following so closely in Frank's footsteps that it was scaring him?

Or was he Dimitri Kostopoulos, son of a cinematographer, left to fend for himself when his own father wanted nothing to do with him?

Or did he?

"I have this letter, from Aunt Sheryl. I haven't read it. I guess..." He wiped his eyes once more. "I guess I'm afraid to. I just want to know why, Brian. Why couldn't you stay for me? Did you hate me that much, too?"

They all seemed to hate him.

Frank could find nothing right about him.

His mother was turning out the same way.

Catherine was done, in all of her glory, pushing him aside as soon as she had the status she was longing for.

He wasn't good enough for anyone to stick around.

"You asshole," he cried as another sob ripped through him. "You asshole, why didn't you stay?"

What was left of his resolve crumbled and he laid his head against the ground, tears wracking his body with the force that they left him.

"What do I do, Bri? I don't know, and... and you're not here to help me, and I don't know what to do."

"What you need to do is get to the car so I can drive you back to that house."

Frank's voice startled Brody, catching him off guard. He recovered quickly and moved to his feet, hating the tears that he just couldn't stop. "Leave."

"I'm not leaving until you get in that car."

"You think I would go anywhere with you?" Brody's voice was loud, forceful, the way that Frank used so often with him. "Do you *really* think I'm going to get in that car when you'll probably slam my head against the fucking window? Or hey, maybe you'll try to twist my arm back. Maybe... just maybe you won't wait until we're in the car and you'll slam me up against it with a punch in the gut. Yeah, motherfucker... I'd like to see you try."

"We've been everywhere looking for you."

"Well, you found me. Now leave me with my brother."

"Go get in the car, Brody."

"Fuck you!" Brody shoved Frank hard, but the man barely budged. "Look at me! I am you. I am the product of *you!*"

"You don't know what you're talking about."

"The fuck I don't." Brody stood up taller. "Tell me, Frank, are you going to turn on Tyler like that? Are you going to slam Tyler's head in the door if he misses the bus?"

"I,"

"What about Sammi, huh? Hey, let's take that famous Frank Harris temper out on Sammi. Let's slam *her* head into a car window when she says something that you don't like."

"Stop making me out to be,"

"A monster?" Brody interrupted him. "*You are a fucking monster!* I don't care who hears or who sees because that's what you are. That's what you taught me. I was a kid when you started beating the shit out of me. A fucking kid! Why do you hate me so much, huh? Tell me that." Brody waited a beat as he watched Frank's face, which paled. "Tell me!"

"I don't hate you."

"Then *why*? Why did you treat me like shit when Brian could do no wrong? Why did you think that I was so unloveable?"

Frank's refusal to answer, to even react to Brody's words infuriated him.

"Come on, Frank, tell me." He pointed towards the headstone, determined to get an answer. "How many times have you wished that was me?"

"I've heard about this asinine idea, Brody."

"Okay, wonderful!" Brody threw his hands up. "Answer me, then."

"Never."

"Is that a lie, or because you wouldn't have anyone to beat the shit out of?"

A muscle twitched in Frank's jaw. "Get in the car, Brody."

"What the fuck is wrong with you, Frank? What... no, seriously, what is that all about? Because I and all the bruises you've left on me need to know."

"Brody, I'm warning you,"

"You really think you can take me now?" Brody stepped up, looking Frank directly in the eye. "Bring it, asshole."

"This is precisely why your mother and I have chosen this facility for you."

"A facility you couldn't afford if you hadn't knocked up Theresa Garner."

"That's about enough out of you."

"How does that work exactly? Are you splitting time between Theresa and Sandra?"

"You are going to learn respect."

"That's just it, Frank... I *am* you, aren't I? You look at me and you see yourself because that's what you've made me. What if Sammi starts dating someone just like you, huh? What are you going to do then?"

"You don't know what,"

"I do know! Look at me, Frank. Look at him!" He gestured to the gravestone. "Look what the pressures of being the golden boy did to *him*. LOOK AT HIM!"

"Hey, hey... hey!" Coach was suddenly there, standing before Brody as he pulled Frank aside. He placed his hands on Brody's face. "Look at me, Brody, not at him. Look at me."

Brody's eyes filled with tears as Coach's face became clearer. "They're sending me away, Coach. They don't want me."

"That's not true, kid. They just want to help you."

"I don't know what to do." Brody's voice cracked with emotion. "This is all I know, Coach. It's all I know."

When Coach Garner pulled the boy close, telling him over and over that it wasn't his fault, Brody allowed the tears to come again.

It wasn't his fault that he was turning out just like the monster that raised him.

It wasn't his fault that Brian was dead while he was not.

It wasn't his fault.

It wasn't his fault.

Even with those words reverberating in his head, Brody didn't believe them.

CHAPTER 33

Good

"**M**an, this is fucking bullshit," Max was saying as he tossed clothes into the opened suitcase. Brody pulled them out and re-folded them, stacking them neatly in rows. With his mother looking for him the previous day, word had spread quickly that Brody was in trouble.

Again.

And that he was leaving.

Again.

Still, nothing from Catherine.

"I mean, I'm assuming what you said at the store about Mitch is true," Max continued, "since you never lie. Seriously, though." He tossed more clothes back, which Brody caught and folded. "Dude, you're weird. Anyway, it must have been fucking awesome to deck that fuckhead."

"I should have done more," Brody replied, his voice flat, emotionless.

"You sound like a robot, and it's really fucking creepy."

Brody shrugged, catching more clothes that Max was now tossing directly to him.

"And you're neat, like a chick. You always have been. You're... an old soul. That's what Catherine said one time. You remember, at the pool?"

"Not really."

"Alright, fucker, stop. I know you and your girl had a fight, and supposedly broke up."

"There's no supposedly to it."

"But it's you and Catherine," Max went on, ignoring Brody's words. "She'll come back around. Sarah said she's at practice today. We could crash, since it's at my girlfriend's house."

"No." He wanted desperately to, but he couldn't.

He couldn't deal with her rejection again.

"In the meantime, we need to throw you a little bash before you go away."

"Yeah, no thanks."

"Yes, thanks, because this is bullshit. Besides, no one got to say goodbye to you last time. We have, what? Two full days."

"Not today, Max."

"Fine. Tomorrow, then. Pool, JJ's, the whole nine. And dude?"

"Hmm?" Brody's eyes were focused on his task of folding clothes, placing them neatly, adding a book here and there, the row of pictures of him and Catherine that he'd used for a bookmark.

"You know you've got a place to stay when you get back. No more bullshit from Frank, no matter what."

Brody nodded. "Thanks."

"That's it." Max tossed another shirt in Brody's direction before he pulled his phone out. "I'm getting reinforcements in here."

"Sarah is,"

"Sarah's too accommodating." Max grinned. "I'm getting Emily."

Brody's shoulders deflated even more. "Really?"

"She doesn't put up with your bullshit anymore than I do, but maybe she can snap you out of this."

"She's just a kid. She doesn't need to,"

"She's on her way."

"Max?"

"Yeah?"

"You're an asshole."

Max threw another shirt at him as he grinned. "Yes, I am."

"What's up with the third degree from your mother?" Emily asked about fifteen minutes after Max had sent her the text. She shut the door that she'd pushed her way through and crossed her arms. "She starts asking where I'm from, and when I told her we met at the center, she really had her panties in a wad. And is that Frank out there? He's creepy. Anyway, so... dude, you pack like me."

Max threw his head back in laughter, but Brody couldn't even muster up a smile. "Hey," was all he said before he began pulling out his favorite books to put in his duffel bag.

"Planning on living out of your suitcase, I see."

"Not necessarily."

Max announced that he needed to take a piss and he left the room leaving Emily staring at Brody, her brow furrowed. "I hear you and the princess broke up."

Brody nodded, not wanting to talk about it at all.

"Good."

"What did you just say?" Brody asked incredulously, and he almost swore he saw one corner of Emily's mouth lift.

"I said good. You need to figure this shit out on your own, and you don't need to rely on someone else to do that."

"I didn't..."

But he stopped himself from finishing his sentence.

Because he did.

He did.

"Now that I've got your attention," Emily continued, "yeah, it sucks that you're being sent away. But you can use this time to really get your shit together."

Just like Catherine had said he needed to.

"I don't want to go," Brody admitted. He didn't want to leave his friends, he didn't want to start his senior year being schooled in a locked-down facility.

He didn't want to take that chance that in 90 days Catherine could find someone new, someone whole.

Someone who wouldn't drag her down the way she said that he was.

"You'd be a dick if you wanted to."

"But I don't have anything left here right now."

"And now you're being a dick." Emily tossed a pillow at him, which he promptly grabbed and set back on the bed. "You have friends here, you know. Friends that are going to be here for you no matter what. This is the closest thing to friends I've ever had, and you've known them most of your life. Do you know how lucky that makes you?"

He heard the front door slam.

Frank must be leaving.

How many times had his friends been there for him when he was at his lowest point? When Frank had made him feel like he was less than nothing?

"Yeah, I know I'm lucky." He picked up the book that he'd been reading with Catherine, its bookmark now one that Sammi had colored in Kindergarten. "It just doesn't feel like it right now."

"And it's not going to for awhile. But, hell, you'll have 90 days away from their shit drama. Your parents, I mean. Yeah, I know, he's not your father," she cut him off, "but you know what I mean."

He understood that all too well.

He'd wished to be away from it all.

He just didn't think that it would be like this.

"Man, Frank's got issues," Max announced as he came back in.

Brody let out a short laugh.

Followed by another.

And another.

"See?" Max said with a full grin. "Em's a godsend. You're stuck with us, especially for getting ol' Broody here to laugh."

"I didn't do that; you did."

"What did I do?"

"Ah, Max," Brody said, his voice still lacking much emotion. "You have no idea the issues that Frank has."

"Sure I do."

"What's this about us going to a pool tomorrow?" Emily asked.

"Ah, the community pool. You haven't been," Max was saying as Brody resumed packing.

The community pool.

Would that be his last time there?

Would Catherine come?

"You have mail on the table," his mother announced with a knock on the door that was more like a *bang*, but even that didn't cause Brody to jump.

"Wow, she's a joy," Emily muttered. "And I know that look on your face. She may not show, but it isn't about her. This is about you."

"You did get a little whipped there, Brody," Max chimed in. "Just sayin."

"I did not get whipped," Brody replied, knowing that whipped wasn't the proper word.

Dependent.

He'd become dependent on her, on the comfort that he only found in her presence.

How was he going to get through the next couple of days without her?

How was he going to get through any of it without her?

But she'd left him no choice.

"Listen," Emily began as she sat on his bed with a bounce, "don't let my age fool you. I've seen a lot of shit, and I can read people like no one else can."

"You going to be a detective?" Brody shot at her.

"Fashion designer, if I can help it, but this is about you. I know that you have a lot of heart, but... what was it that Dick said about empty cups and pouring? You know where I'm going with this."

"Can't get blood from a turnip," Max offered.

"That's about money."

"I'm trying to insert a little bit of humor into a tense situation here," Max added.

"So we're supposed to humor you so you can humor us?" Emily asked.

"Yeah, something like that. Oh! I need to go tell your mom that I'm stealing you for tonight. And tomorrow, too."

"You're done packing," Emily said. "That's about all you can bring with you anyway. You wanna get outta here?"

"Don't know if I can." He didn't know if he wanted to be around anyone, not then. He wasn't sure about the pool, or JJ's, or anything the next day.

It was bad enough when he lost Brian.

Now he was without the girl who'd captured his heart.

Had she been an illusion? She'd flipped that switch so easily, turning cold, heartless.

Had she ever loved him?

People don't just abandon those they love.

"I'm going to let your mom know I'm kidnapping you for the evening. And tomorrow," Max added, exiting the room yet again.

"Fuck," Brody muttered as he sat on his bed, his hands reaching for his hair, but he stopped, choosing to fidget with a string in the hole of his jeans instead.

"I know you're in a bad place," Emily said as she sat beside him. "Get out of the house. Don't isolate yourself. Spend time with your friends before you have to go. And Brody?"

"Hmm?"

"Don't run."

"Wasn't thinking about it."

"And don't... don't reach out to her. Give her some time. Maybe that's what both of you need."

"How'd you get so smart?"

"Grew up too fast," she replied with a shrug. "Maybe I'm just an old soul."

An old soul.

What Catherine had referred to him as, even though he didn't remember it.

"Yeah," he said. "Maybe we both are."

"It's a go," Max announced, and he tossed an envelope in Brody's direction. "Grab a few things and let's get the fuck out of here. Oh, and Emily, you're coming with. We need to get you on our team."

"Team, what team?"

Brody opened his mail as Max explained the video game, and how he was losing his partner in crime and that Matt wasn't interested in the game. Brody's eyes widened as he took in the sight of the check in his hand, and his heart began to pound wildly.

Coach must have been one hell of a deal maker.

"Hey, Max? My pictures…"

"Yeah, they were everywhere. Went national, too. You're the star of this community, and… whoa." Max looked at the check, then back at Brody. "Beer's on you. Let's go."

"I…"

"We'll stop at your bank, big shot," Max said when Brody's voice trailed off.

He could use this money to get a head start in life.

He could use this money to find his father.

He could travel, take pictures, sell them like he had these.

He knew he had to go to the program, but he would turn 18 during that 90-day stay.

"You in there?"

"Hmm? Oh, yeah." Brody stood, choosing to bring his entire suitcase. "Let's go."

Nighttime was the worst.

This was his second night since losing Catherine—losing everything—and sleep was as elusive as ever. It didn't help that he was at Max's on the couch, without the comfort of his own room or roof.

They'd played their game until nearly midnight.

Queen C never showed.

Max had tried to assure him that all would be well and that Catherine would see him, talk to him before he had to leave. But when text messages went left unread, phone calls went straight to voicemail, and he'd been blocked on messenger, he knew better.

She could be so cold.

He'd seen it before.

He turned on the lumpy sofa and adjusted his pillow in yet another attempt to get comfortable, to finally succumb to sleep, but both remained elusive as he stared at the wall. The pictures were hidden in the darkness, but he still knew them by heart, with their smiling faces not faked for a camera.

Max was happy.

Max was always happy, always joking.

Max had even tried to cheer up Brody at Brian's funeral, although nothing quite worked.

Brody wondered in silence if Max's happiness was as faked as Brian's had been.

Brian had always told Brody that things could be worse. He always made excuses, reminded Brody how lucky they were to have him to help with bills when he was working, or to help with the kids when he wasn't. He could always recall happy events, ones where Frank would treat Brody like he mattered.

That was the last thing he felt like now.

He should be celebrating this victory of having his pictures published. Without Catherine, though, his mood darkened, leaving little to celebrate with the memory of her being the one who submitted the photos with her father's help.

He shouldn't be staring at the door wondering if anyone would notice if he stepped out for a middle of the night run.

He shouldn't be wondering if his mother would miss him if he went on that run and never returned at all.

One glance at his messenger gave him a glimmer of hope.

His messages had been read.

She'd read his words.

With a sigh and the smallest of smiles, he closed his eyes and sleep overtook him soon after.

CHAPTER 34

Over Him

A s the cheerleading squad arrived fashionably late at the pool the next day, Brody noted with a heavy heart that Catherine was not among them. He hadn't expected her to show; she still left him on 'read,' failing to respond. The news of his impending departure had spread, so he knew that she was aware.

Did she simply not give a damn?

"Brody, my man." Randall walked up to him and clapped him on the shoulder. "Looks like most of the student body has come to bid their farewells."

"Or they're just here to escape the heat," Brody replied with a tight smile. Even the breeze was oppressively warm.

"It's not the same without Ty and Sammi to toss around," Max noted as he passed. "But break's over. See who can jump the furthest?"

"I'll sit this one out," Brody said, and he gestured towards the concession stand. "Line's finally short enough."

"Be a good man and get me a drink," Max called to him with a grin, unwilling to let Brody forget that he had the money to do so.

He had the money to get his passport once he was eighteen, just like he'd always wanted to.

He had the money to get started on his journey, away from this place.

And he knew that he could, with Tyler and Sammi safe in Chicago with Sheryl and her husband.

He knew that he could with Catherine not waiting for him to come back.

"Hey." Audrey was beside him in line, smiling. "How's our local celebrity doing?"

"I'm hardly a celebrity."

"Eat those fifteen minutes with a spoon, Brody. You deserve it. The pictures are amazing."

"How are you?" he asked, uninterested in talking about himself.

"Well, my home was torn to pieces, but luckily I was able to stay with Sarah while they rebuild it. Dad says it should be done in a couple of months."

Brody's smile was genuine. "That's wonderful. How's your sister?"

"They're still in Kentucky with my dad's family. He says we're one of the lucky ones, whose insurance company isn't fighting. We got people working on it almost right away. But there's no way I was going to Kentucky, missing out on my senior year, having to give up my spot on the squad. Speaking of, your girl is amazing."

Brody's smile fell and he turned his eyes back to the concession stand. Only three more people ahead of him. "She's not my girl, Audrey."

"She's hurt, yeah, but trust me, she's still your girl. She's done nothing but cry since she heard the news, even more than she did when you broke up."

She cried over him?

She cried over him.

"Where is she?" He tried to keep his tone conversational, light.

"At the studio."

"Working?"

Audrey nudged him. "Pry much?"

"Just curious." And hoping that she had a reason to not be there, to not spend part of his last days there with him.

"Sure you are."

One side of Brody's face lifted in a grin. *Put on your happy face. Don't let them see it's tearing you up inside.* "You know me, Audrey."

"I do, Harris. I most certainly do." She looked around "Where are the kids?"

"They're with my aunt." Most likely permanently, especially if he didn't come back.

"What, you get to be a kid finally?"

Again, he mustered half a grin. "Something like that."

"Well, your mother wasn't much into mothering. It was all you and Frank. And Brian, when he was here."

Brody opened his mouth to protest, to protect his mother, only this time he couldn't.

Audrey was right.

"I hear you had a screaming match with your father."

"He's not my father," Brody stated for what felt like the millionth time. Only one person was ahead of him in line now.

"He did raise you, though. Maybe you can form some kind of a truce."

Brody scoffed. "Yeah, I don't see that happening."

"What if he extends that olive branch, though?"

He turned his gaze to Audrey and sighed. "I can't."

"But you should."

"Audrey…" He stopped as she placed her hand on his arm.

"Life's too short, Brody."

That was a lesson they'd all learned at far too young of an age.

"And you never know." She shrugged. "Forgiveness may set you free. I'll see you later."

"See ya," he mumbled, then he turned to order as her words swam in his forever racing mind.

The smell of chlorine clung to Brody's skin as the day wore on. No one there seemed to know that he wasn't leaving on his own, and Max confirmed that he didn't tell the circumstances of Brody's impending departure.

"Why not?"

Max shrugged. "Because that's your business."

So Catherine may think that he was leaving because he wanted to. "Shit, where's my phone?"

"Over by our stuff. Dude, don't message her again."

"Max…"

"Ah shit." Max hit his forehead with his palm. "Dude, go message her."

Brody hurried over to his bag, rummaging through it until he found his phone. He scrolled through his messages, finding her name. She still hadn't replied to him, but he knew he hadn't told her why he was leaving.

He'd wanted that conversation to be face-to-face.

Maybe if she knew…

He was distracted by a pair of toned, tan legs walking towards him.

He'd know those legs anywhere.

His heart pounded in his chest as he looked up at Catherine, who stood before him, hands on her hips, her white bikini glowing against her skin. Despite her agitated expression, she looked like an angel.

One of her eyebrows shot up as she caught a glimpse of his phone. "No need to message *again*. I'm standing right here."

With several of the other cheerleaders with her.

With an air of superiority.

Lady Catherine was in all of her glory.

"Can we talk?"

"We're talking now," she shot back as she crossed her arms.

"Alone."

He was so sure he'd noticed a break in her resolve, but she quickly recovered.

"You're leaving. Congratulations. No need to talk alone."

"I know you feel betrayed,"

"I have been."

"Cat,"

"Okay, we're done here," she said, and with a flip of her hair over her shoulder, she turned to walk away.

"They're sending me away, Cat."

His words had her pausing, looking over her shoulder at him with an icy stare. "Good," was all she said, then she continued her walk to the opposite side of the pool.

He couldn't fool her, though.

Not when he could read her body language with the way she sat on her towel and leaned back, her head upwards towards the sun.

She was relieved.

And now, so was he.

Matt and Emily arrived at the pool during another break time, with Emily avoiding going over to the side where JJ was playing his guitar. "Okay, my foster sisters? Annoying. Totally fucking annoying. So glad they're moving me again."

Matt nudged her. "Tell them who you're moving in with."

Emily rolled her eyes. "My ex-stepmother. Plus side? The sisters there are actually related to me. And they damn sure won't be as annoying as tweedle dumb and tweedle dumber."

"I'll need your new address," Brody said, and she nodded.

"Yeah, I'll get that to you. I see your girl is here."

Brody frowned. How many times did he have to say it? "Not my girl, Em."

"Then why does she keep looking at you when you're not looking at her?"

A grin threatened to surface on Brody's face. "Don't know."

But she was looking.

And she was *there*.

He didn't know if she was going to be joining the majority of the crowd when it migrated to JJ's, but considering it was a majority, she probably would. Appearances mattered to her, after all.

"I baked goodies," Max piped up as he and Sarah joined them. "She'll show." He grinned at Brody. "I even have some set aside for when you're on the road."

"On the road?" Em asked. "Dude, are you running?"

Brody shook his head. "It's a six hour trip that I need to make sure I have my phone charged up for."

"And you charged up for, hence the goodies." Max grinned proudly. "I made brownies."

Brody's gaze showed his wariness. "Tell me they're not."

"They're not. You'll piss clean. But dude, these are triple chocolate. Make sure you have something to drink, they're that rich."

"You, like, *bake* bake?" Emily asked incredulously, and Max turned his grin to her.

"Yep, and you're coming to JJ's to try some."

She hesitated for a moment, then sighed. "Fine, I'll come try some of your goodies."

The look on Max's face had both Brody and Emily laughing. "You two are fucking weird," he said with a grin. "I'm gonna go do a cannonball at the whistle blow. You in, Brody?"

"Fuck it," Brody said with a shrug, the thought of being close to Catherine, who was on that side of the pool, making him warm with anticipation.

"Hey, I'm in, too," Emily spoke up as she stood. "Looks like it's about time."

The three of them walked nonchalantly past Sarah's station, Brody's stomach in knots the entire way. He chanced a glance at Catherine, noting how she quickly looked away from him.

She'd been watching.

The knowledge had him smiling as the whistle blew and he took off in a dead run, his cannonball further than the others.

"Jeez, this place is packed," Emily said as she elbowed her way through the crowd at JJ's.

"Yeah, well, I'm not kidding myself into thinking they're all here to say goodbye to me," Brody said with a half grin.

"Of course we are, dick," he heard someone say, and a genuine laugh left him.

"It's always like this when word gets out," Brody said to Emily, who grabbed a cola from the fridge.

"Where's your girl?" Nan asked as she entered and threw an arm around Brody's waist. "She beat me at beer pong. I want my damn title back."

Brody's smile faltered. "Um… we broke up, so I don't know if she's coming."

"She's been milling around here, sweetie. She's been here for awhile. Mostly out back, but she's not there. That's why I asked you." Nan gave him a squeeze. "Maybe it's for the best, though. I know how long distance doesn't work out."

"I'm only gonna be gone about 90 days, Nan."

"Honey." She reached up and took his face in her hands. "I've known you since you were knee high to a grasshopper. You've got that far away look in your eyes, baby boy. You're not coming back."

Brody grinned at her, although he didn't feel it. "Of course I will. Where else would I go?"

"Everywhere." Nan patted his arm. "I know you." With her proclamation stated, she walked away in search of Catherine, who Brody hadn't even known was there.

Maybe he should be outside, where she would show off her moves.

Or maybe he should stay in the kitchen, where he had clear vision of the beer pong table. Nan was sure to challenge Catherine, who wouldn't dare turn up the competition.

"Listen," Emily said over the noise, "I really can't stay."

"Curfew?" Brody teased, then mussed her hair. "Kidding. I know, it's best you're not here. No need to stay around temptation." He held up his beer and Emily smiled.

"Thanks for understanding." She stood there for a moment, then reached in and gave him a hug. "And thanks for being my new big brother."

"Damn straight," he said, returning the hug. "Now get your ass home."

"Brody,"

"I'll be back. And I'll write only if you promise to write back."

"Cross my heart."

"I'll see you soon, I promise."

"Don't make promises you can't keep, Brody." Emily smiled sadly. "See ya," she added, then she pushed her way into and through the crowd, heading for the nearest door.

Brody didn't understand what was up with her, or Nan. He was coming back; this was his home, his school.

And Catherine was there.

She took the side of the beer pong table where her back would be to him purposefully, but she was there.

That was all he needed.

Wasn't it?

CHAPTER 35

Goodbyes

"Man, I hate this." Max poured three shots and handed one to Brody, then another to JJ. Raising his, he took a deep breath, and exhaled shakily. "We're always brothers."

"Are you going soft on us Max?"

"Fuck you, JJ. You'll always be JJ to me, by the way. Just so you know. You two ass clowns are leaving me alone my senior year."

Brody raised his hand. "This ass clown will only be gone for 90 days."

"Not the point, and put your hand down. No more interruptions. We're always brothers, no matter what. Promise."

"Scout's honor," JJ quipped, then his smile faltered. "Yeah. Always."

"Always," Brody agreed. With a raise of their glasses, they downed the last of the bottle they'd found stored away. The three of them were in JJ's bedroom, away from the noise of what few stragglers were still hanging about, surrounded by the same posters that had adorned the walls for years.

"I can't believe that nothing in this room has changed," Max commented. "Aside from your clothes, and all the beer bottles."

"No, that hasn't changed much, either," Brody said.

"Nan says she's leaving everything in here just as it is." JJ's grin held an edge of sadness. "It's just a room."

"It's the most stable room you've had," Max pointed out. "I want to see you make it, but damn, I'm gonna miss you. We both are."

"Is that so?"

"Yeah," Brody replied as he leaned back against the wall. "It's so."

JJ nodded briefly, then sighed. "So many memories in this room."

"Still got the GI Joes?" Max asked.

"I imagine Nan has put those back for great grandchildren. Don't think that's coming from me, though."

"What, Kaitlyn doesn't want kids?" Max quipped, and JJ flipped him off.

"We're not like that."

"C'mon, dude, Audrey told Sarah she keeps going on and on about Jason. Don't tell me that isn't you."

"It isn't." JJ reached for his beer and took a drink.

"What about Twister?" Brody asked, and JJ let out a soft laugh.

"Fucking hell we had some fun with that. Remember the Paisley twins?"

"Which one of them did you date?" Max asked.

"Neither. That was Brian."

Brian.

The one who had more stories then all of them combined and wasn't there to share them.

"Remember that time he triple dog dared you to down that bottle of tequila?" Brody asked, and JJ groaned.

"I remember puking until I thought my balls were permanently imbedded in my throat. What about the time he got Max to sing The Itsy Bitsy Spider in nothing but his skivvies?"

"I one-upped all you pussies when I went into that restaurant there and ordered."

"I can't believe they didn't kick you out," Brody said to Max.

"I ended up dating the cashier." Max shrugged and grinned. "Totally worth it."

"What about Brody's 15 stitches in his face when he drove his bike off the roof."

"Twenty," Brody corrected him. "And chicks dig the scar."

"Man," Max said, "I'm glad I waited until you were done. There was no way I was gonna try it then."

"I think we were all too busy making sure Brody wasn't bleeding to death," JJ reminded him.

"Yeah, and Brian felt like shit for saying you wouldn't."

The room fell silent upon the mention of Brian's name.

Brody's smile was sad as he remembered that day.

"Shit... shit, Brody, I'm so fucking sorry."

"Yeah, it was pretty stupid."

"You could have fucking died all because I dared you."

"I wouldn't have done it if Jill hadn't been there. I think JJ would have joined in if he'd had Kaitlyn to impress. What about you?"

"I was just being an asshole," Brian said, defeated.

"That's why we love you, Bri."

Brody's eyes closed as he wished he could take it back.

Brian wasn't an asshole.

But he'd apparently seen himself that way.

"How does Kaitlyn feel about you leaving?" Max asked JJ, who shrugged.

"She thinks I'll be right back."

"Ouch."

"Yeah, well, she's pissed that I'm leaving, so..." JJ's voice trailed off as he pulled out a cigarette. "Hey, Brody, could you open the window?"

"Nan's gonna kill you," Brody said with a laugh as he stood and stretched before opening up the window. "Don't act like you haven't loved every minute of Kaitlyn living here while her home gets rebuilt."

"The further up Jason's ass Kate's head goes, the more I can't wait to leave," JJ replied. "I don't even know if I'll wait until her house is ready at this point. Gram will still let her stay."

"Don't let her hear you call her that, either," Max added with a laugh. "Nan would be more pissed over that than you smoking."

JJ exhaled smoke rings. "True."

"You're the only one of us who kept smoking."

"Brian did, occasionally," Brody said. "He got caught with them. I said they were mine."

"Why did you always do that shit?" Max asked. "It could have saved you a lot of trouble if you just admitted you weren't *all* of the trouble."

Brody shrugged. "Because I could handle it."

Until he couldn't, and he'd fought back in that house on the hill.

A soft knock interrupted them, and Kaitlyn asked if she could be let in.

"Is Nan in the hall?" JJ called out.

"No."

"C'mon in."

Kaitlyn looked as if she'd wanted to convey her message from the hallway, but noting the lit cigarette in JJ's hand, she decided otherwise. "Are you out of your mind, Jason?"

"What? It's not like I'm going to be here that much longer." He grinned as Kaitlyn shut the door.

"Anyway, I don't know how much longer all of this will be going on, but I need some sleep."

"I'll ensure you get your beauty rest," JJ said to her. "Everyone will be gone soon."

"It's just a big day at work tomorrow."

"I said it's fine." JJ's grin didn't meet his eyes.

"Oh, Brody? Catherine left a little bit ago. I thought you should know."

Without saying goodbye.

Brody didn't know if he'd get another chance before he left.

"Thanks," was all he said, unwilling to show how much it hurt.

How it made his stomach clench.

How it made his heart ache, sitting like a rock in his chest.

It hurt to breathe.

It hurt to breathe.

"I better get going," he said as he stood back up and stretched.

"Are you sure, man?" Max asked. "It's only midnight, the night is still young."

"I'm sure."

Max and JJ both stood with him, and Kaitlyn gave Brody a long hug. "Take care of yourself," she whispered to him, then left the room with a soft smile.

"You're gonna be gone before I get back, aren't you?" Brody asked JJ, who shrugged.

"Hoping so. No offense."

Brody smiled. "None taken." Without waiting for JJ to protest, Brody pulled him in for a hug. "You meant the world to Bri. He's looking out for you. So is Michael." He stood back, still smiling. "You're gonna make it, Jase Warner."

"I still can't call you that," Max piped up, and JJ laughed as Brody and Max exited his room. Brody didn't have to look back to know that JJ wasn't following. He wasn't big on goodbyes.

The crowd was even smaller as Brody and Max exited the house where Nan was collecting trash in a large black garbage bag, which was normally the cue. "You headed home, too?" Brody asked, and Max shook his head.

"I promised to be part of the cleanup crew."

"So you need to get back in there."

"Yeah... hey, listen." Max rocked back on his heels. "It sucks that you're going, but I'm kinda glad that you are. Don't kick my ass for that, though. I'm just..." He sighed. "You've always been the bookworm, the one who looked out for all of us. But hotheaded? You? Losing your shit and all?" He shook his head. "I don't know, but I can guess that it's what you've seen."

"My whole life," Brody admitted. "Or most of it."

"I don't know how they could afford this, but I'm glad they're doing it. Or your mom, or.... You know what I mean."

"Yeah," Brody said softly, not adding that it had to have been Catherine's grandfather, so desperate to tear them apart.

Little did he know, they already were.

"So you take time away, you learn how to not beat things and people up, and leave the shitty temper to JJ. That's always been his thing."

Brody let out a short laugh. "True. And hey… I appreciate you looking out for me, Max, but if people ask, tell them."

"Are you sure?"

Brody nodded. "Maybe some good will come out of it."

"Besides you, you mean."

"Yeah. Besides me."

Max pulled him in a tight hug, his second since the tornado. "I'm gonna miss you, asshole."

"I'll miss you, too." He stood back. "I think I can write letters."

"You're a senior, dick, I hope you know how."

"So I'll write you."

"Ma was serious, you know. About you coming to stay with us when you get back, I mean."

Brody's smile was sad. "Tell her thank you."

"You tell her when you come back."

"Deal," Brody said. "I really do need to get back before Sandykins thinks I've run off and she sends the cops after me."

One last goodbye, and Brody turned to walk away, the sounds from the house growing ever fainter the further away he was.

The night air held an unseasonal chill to it, its breeze pushing early fallen leaves across the ground as Brody walked home. The soft floral scent as he would pass flowering bushes was another reminder to him that Catherine was gone, had left without saying goodbye. Yes, he had one more day, but after she'd made the comment about his messaging, he didn't dare try again.

He paused as he passed Max's house, with its immaculate lawn. Could he give in and live here with them?

Should he?

With a heavy sigh, he continued on, pausing only to gaze at his own front door for a moment before going in.

How had it come to this?

He pulled out the key he'd had —the one that set this latest string of events in motion—and let out a relieved sigh when it worked. She hadn't changed the locks on him again. Only the kitchen light was on when he entered the house with its new furniture that his mother was so proud of. He didn't trust knowing his way around without the light, so he walked the short hall and turned his own light on before going back out into the kitchen to darken the rest of the house.

Tyler and Sammi's things should be out, scattered around, waiting for him to pick them up as his mother never would.

He knew they were safe, though. Safe and loved.

Safe and loved were what he'd wanted most for them.

For himself.

He stared at his bed for the longest time. Only two more sleeps in it before he left. Maybe he'd sleep most of tomorrow away, with nothing to do, having said his goodbyes and packed already. As he pulled his phone from his back pocket, it buzzed twice, letting him know he'd received a text message.

His heart pounded as he saw Catherine's name.

And as he read her short message, warmth engulfed him.

Meet me on the roof.

CHAPTER 36

I Still Could

Catherine was waiting for him on the roof, the moonlight illuminating her as Brody climbed up. He watched his footing, keeping his eyes downcast even as he sat beside her.

"I'm sorry."

"You should be."

Their voices were low, barely heard above the crickets on the ground. He raised his eyes to hers then, expecting the hardness that Lady Catherine often showed.

There was none.

Only a profound sadness.

"I figured I had time for you to grovel and beg for forgiveness," she said. "Turns out I was wrong."

One corner of his mouth lifted. "I still could."

"Make it quick."

He took her hand in his, interlacing their fingers. "My anger was no excuse for what I did; I know that. I'll be forever remorseful that it went down that way. Just don't ask me to apologize for decking that asshole."

"No, that part is fine."

"And I'm sorry I fucked up the rest of our summer plans."

"You mean our picnics and ice cream parlor visits? We're doing those tomorrow. Today, but... after we've both had sleep."

His heart soared.

"I was so angry with you, Brody."

"It's justified."

"But lashing out to hurt you back wasn't."

"If it helps, I understand."

"Good, because I don't grovel well. It doesn't go with my complexion. I turn all red and splotchy, and,"

"You're beautiful."

"It's dark."

He reached up with his other hand, cupping the side of her face. "You're always beautiful, Cat. Always."

"Being a bitch isn't beautiful."

"I was hoping my girl was still in there."

She leaned into his hand. "That was the hardest thing I'd ever done. That's how I knew it was both right and wrong. How I handled it was wrong, but I meant it when I said you need to get your shit together, Brody."

"Even when you went all Padme on me?"

She laughed softly. "Especially then."

And then she kissed him, just the softest of kisses leaving him with a song in his heart.

"I love you even when you're being a shithead," she said.

"And I love you even when you're letting Lady Cath-er-ine out to play."

"Oh, she wasn't playing. And neither was I."

They shared another kiss beneath the moon and stars.

"I didn't see Jen at JJ's tonight."

"Way to deflect," she teased.

"Not deflecting. Observing."

"You and Max with your justifications for everything."

"That's a Brian thing, actually."

Another kiss, another piece of his broken heart mending, fusing back together.

"I'm spending the night there tonight, actually. She didn't think bringing Bethany around me when I'm 'in a mood' was a good thing."

"Good call."

"I'm sorry I doubted you about that. You never lie to me."

"No, I don't."

"So you really aren't going away because we broke up?"

"I'm going away to get my shit together. Unwillingly going, but going just the same."

"Use that time wisely."

"I will, I promise."

"I have to go," she whispered against his lips, and she shivered when he kissed her again.

"Before we're caught and tomorrow doesn't happen," he added.

"Exactly."

One more kiss and she was reluctantly moving away. "I love you, Brody Harris."

He knew in that moment all was going to be okay.

Just as he knew he'd never take back his birth name.

The morning alarm going off on Brody's phone didn't bring the groan from him that it usually did. There was far too much for him to look forward to that day, despite the bittersweetness of it all.

One last day with Catherine before he didn't see her for the next three months.

The coffee had already been brewed, and he was sitting down at the dining room table having his first cup when his mother walked in. "You're up early."

"I have things to do."

"These things don't involve being on the roof at god knows what hour, do they?"

He took a sip of his coffee. "Spy much?"

"My window was open. It was a beautiful night."

His smile into his cup showed how much he agreed with her.

It had been.

"I'm glad to hear that you're not fighting me on this decision anymore."

He shrugged. "I can't. I'm a minor, and up until I turn 18, my life is centered around your decisions."

She sat across from him. "Yes, Brody, it is."

"Does that mean you're moving Frank back in?"

She reached for her half cup of cooled coffee. "I haven't decided yet."

"What about me?"

"You don't get a say-so in the matter."

Of course he didn't. He hadn't expected as much. "I mean... what about me? What about when I do turn 18? Do I get to leave the facility? And even if I stay the full 90 days, do I have a home to come back to?"

He watched Sandra raise her eyes to him, ones that should contain love and warmth but were somehow devoid of both. "I'm not sure."

He nodded, knowing that she was lying to him.

She was absolutely sure.

He wasn't welcome back.

"What did I do to make you hate me so much?"

"You're my child. Thinking that I hate you is absurd."

"You don't love me, though."

"I don't know you anymore."

He nodded again as he stood, coffee still in hand. Sandra Harris was not going to ruin this day for him.

She wasn't going to ruin his life for him.

She could stick to ruining her own.

"I gotta go get ready," he said, his tone light, conversational. "My girlfriend and I have plans for today."

Without waiting for another word for the woman who should love him above everyone else, he walked down to hall to prepare for his day with the girl who did.

He went straight to his room to look through his suitcase for clothes to wear when he happened to see an envelope half sticking out from under his bed.

The letter from his aunt.

He still hadn't read it.

He placed his coffee atop his dresser and leaned down to pick up the envelope, searching first for signs that it had been tampered with. Finding none, he was going to place it aside.

But he had placed it aside for too long.

He opened the envelope finally and pulled out the letter he should have read the night she'd given it to him.

Brody,

Please don't feel any guilt over what happened with Brian. He was dealing with his own demons, ones that he rarely told a soul about. He'd promised me that he was getting help, and I promised him that I would keep his secret safe.

But I can tell you.

Sweetheart, your brother was in love with a boy, and this boy loved him, too.

I don't think that anyone else knew, not even JJ. I don't know if your mother or Frank found out about it, if it ended badly, or if his own depression did him in. I don't think we will ever know. I did read his letter, and I promise you it didn't say anything that would give us a clue as to what happened.

I am sorry that I failed him, and I'm sorry that I failed you. I should have taken all of you away the moment that I could. As soon as Sandy told me that she was speaking with Frank again, I put that in motion. Unfortunately, she left me with an ultimatum. I could take Tyler and Samantha as long as I didn't take you with them. She never told me why. I suspect that it's to keep you as a buffer, and I hope for your sake that you leave the moment you can.

I will help you leave. All you need is ask.

Your father—your real father's name is Nikos Kostopoulos. He goes by Nicholas Paul. I am enclosing his address in Toronto. Honestly, I never got to know him well. I'm unsure what was said or done to make him give up his rights to you and your brother. If I did, I'd know whether or not you should contact him. Actually, no. That decision is entirely up to you. Whatever answers you seek lie with him. I hope that you find them, and that you find peace.

I love you, Brody. I promise that Ty and Sammi will always be safe and loved, and that my home is open to you whenever you would like to come visit. I meant what I said; if you need help getting out of there, let me know.

Love,

Aunt Sheryl

Brody stared at the letter for a moment after reading it and holding his father's address in his hand.

Would he go in search of answers or not?

He already knew better, and pulled out his phone, opening the Facebook app with his thumb. He typed Nicholas Paul into the search bar.

And there he was.

He clicked on the messenger button, typing *You know me as Dimitri. I would like to talk to you.*

Then he hit send before he could change his mind.

"Guess what!" Catherine jumped into his arms the moment he opened the door and kissed him fully on the lips. "My dad is totally dating the school secretary."

"Is that so?" Brody asked with a smile as he carried her outside. "You got your dad's car and everything today."

"And I made us a picnic lunch for the park."

"What is it?"

"A surprise."

"Speaking of, now it's my turn," he said as he placed her on the ground beside her father's SUV. He pulled his phone out of his pocket and opened messenger to show her.

"You totally found him!"

"He totally hasn't read this yet, but yeah." He grinned. "Aunt Sheryl let me know how."

"So you talked to her?"

"Actually," he held her door opened, "I finally read the letter."

Her smile fell. "Just now?"

"This morning."

"And it had that in it?"

Brody kissed the tip of her nose. "And so much more. Where to first?"

"The park, duh."

He took the keys from her outstretched hand. "Park it is."

CHAPTER 37

He Loved This Girl

Brody did his best to ignore that this was his last day with Catherine before being sent away. Her infectiously cheerful mood helped facilitate his own, and he found himself enjoying every moment. He cheered her on as she showed him her newfound Valley High skills, down to the tumble that ended in the splits.

"All goes well, I should get to see that in person," he said, smiling as he brushed a tendril of hair back that had fallen from her messy bun.

"You think Valley will make the playoffs?" She was genuinely excited—giddy, even—over the prospect of Brody being back in time to see a game.

"They at least make regionals most years."

"Fantastic." Her smile was beaming as she took down her hair and it fell in waves.

She was the most beautiful girl he'd ever seen.

He loved this girl.

"You said that Brian had art somewhere here?" Catherine looked around the park, puzzled, and Brody pointed to the closest bench.

"Table top."

"Well, then." Her smile was beaming. "I suppose that's the perfect place for lunch."

"You were serious." He followed after her. "You made us a lunch."

"Remember those Italian sausage sandwiches that Greta used to make for Sundays when she wasn't there?"

"Holy fuck do I ever," Brody said as his stomach growled softly. He hadn't eaten yet that day, as he rarely did in the mornings, but it was more the reminder of Greta's cooking.

Catherine turned on her heel, walking backwards effortlessly. "Guess who learned how to use Facebook and gave me the recipe."

His mouth opened in surprise as he caught up to her, and she turned to walk beside him. "No fucking way."

"Yep! She's not far from the old house, and get this—her new employer is helping her get her U.S. citizenship."

"Tell her I said congratulations."

Catherine smiled up at him and placed her hand in his. "I will. These sandwiches have passed my father's seal of approval, by the way, and he had one hot."

"They're better cold."

"Agreed."

An easy silence fell as they walked back to Coach's vehicle, where Catherine pulled out a cooler that she'd had behind the driver's side seat. Their silences were often easy, with nothing left unsaid between them, even on this day when his departure was imminent.

Temporary.

But imminent.

They sat at the table, the same one where Brody had cried for the loss of his brother, with Catherine admiring his art.

"He was talented."

This time Brody's smile was full of pride. "Yes, he was."

And though Brian should still be with him, though he missed him terribly and at times his absence was unbearable, this day when Catherine spoke of him, Brody could answer with ease.

"Audrey said that he was in drama club."

"The best actor they'd seen is what he was told. And he never let it go to his head, either... or at least he said he didn't. Damn, Cat, you nailed the recipe. This sandwich is amazing."

"Thank you."

"Sandra says that Brian was the best actor off stage as well, which I suppose is true."

"How so?"

Brody shrugged. "I never knew he was hurting the way he was. Hell, I never knew he had a boyfriend. And yeah, it's not my story to tell, but he's not here anymore so I do what I can to make sense of it."

"Not,"

"No, not JJ. I don't want to guess, honestly, because my bet is they don't want anyone to know right now." He frowned slightly. "I am sorry, Cat."

"I know." She smiled over at him. "And we're past it. So keep going! I want to know as much about him as I can."

"Why is that?"

"Because he'll always be a part of you."

"That he will, Cat. That he will."

His stories of his twin that day were lighthearted, touching on his mischievous side that Catherine decided Brody shared with him. He told her of the whole plot to drive the bikes off the roof, and even of Brian's bedtime confession that night where he thought he was an asshole.

"Well, he could have killed my boyfriend."

"I wasn't your boyfriend at the time," Brody grinned, his stomach taking a dive as her fingertips traced the small scar left behind.

"But you are now."

His smile was warm, and he leaned across the table to kiss her softly. "Yes, I am."

"I wish I could see more of his art."

"Silly girl," he said, drinking in her comfort. He gently touched her hand. "I'll only be gone three months."

"It's three months too long."

Her eyes conveyed the same emotions churning inside of him, with his sadness and fear of the unknown warring. Suddenly, though, her smile was bright. "C'mon, rebel. Help me clean up. I want to see the hangout in the daylight."

The hangout.

The place they'd declared their love for one another in more ways than one.

He returned her smile.

He carried the boombox for her as they took the trail into the woods. Her mood was jovial as she recounted everything she'd found out about her father and his new girlfriend, and jovial still as she discussed how she and Jen were planning on spying on their date to see 'how familiar' they seemed with one another.

Her laughter was a song in his heart.

Her smile a salve to heal his wounds.

She had no idea the vision she made as she walked along, carefree. It was one he would carry with him during his time away.

He loved this girl.

He even loved her stubbornness and the way she fought for respect from him, though he'd had it all along.

He loved the forgiveness in her heart.

Their hands were clasped, holding on perhaps a little too tightly, their fingers entwined, unwilling to let go until they absolutely had to. He held her hand the whole way through the woods, steering her off the trail at just the right spot to head to the 'hangout' spot. Still she talked on, telling him bits and pieces of her life before him, adding "Wow, I was such a bitch" more than once, making him laugh.

He couldn't say the same of her now.

When they finally reached the clearing, he set the boombox down and took her into his arms, kissing her the way he'd wanted to all day long.

Soft.

Sweet.

Promising.

"You keep kissing me like that and I will totally forget the surprise I had for you."

"What, are you gonna strip for me? Ow." He rubbed his forearm. "Okay, that was warranted."

"Damn straight it was." She was grinning as she walked over to the boombox and hit the power button, then the arrow a few times until she was satisfied she'd found the right one.

"Is it more of your routine?"

"Brody..." She turned to him with her hands on her hips as a familiar song began to play.

To Love Somebody.

She held her hand out to him and her smile was beguiling. "Dance with me."

One corner of his mouth lifted in a half smile. "Is that any way to ask?"

"I'm not asking, shithead."

He threw his head back in laughter before he took her into his arms and swung her around. "There's my girl."

They settled into a slow rhythm, swaying along with the music as they smiled into one another's eyes. "I am your girl, you know."

He kissed the tip of her nose. "I know."

He knew it with everything in him, just as he knew that he was hers.

He couldn't help but kiss her then.

And they danced.

Their hearts beating in sync, their souls crying as their faces smiled for their last day together. He knew he would always remember this moment and every detail about it.

The sound of the leaves beneath their feet.

The softness of her cotton t-shirt.

Her floral scent mixed with impending summer rain.

There would be no regrets between them, not as the song ended just as sure as the day would draw to a close.

They smiled through shared stories of years gone by, of first crushes, of most embarrassing moments.

They laughed as the sky opened up and began to rain.

They ran hand-in-hand towards her father's car, only to realize they'd left the boombox—and her keys—and had to run all the way back.

He held her as they shivered together once inside the dry car, their laughter echoing within.

"Promise you won't forget me," she whispered against his skin.

"Hey." He pulled back and pushed her dripping hair back before he kissed the tip of her red nose. Even like this, with soft smudges of black beneath her eyes, she was beautiful. "I could never forget you. And stop talking like I'm going to be gone forever, Cat. I'm not."

"I know." She sniffled. "Sorry our day got ruined."

"It's far from ruined." He kissed her lips softly, lingering there as he wished the kiss could last forever. "I'm with you, aren't I?"

"But you won't be."

"But I'll be back."

"Because our story's not over."

"Not even close."

And he meant those words with everything in him.

He just never dreamed it would be years before he saw her again.

RESOURCES

This book is a work of fiction. In no way do I condone any of the acts within. They are, however, important issues that many people face, no matter their age, gender, or social status. If you or someone you love has dealt or are dealing with any of them, please reach out. Help is available. You can look for local resources or contact one of the national centers below.

National Suicide Hotline
1-800-273-8255
https://suicidepreventionlife.org/
https://www.crisistextline.org
Text HOME to 741741

National Sexual Assault Hotline
1-800-656-4673
https://www.rainn.org/get-help

National Domestic Violence Hotline
1-800-799-7233
https://www.thehotline.org

The Trevor Project (for LGBTQ)
1-866-488-7386
https://www.thetrevorproject.org

ENTRAPPED

COMING SPRING 2020

The final installment in
the Entangled series

Enlightened
(Entangled Book 3)

OTHER BOOKS BY AUTHOR

Entitled (Entangled Book 1)

STALK ME!!

(Just follow, but that's catchier)

www.thatonewriterchick.com

www.facebook.com/thatonewriterchickakacarlie

www.facebook.com/groups/theauthorstable

www.instagram.com/thatonewriterchickakacarlie

www.goodreads.com/thatonewriterchickakacarlie

ACKNOWLEDGEMENTS

James, Glacia, and all of my fellow authors at TAT- Thank you for giving this chick a chance and making me feel loved and accepted. I hope that you all know how much I love and appreciate each and every one of you! And to **All TAT members-** THANK YOU for your support. We wouldn't be a success without you!

Rose- You know Brody better than I do at times! Thank you for EVERYTHING.

Tami- The T to my J. Thank you for getting me unstuck and helping make those pivotal scenes come to life.

Cody- Book 2… what?! Thank you for understanding my vision or lack thereof and making beautiful book covers.

Stephanie- Your eagle eye has saved me once again! Thank you so much for being YOU.

Amber- Look at us go!!! I am so incredibly proud of you, more so than I could possibly convey

My family- Thank you for your support and your belief in me, especially when I had none in myself. It's changing, I promise.

My PJ family- Your Tee-Dub is living her dream! Thank you for pulling me out of such a dark place that I'd gone down. You're forever in my heart.

My Dash/Illusions/Visions et al family- Thank you, all of you, for believing that your sunshine actually had it in her to do this.

Jules- I say we plan another 5-day slumber party. Rose won't mind, right?

Nellie and all at MM19- Your love and support has me realizing my dream TWICE in one year! Thank you so much for EVERYTHING!

Crissy- Talk about bringing my visions to life! The website, the graphics... you are a true web goddess!!!

My BDC family- SEE?! I told you I was actually writing novels!! I wish I hadn't been in such a horrible headspace the majority of my time there and had trusted that I could truly find the kinship that I eventually did with you. You're all in my heart always!

My readers- Yes, YOU!! You're what keeps me going, continuing to let my imaginary friends talk to me. I hope you enjoy reading as much as I enjoy sharing their journeys with you!

And finally... typos- If you're still here, you're the MVP. But keep hiding. I'm not in the mood for you.

Authors (especially indie!) rely on your reviews. Please take a moment to review this novel on the platform that it was purchased from. It is appreciated more than you will ever know!

ABOUT THE AUTHOR

Carlie Yates (That One Writer Chick) has been writing stories since she was in the fifth grade, convinced that if she didn't get her thoughts and characters down on paper, her head would 'plode; it could be ex- or im-, but either way, it wouldn't be pretty. Inspired by S.E. Hinton, she always said when she grew up that she would be a published author. She is currently renouncing her pledge to grow up. This Midwest mom of boys has addictions to reading, road trips, hair dye, and the Oxford comma, and is thoroughly convinced at any given time the theme track to *My Three Sons* will start playing in the background of her home.